The King and the Slave

Tim Leach

ATLANTIC BOOKS

London

First published in Great Britain in 2014 by Atlantic Books,
an imprint of Atlantic Books Ltd.

This paperback edition published in Great Britain
in 2015 by Atlantic Books.

10   9   8   7   6   5   4   3   2   1

A CIP catalogue record for this book is available
from the British Library.

Paperback ISBN: 978 0 85789 923 1
E-book ISBN: 978 0 85789 924 8

Printed in Great Britain

Atlantic Books
An imprint of Atlantic Books Ltd
Ormond House
26–27 Boswell Street
London WC1N 3JZ

www.atlantic-books.co.uk

For Maureen

An Endless Plain

I

There is a place, far to the north of Babylon, through the rock and stone labyrinth of mountains that bear no name and many *parasangs* to the east of the great Hyrcanian sea, where a great plain stretches out to the horizon and beyond. Were one to be born at the centre of this steppe, one would never imagine that such a thing as a mountain or a sea could possibly be, and could believe only that the world was an infinity of earth and rivers and horses. It is here that the Massagetae make their home.

Most of these nomads have never seen a temple or a watch-tower or a great city wall. They shun cities as tombs, think of those who live in them as devils who have traded away their souls in the market squares. But there are a few amongst them who make great journeys to the south and west, taking herds of tall horses with them and coming back with treasures – necklaces in lapis lazuli, recurve bows that only the strongest men can pull, clay jars of honey, and, rarest and most valuable of all, the occasional small piece of iron.

These travellers come back with stories too. They tell of mountains that are still capped with ice beneath the summer sun and that steal the air from your lungs when you walk across them, of distant seas that are as great as the plains and are crossed by men in fifty-oared

3

ships. And, sometimes, they speak of places where tens of thousands live crowded together in tents of stone.

The only city that the Massagetae understand is the one that comes and goes in the passing of a single day, when two tribes chance to meet at a good grazing ground. The foundations of the city are laid in moments: a forest of wooden poles, unrolled and joined together with twine, set in a series of circles. Then they are covered with white cloth, so that from a distance the circadian city seems more like a snowfield than a gathering of people. And if it threatens rain during the brief life of the city, it will suddenly change colour, as ten thousand brown horsehides are laid out on top of the tents.

All life is here, if only for a moment. A chanting circle marks a knife fight, two men settling a dispute over livestock or a woman. Children run free in feral mobs throughout the encampment, while all around them men and women drink and talk and argue and barter and make love. A trade pact will be struck, reach a profitable fruition and be broken in bad faith in a matter of hours. A man and a woman meet for the first time, conduct a forbidden courtship and elope from one tribe to another during one passage of the sun. All the life of a city year takes place in a single day and night. The next day, the city is gone, worn ground and horse tracks all that remain to suggest that thousands spent a night and lived a life in this place.

The plains stretch on, cityless, but by no means unchanging. Cutting through the plains in one place is a broad, deep river. The Hellenes called it the Jaxartes, the Persians knew it as Yakhsha Arta. The Massagetae saw no reason to give it a name. There were many smaller rivers, but this was the great barrier of the plains. It and rivers like it had divided kingdoms for thousands of years, until men learned to build boats and bridges, and discovered that one could rule beyond the natural markers of mountains and rivers, that there were no frontiers left, only temporary obstacles that could be washed aside with blood.

Approaching that river, on a warm, calm summer day, came a city of a different kind. The walking city of the Persian army.

Once it had been little larger than a town; a ragged band of archers and horsemen from many different tribes who had gathered together and overthrown the king of the Medes. Now, after twenty years on the march, swollen with tributes from a dozen kingdoms, it was more populous than the greatest cities of the world. Once, it had been filled only with warriors. Now, marching alongside the spearmen and the cavalry were the women held in common by the soldiers, and children dashed along the army's flanks, like scouts or outriders.

The army had been on the march for so long that there were young men who had been born, raised and now fought alongside their fathers, young women who had grown into their mothers' sad trade. Some said that this army might march on for generations, replacing soldiers and kings alike with those who were born within it. Perhaps it would still be marching long after Babylon and Sardis and Ecbatana had been conquered and forgotten.

It was a nomad city, marching from the south to tame a nomad people. Somewhere, deep within the plains, the Persians knew that an army was gathering to face them. They had merely to find it and destroy it, and these vast plains that had never seen a master would belong to them.

If you were to ride towards this army, amongst them, against them, like a fish that swims upstream, what would you see? To pass so freely, you would require some conferred immunity to this force that had broken cities and toppled empires. Let us say that you have a mark of the gods upon you, or you bear some diplomatic seal that even Cyrus of Persia, who has made the great kingdoms of Babylon and Lydia and Media bend to his will, must still recognize.

You would ride past the common spearmen bearing their tall wicker shields, the horsemen riding bareback with short bows across their shoulders. You would see a few bands of bronze-armoured

Ionians, the mercenaries who sang as they fought and never broke formation. In the midst of the ten thousand Immortals, the elite spearmen whose weapons are marked with gold and silver, you might catch sight of a man riding a tall white horse. Cyrus the Great, the king of Persia.

But your business is not with the king.

Riding further, past the last of the slingers and archers who trail behind the rest of the fighting men, past the concubines and children, you would see a second army following in the wake of the first. Here the slaves and servants, cloths tied over their mouths to ward off the clouds of dust kicked up by the army in front, drive cattle and carts loaded with grain and water and weaponry. As you glance over these ragged thousands, your eye might be caught by one man in particular, somewhere near the centre of this second army. He is the only one riding rather than walking, a distorted mirror image of the man on the white horse, appearing as a king amongst the slaves. But he rides a mule, not a warhorse, and wears the simple robes of a slave, not the bronze and gold armour of a ruler of men.

His hair and beard are silver touched with black, close cropped against skin that is deeply tanned. This man has passed six and a half decades on this earth in a world where few men live to see forty, and half that life has been spent walking and riding in the wake of one army or another beneath the heavy sun of the East. To survive so long as a slave would be remarkable, but he has not always been the property of another man. Once, hard as it was to believe, he had been one of the great kings of the West: Croesus, ruler of Sardis and Lydia, whose empire had stretched from the Ionian coast to the banks of the great Halys river.

You might try to find some remnant of the king in his bearing, but time has erased almost every trace of rulership from him. There is no hint of arrogance in the way he sits on his mule – he looks rather like a farmer leading his herd to market, constantly leaning down to plead and threaten and coax the stubborn beast forward. He has the hesitant eyes of a slave who must be careful what he does and does not see, and moves with the wary, small motions of one who seeks to remain unnoticed. Yet, from time to time, some ghostly gesture from his past returns to him — a kingly tilt of the head as he listens to the men who walk at his side, an imperiously raised hand to greet a distant companion. And when he lets his gaze drift over the plains, for a moment he still looks upon the world as one who seeks to possess it, reshape it. Then he drops his head and is once again the slave. A man who can change nothing, and who will be forgotten.

When they had almost reached the river, the air suddenly cleared of dust. They had come to a sudden halt, and Croesus reined in his mule, which was as reluctant now to stop as it had been to move forward a moment before. He wiped the sweat from his beard and brow, threw back his head and closed his eyes against the heat of the sun, enjoying a rare moment of peace and stillness.

He waited, and let the rumours pass down from the front of the column and flow over and about him like water. An omen had been seen, one slave said, a horse eating a snake, and the priests had ordered a halt to determine what it meant. Another insisted, more prosaically, that there had been a sighting of the Massagetae army across the river.

Up ahead, a distant flash of red cloth; the king's tent was being erected; it seemed they would be stopping for some time. Croesus saw a band of riders begin to work its way back along the flank of the army. He assumed that soon they would peel away, that they were scouts dispatched on reconnaissance, but they rode straight on, until they were amongst the carts and cattle of the supply train. As the horsemen drew closer, Croesus heard those around him begin to mutter to each other. He squinted and leaned forward, for his eyes were not as strong as they once had been. At last, he recognized the man who approached, flanked by bodyguards. It was the general of the army, Harpagus, and Croesus at once understood the fear of those around him.

'Do not worry,' Croesus said, as he nudged his mule forward once again. 'He is coming for me.'

2

They rode in silence for a time. Harpagus sat with the easy grace of a warrior who has spent more of his life on horseback than on his own feet, Croesus moving awkwardly on his bad-tempered steed. Harpagus gave no word or sign of what the summons might mean; his sharp-boned face was without expression, his eyes as blank as those of a dead man.

'So,' Croesus said, at last. 'What is it that the king wants from me?'

'The Massagetae have sent us a messenger.'

'From Tomyris?'

'Yes. That queen of a leaderless people,' said Harpagus. 'Their army is on the other side of the river.'

'It is time, then?'

'Yes,' Harpagus said. 'It is time.'

'You should not come back amongst the slaves and servants, you know.'

'What? Why not?'

'You make them nervous.'

'I do not make you nervous?'

'Not any more,' said Croesus. 'But they do not know you as I do.'

'Perhaps I shall send a messenger in future, to spare their delicate feelings. And yours.'

'Do not even send the messenger next time,' Croesus replied. 'I do not know if this is my hundredth, or thousandth, or ten thousandth counsel of war. I wish he would not command me to be at these meetings.'

Harpagus did not answer. Croesus looked at the general, and was surprised to find a crack in the blankness – a certain hesitance there.

'Harpagus?' Croesus said.

'The king did not ask for you,' the general said slowly.

'What?'

'He did not think he would need your advice. But I want you to be there.'

'Why?'

'The king is not himself.' Harpagus paused. 'Perhaps he will speak to you. You are the only one he talks to in that way.'

'In what way?'

'As though you are his wife.'

'He should have brought Cassandane with him,' said Croesus. 'He misses her.'

'That may be. You will have to do instead.'

They drew close to the king's tent, passing through the ranks of the Immortals, Cyrus's personal bodyguards. Croesus looked at them, trying to pick out men he recognized, to see the new faces there. Any who fell in battle were replaced before the next setting of the sun, and the Immortals had never gone into night with less than ten thousand standing in their ranks.

'That is an ugly beast,' the general said, looking at Croesus's mule.

'Stubborn too. Still, it makes me a prince amongst the servants and the slaves. You should hear them complain.' Croesus leaned forward and gave the mule a rare, affectionate scratch between the ears. It spat on the ground. 'It was kind of Cyrus to let me have him. A kindness to an old man.'

'He just wants to keep his property intact. His talking curiosity, a slave who was once a king.' He nodded at the mule. 'What do you call it anyway, your ugly little steed?'

'I call it Harpagus, of course.'

The general threw back his head, and gave a dry-throated chuckle. 'Very good. I like that.'

They drew up before the king's tent. It was a vast, many chambered structure, a palace on the plains. Even in all the years that he had served the king of Persia, Croesus had seen perhaps a quarter of its contents. Only the king knew all the secrets that it contained.

Croesus swung himself down from his mule, wincing at the cracking of his knees. He lifted the heavy cloth of the tent, and stepped through.

It took his eyes a moment to adjust from the glare of the sun to the dim reddish light inside. Within, gathered in a semi circle, he could see the men whose decisions controlled the fate of millions – the captain of the Immortals, a high priest of the Magi, the king's eldest son, Cambyses. On the far side of the tented chamber, a cushion serving as his throne, Cyrus, king of Persia and many other kingdoms, sat cross-legged on the ground, resting his chin on the palm of one hand, the other toying with the tassels of the carpet.

There were none who could say for certain how old this man was, who had broken the greatest kingdoms of the world to his will as a nomad will break a horse to ride. His face was ageless, the body still that of a young warrior, though Croesus believed him to have lived nearly half a century. It did not seem enough time to have done all the things that Cyrus had done. The world had never seen a king like him.

'Well,' Cyrus said. 'I suppose we can begin now.'

Croesus knelt and touched his forehead to the ground. 'My apologies, master.'

'Harpagus is the one who should apologize. But no matter.' The king gave an elegant wave of his hand. 'Sit down.'

Croesus found a place next to the king's son, Cambyses, the young man reluctantly shuffling aside to give him space to sit. Cyrus nodded to one of his bodyguards. 'Bring him in.'

The entrance parted again, and the messenger entered the tent, his hair pooling around his waist, a wolf-fur coat slung over his shoulders. An emissary from a different world.

The nomad gave a small nod to the king, then closed his eyes and began to repeat his message. 'I bring my words from Queen Tomyris of the Massagetae. King of Persia—'

'*Just* Persia; you note that?' Cyrus said, and the messenger fell into silence at the interruption. 'No mention of Babylon, the Medes, the Ionians. Or Lydia for that matter, Croesus.' He looked back to the Massagetae. 'Go on.'

'Rule your people, and try to bear the sight of me ruling mine. But of course, you will ignore my advice . . .'

'That much is true.'

'. . . for the last thing you want is to live in peace.'

Cyrus opened his mouth again, as if to deliver another retort. But he had no answer to this.

'Listen then,' the messenger continued. 'If you want to face the Massagetae, we will withdraw three days' march from the river and send you boats for the crossing, and we can settle things in the way you have become accustomed. Or, if you prefer, withdraw three days yourself, and let us meet on your side of the river. The choice is yours.'

There was silence for a moment.

'Very well,' Cyrus said. 'Leave us. My men will give you food and wine—'

'No wine,' the messenger said. 'Just water.'

'As you wish. You will have your response soon enough. Now go.'

Croesus watched the messenger walk away, his gait the strangely awkward one of a man whose legs and hips had shaped themselves to a horse's barrel chest from a lifetime in the saddle.

'What do you think?' the king said to his council, and it was Cambyses who spoke first.

'We can defeat them wherever we fight under your leadership,' the king's son said. 'Why worry about which side of the river the battle is held?' Cambyses smiled. 'You and I could fight them alone, Father, do you not think?'

Croesus could not help but wince at this. This council, which had fought and won a hundred battles without loss, approached war with respect to the gods and careful planning, not the empty promise of heroics. And Cambyses, feeling the quality of the silence and knowing that he had blundered, dropped his head and looked to the ground.

'Thank you, my son,' the king said slowly. 'Your bravery, it is commendable. Now, Harpagus? What were you going to say?'

'Let them come over to this side. When we defeat them, we shall drive them into the river.'

There were nods from the other men in the room. Cyrus looked to his slave. 'Croesus? What do you think?'

'I am not much of a strategist.'

'Surprise me. Give me some of that original thinking.'

'Very well. No one has mentioned the possibility that we might lose.'

The king did not reply for a time. 'Well,' Cyrus said at last, 'that *is* an original thought. We outnumber them. They fight with brass, we fight with iron. We will not lose.'

'But we could. It may be bad strategy to fight with your back against a river. But if we lose on that side of the river, your empire is protected. If we lose on this side, there's nothing to stop them from sweeping down through the northern kingdoms as well.'

Cyrus laughed. A hard-edged, mocking laugh that Croesus had never heard before. 'I asked for original thinking,' the king said. 'Not something that a child might say. We have fought the greatest armies in the world, and you think we will lose to these horsemen? That is the kind of thinking that lost you your own kingdom.' Now laughter broke around the tent, Cambyses loudest of all.

The king turned to Harpagus. 'We will bring them to our side, as you suggest. Give the word to the army—'

'Very well,' Croesus snapped. 'Let them say Cyrus the Great gave ground before a woman. If that is how you want to be remembered, so be it!'

Silence followed. The sharp silence that is a prelude to disaster.

'Out,' Cyrus said softly. 'All of you.'

The others filed slowly from the tent, and Croesus got to his feet, clasped his hands behind his back. He waited for the rebuke and the announcement of his punishment. But no words came. He lifted his head, and saw that the king was not looking at him, but was still sitting and staring listlessly into thin air.

On their last day in Babylon, before the long march to this northern frontier, Croesus remembered that he had been called to the king's chamber, and had found Cyrus arguing with one of his wives, Cassandane. Dark-eyed and beautiful, she spoke insistently, in some dialect that he did not understand. Whether she were trying to dissuade him from marching, or seeking some last gesture of love, he did not know.

The king had said nothing to her. Not a single word. It was only when he had turned away from his wife that Croesus had seen that Cyrus was not angry or sorrowful. He had been blank-eyed, as he was now. He seemed driven not by thought or desire, but by some irresistible compulsion.

'Why are we here, master?'

At last, Cyrus looked at him. 'There was a time when you would not have dared speak to me like that,' he said.

'Call it the privilege of age. A king's wrath is less intimidating to an old man.'

'You are angry at me?'

'You told me once that the wars were finished. That we would stay in Babylon. And now, we are here. I just want to know why.'

'I do not know, Croesus. I am sure there was a reason, once. But I have forgotten it. Perhaps we should not be here. I think that God has punished me for it.'

'Why, master?'

Cyrus bowed his head into his hands. The king had always had an energy to him that was almost tangible. Now, Croesus thought it was still there, but much diminished. It is possible to feel the cold more acutely in the presence of a dying fire than in front of no fire at all. That was how Croesus felt in front of Cyrus, like a man shivering in front of a failing fire.

'Another message came today,' the king said, his head still in his hands. 'From Babylon. I have told no one of it.'

'What does it say?'

Cyrus looked up at him, and his eyes were without hope. 'My wife is dying,' he said.

Croesus did not reply. Some of the king's wives had been taken for passion, some for diplomacy. Before he had marched the army north to the plains, he had even sent a proposal to Tomyris of the Massagetae, seeking to win her kingdom through marriage. But there was only one woman that he could be speaking of now.

'Cassandane has caught a fever,' the king said. 'The surgeons say that it will kill her. I love her, more than any of the others. More than I have ever loved anyone. I never said that to her. I thought I would have more time.'

'I am sure that she knows, master.'

Cyrus did not seem to hear him. 'I wonder if she is dead already,' he said. 'It has taken that rider many days to reach us. I think that she must be.'

'I am sorry, master.'

'Tell me what I should do. I know what to do when t'

against me. I've fought many battles that way. But I do not know what to do with the impossible.'

'You think that I do?' said Croesus.

'You were a great king once. Now you are a slave. For you to still be living is an impossibility. And yet here you are. I think you have found your way out of many impossibilities in your time.' Cyrus tried to smile, but there was no joy in it. 'What should I do?'

Croesus tried to remember his own wife. She had taken her life the day his city had fallen, the day he lost his freedom. The truth, he realized, was that he could not remember her, and he knew that this was the truth that Cyrus was not ready to hear – that he would forget Cassandane, would be glad to forget her and the pain of her. That he would be left with only an absent hollow, like a lake that has been lost with the passing of time and leaves nothing but a scattering of stones, the worn bones of fish that drowned in the air, to mark where it once was.

'Write to her,' he said. 'Think of all that you want to say to her, and write it down.'

'She will never live to read such a letter. What good can that do?'

'None. But write it anyway.'

Cyrus gave an almost imperceptible nod. 'I will. And I will think on what you said.' The king turned his head aside, and Croesus knew that he had been dismissed. He bowed deeply and left the tent, glad to go back into air, and light.

Back inside, the king sat still and alone in silence for a time. He beckoned to a servant to bring him a small table, clay and a stylus. When they were laid in front of him, he placed his hands on the clay and closed his eyes for a moment, like a man at prayer.

He opened them again, and began to write.

3

Near to the river, there was a point where the ground sloped up slightly. It could not be called a hill, but it was as close as the plains came to such a thing. It was from this point that a solitary nomad watched the Persian army.

The Massagetae feared the lone rider on the plains more than a marching army. It was the mark of a madman if he rode hard, driving his horse to death to run from the phantoms of his mind. If he rode hunched low on his saddle, he had been flogged and cast out of his tribe for some crime or betrayal. Either way, to ride alone was a death sentence for the nomads. No man could survive on the plains alone for long, and no other tribe would take in a rider with scars on his back or a madman's words falling from his tongue. They made an exception only for the mystic, who wanders between tribes the way a river meanders through the plains, belonging to all and none at the same time.

This lone rider was such a man; he had gone to the high place by the river to fast and meditate. Every few years, he would ride out from the tribe he had adopted to spend some time in contemplation; then he would wait and see what other home he could find, taking up with whatever tribe happened to come along first.

He had heard of the call to arms that Queen Tomyris had put out, summoning every warrior of the plains to gather together and resist the Persian advance. Such things held no interest for him. What was a man's attempt to carve up the land one way or another, when the Sun proclaimed his sole mastery at every dawn?

The army below might mean his death. Not through direct action; even if their scouts had come across him, a solitary man would be of no interest to them, his old horse not worth stealing. But they had driven away every tribe that might have given him shelter for ten *parasangs* in every direction. The plains were filled with the skeletons of holy men who had cast themselves into the sea of the steppe and had not found safe passage with another tribe. He might join them soon, yet he bore the army no grudge. If it was his time, it was his time. His dreaming life would be over, and his spirit would sink into the grasslands that he had made his home, would travel to the next world. As a mystic he knew what the afterlife looked like; he had seen it in his dreams. It was an endless plain, a mirror of this world. It held no fear for him.

He meditated and waited for several days, watching as a group of Massagetae boats arrived to meet the Persians, as the army gathered itself and prepared to cross the great river. On the third day, he saw that the dawn was the deep shade of red, the colour of omens, that told him it was time to move on. He would ride south with the sun at his left hand and see what his fate held for him.

Though the war between the Massagetae and the Persians did not matter to him, on a whim, the mystic decided to cast an augury before he rode out, more for practice than out of any genuine curiosity. He carved the sigils into the earth in blessing of the Sun, carefully wiping the blade free of dirt and muttering an apology to the god that he had no better sacrifice to offer. He took up the rabbit he had snared that day. It kicked weakly against the leather thongs that bound it, trying to squirm free of his hand. He knocked it between the ears with the butt of knife and opened its throat with the bronze blade. He let the blood soak into the marked earth, then opened its belly and spread its entrails cleanly.

Looking down into the red knots of flesh, he read the outcome of the battle that would soon be fought. He clucked his tongue in surprise at what he saw. Then he swung into the saddle and rode south, leaving the army to its destiny and going in search of his own.

Beside the river, Croesus watched the boats come from the other side, dozens of sturdy, simple craft made from bone and leather. He watched those Persians who had experience of river and sea come forward to check that the boats had not somehow been rigged to sink. One by one they disembarked, signalling to their companions that there was no trick. The captains moved back through the army, shouting and gesturing, trying to impose some kind of order, to move close to a hundred thousand people across the water.

Croesus looked away. Down near the river's edge, he saw a figure sitting by himself, tearing up clumps of rushes and throwing them into the fast-flowing water, a pair of bodyguards sitting a discreet way off.

When Croesus drew close enough for his footsteps to be heard, Cambyses turned his way. The young man leaned forward, blinked and stared, but it was not until Croesus was very near that the prince seemed to recognize him. His eyes were growing weak as the years passed, and already he had the frail vision of an old man three times his age. Cyrus had brought doctors and medicine men from countless different lands, but none of their treatments had worked. Croesus had heard rumours that Cyrus had sent emissaries as far as Egypt, hoping that their old knowledge could provide some kind of a cure. None spoke of it, but all feared that the prince would one day be blind. And a blind man could not rule.

'May I join you, my prince?'

Cambyses shrugged and turned back to the river. Croesus sat a respectful distance away.

'I am sorry that I laughed at you,' Cambyses said. 'Before, in my father's tent.'

'You never have to apologize to me, Cambyses.'

'I know. But I wanted to, anyway.' He tossed another piece of grass into the river. 'Anyway, he took your advice. I embarrassed him, and so he ignored what I said.'

'A whim of the king. A favour to an old man. It means nothing.'

'No,' Cambyses said. 'He did what you suggested because he respects you. He does not respect me. I disappoint him. That is true, is it not?'

'We all disappoint our fathers. But they forgive us.'

'I do not want to be forgiven.' Cambyses looked out across the river, at the plains. 'I hate this place,' he said, and Croesus wondered just what the other man could see of the plains, with his eyes as weak as they were. Perhaps in mountainous country he could still see the ridges and peaks, and near the sea he could hear the sound of the rolling waves. A city would be alive with sound and colour, and have its own appeal to the near-blind man. Out here, he saw only an empty world.

'I wish I was with my family,' the young man said.

'I understand. I miss my friends as well, master.'

'You have friends?'

Croesus almost laughed at the baldness of the question, but saw that Cambyses was quite serious. 'Yes, I do,' he said. 'Two slaves, like me. Hellenes, from the coast and the islands. Isocrates, and Maia.'

'Where are they now?'

'In Pasargadae. They are helping to build your father's palace there.' He thought for a moment, and smiled to himself. 'Isocrates will be organizing things as usual. He would have made a good king, if things had been different.'

'You have told him this?'

'Oh, no. He would be insulted if I did.' He paused. 'I do not know what Maia will be doing. But I am sure she will find some way to make herself useful.'

'You will see them again soon?'

'If the gods will it.'

'I hope I will see my mother as well. I miss her.'

'Yes,' Croesus said slowly. 'I hope you do.'

'Why did you come to me, Croesus?' Cambyses said. 'None of the others want to talk to me.'

'They do not presume to intrude on your time as I do, master.'

'No,' Cambyses said flatly. 'That is not it. Perhaps soon I will understand why they hate me.' Then the prince stood, and strode off without another word.

Croesus sat on the bank alone for a time. He thought of his own sons.

One he had buried long ago. The other, Gyges, a mute Croesus had mistaken for a madman, had been taken as a slave when Sardis fell. Many years later, in Babylon, Croesus had sent him away with a family of horse traders so that his son could be free of the city that threatened to drive him insane. Those who took Gyges in had been Massagetae.

Croesus had never thought that Cyrus's army would come this far. He imagined where his son might be, out somewhere in this vast plain. He had no fear that Gyges would be in the army that waited for them beyond the river. He had never done anything that he did not want to. You could no more hand a spear to him and expect him to use it than you could command a dog to eat grass. Perhaps, he thought, that was at the root of the boy's strangeness. What had been mistaken for madness was simple resolve to be who he was, not what he was commanded to be. He wondered whether his son still lived, what place he had found amongst the people of the plains.

Nearby, Croesus could hear a familiar voice calling out orders to his men. He looked over his shoulder and saw Harpagus stalking through the army, leaving shaken captains in his wake, orders ringing in their ears. Croesus waved to Harpagus, and the general looked at the slave with a sour twist in his mouth. He turned, gave one particularly barbed set of commands to the soldier who stood to attention close by, then wandered over to join the old slave on the banks of the channel.

'I see you are shirking your duties to stare at a river,' the general said.

'When I was a king,' said Croesus, 'there was a man in my court called Thales. He seemed to spend all his time staring at the sun and the moon and the stars, and they called him a philosopher for it. I have seen many great rivers in my life. The Pactolus, the Halys, the Euphrates. Now this one. Perhaps I could be a philosopher of the rivers. What do you think?'

'I hope you like crossing them as much as you seem to like staring at them. And I hope you are pleased that Cyrus has ignored my advice to indulge your fantasies.'

'I do not suppose that's what you had in mind when you took me to the council. My apologies.'

'No matter. We shall win either way.'

'I am sure you are right.' Croesus stretched his feet forward, and felt the cool water run over them. 'Why are you here, Harpagus?'

'I came to rescue you from the prince.'

'I needed no rescuing. I am fond of him.'

Harpagus raised an eyebrow.

'That is unworthy of you, Harpagus.'

'He is not a king yet. I wonder if he ever will be,' Harpagus said. 'What do you see in him?'

'Something of my sons, perhaps. I have buried one, and the other is lost to me. I miss them. You must forgive an old man his indulgences.'

'Oh, I shall try.'

They sat for a time on the bank of the river, two old men looking out on the running water.

'I have an interesting plan for when we get to the other side,' Harpagus said, breaking the silence.

'What kind of plan?'

'A trick for the Massagetae. You will like it. Risky, but inventive.'

'That does not sound like you.'

'Your bad influence on me,' Harpagus said. 'I can always say it was one of your daft ideas if it goes wrong.'

'How comforting.'

Harpagus stood, slapping the dust from his tunic. 'Come on. The boats are waiting.' He reached down and offered the slave a hand. 'You cross with me.'

Croesus took one last look at the river, then clasped the other man's hand, struggled to his feet, and made his way slowly towards the boats.

As he walked, motion caught his eye. He watched a single horseman ride down from the high point on the plains, travelling south. A lone traveller, he thought to himself, and paid it no mind.

4

At dawn the next day, a Persian detachment marched out from the encampment on the far side of the river. They hunted, not for water or meat, but for a particular kind of landscape. They did not look for a place to stage an ambush or fight a pitched battle. They looked for a place that would be tempting for other reasons. They looked for a place of beauty.

After some searching, they found a pleasant hollow beside a small river, a tributary of the great Yakhsha Arta. It was a spot where any seasoned rider would stop and water his horses, then be tempted to linger on, listening to the silvery sound of the shallow water, enjoying the sun on his face and the soft earth under his back.

They planted four high poles and strung a heavy cloth covering between them. There were clouds blowing in, and it would not do to have their trap made unappealing by the rain. In the dry space below they laid heavy cushions and unrolled thick carpets that were perfect for bare feet to dance on.

They laid out the gifts, chosen with care. Gold was worthless to the Massagetae. One of their most common metals, it was considered a poor, soft substitute for brass. They would have laughed at jewels as well, trinkets for women of no value to a warrior. Instead, the Persians offered iron daggers with intricately patterned bone handles, bronze spears and axes, light tents that held out the rain and were quick to put up or collapse. Fine treasures for nomads who valued only practicality.

They surrounded these with dozens of amphoras of wine, dark and unwatered. They placed skinned sheep carcasses above stacked wood and kindling, and waited for a north wind to blow. When it came, they lit the fires under the carcasses, watching the cooking smoke blow north, towards the Massagetae.

They should have waited all day and night with no success. The Massagetae, at the great conference of shepherds that had gathered their army together, had been warned against greed and told to be alert to the trickery of the Persians. But, by chance or by fate, a group rode within sight of the camp, and at their head was a captain who had his own reason for taking a foolish chance.

He gave a long, ululating war cry, and swung his band of horsemen back towards the trap.

As Croesus passed through the camp towards the king's tent the next morning, he noted, as was his habit, the mood of the men around him, the way a sailor would study the sky to glean a sense of the day ahead. He had learned to watch for the signs of trouble, the whispering talk, the silent man sitting alone, that spoke of illness or defeat. On this day, he saw spearmen smiling openly, small infractions of discipline going unpunished by the captains, people telling stories with animated motions of their hands. Whatever had happened in the night, it seemed the plan had gone well.

He reached the king's tent, but paused before he went in, stopped by a sound. He listened again, and from within the folds of the tent he recognized one of the many sounds of war that he had almost managed to forget. The soft clink of chains.

The prisoner was a young man, who sat hunched and dirty and miserable, in one corner of the tent. His hands and feet were bound together with iron chains, which moved and rattled as the prisoner lifted them up and stared at them. He stared at his bindings with such horror that Croesus wondered if the young man had seen such a thing before. Perhaps the rough justice of the plains had no use for such things, exile and the whip being sufficient punishment for all the crimes that a man could commit. Confinement was a horror that he had not dreamed of.

'Your trick worked, I take it?' he said to Harpagus.

'Their messenger gave me the idea, when he refused the wine,' said the general. 'Their people are not used to it.' He nodded towards the prisoner. 'We caught them sleeping off the drink.'

'And who is this?'

'The queen's son,' Cyrus said. 'He is called Spargapises.'

At the sound of his name, the one word he could have understood out of what was being said, Spargapises burst into tears and covered his face. Croesus looked away from the prisoner, and noted an absence in the tent.

'Where is Cambyses?' Croesus said to the king.

Cyrus hesitated. 'There are other things that I wanted him to do,' the king said slowly. 'There is no need for him to be here.'

You did not want him to see this, Croesus thought. 'What will you do with him?' he said aloud.

'Tomyris's messenger is back again. No doubt to bargain for the return of her son.'

'What will you do?'

'What do you think I should do?'

Croesus reached out a hand and leaned against one of the poles of the tent, feeling the grain of the wood against his palm as if it were a spear in his hand. He felt something akin to the warrior's weariness, a particular exhaustion born of fear and doubt. 'Keep her son as a hostage,' he said. 'Make peace with her. That is what I think you should do.'

The king's face was unreadable. 'Harpagus?' he said.

'It has been done before,' the general said slowly. 'But she will not surrender fully to you. Not even for her son. You may get a tribute, but that is all.'

'I do not know if I can be satisfied with that,' the king said, almost to himself. 'We have come a long way.'

'No one has ever won tribute from the Massagetae,' Croesus said. 'You could be the first.'

Cyrus fell silent and thought for a time. He looked at the prisoner, who stared mutely back at him, and then nodded to one of the guards.

When the Massagetae emissary entered, he did not bow, and spoke at once. 'I have a message from the queen.'

Cyrus inclined his head. 'You may speak.'

'Glutton as you are for blood,' the messenger said, 'you have no cause to be proud of this day's work. There was no soldier's courage here. Your weapon was the fruit of the vine. Give me back my son and leave my country, and be content with your little victory. If you refuse, I swear by the Sun to give you more blood than you can drink, for all your gluttony.'

There was silence in the tent, broken only by the quiet sobbing of the prisoner, the rattle of his chains.

'She certainly has courage,' Cyrus said at last. 'And a fine way with words. Tell her that her son will be safe if she offers me a yearly tribute, and will swear to a peaceful alliance with me. I will not seek to conquer her people. I do not ask her to prostrate herself before the king of Persia, but she must bend her knee a little.' Cyrus paused, and when he spoke again, there was a different quality to his speech. He spoke as a man, not as a king. 'Will she accept, do you think?'

The messenger hesitated, caught by the king's plain talk, and Croesus wondered if he had sons in the army. If he, like Croesus, confined by the inflexible demands of his ruler, was looking for some

27

way of making peace. 'I do not know,' he said. 'Perhaps. I will try.'

A voice spoke in a language that Croesus could not understand. Spargapises was speaking to the messenger in the tongue of the Massagetae, his palms open in supplication.

'What does he say?' the king said.

'He asks that his hands be freed, so that he can write a reply,' the messenger said.

'He can relay it through you, can he not?'

Hearing the objection in Cyrus's tone, Spargapises repeated his words.

'He wishes to write it,' the messenger said. 'To be sure his message is exact.'

'Very well,' said Cyrus. 'Why not? Free his hands.'

The guard unchained the young man's hands and handed him a wax tablet. Spargapises stared up at the messenger again, and the other man nodded to him. The prisoner gripped the sides of the table, in one sharp motion he brought his head down against the corner.

The snap seemed to fix every man in the room to his place. Every man, except Spargapises. He lifted his head from the table, his movements slow and clumsy, his eyes dull, already lifeless, as if he were already dead and moving by instinct, the way a bird with its head struck off will dance from the butcher's block. He brought his head down again.

His head came up, and in the stillness of the moment Croesus saw his face quite clearly, sheeted with blood, running with tears. A guard stirred at last, stepped forward and reached out a hand to stop the prisoner, but Spargapises brought his head down a third time, and Croesus heard a sound like a dry branch breaking.

No one spoke. Croesus stared at the ruined man, curled up in front of the table like a sacrifice before the altar, and watched the blood run out over the ground. This body would be the first. There would soon be thousands more to join it.

'I think you have your answer,' Cyrus said. 'You can expect us some time after dawn.'

'Very well.' The messenger bowed, and when he stood, he spoke again, offhand, the way one would give advice that had little consequence. 'My people cannot read or write. If you had studied us better, you would have known that. And you would not have let them unchain his hands.'

Cyrus stared at him levelly. 'I should have you killed for your part in this.'

'Perhaps you should. But you will not.'

'You knew what he would do?' Croesus said.

'Yes,' said the Massagetae. 'And I wish he had not done so. Perhaps we could have had a peace.'

'So why did you let him?'

The messenger paused. 'Who am I to get between a man and the death he chooses?' he said, and walked from the tent.

The guards stepped forward to take away the body, but Cyrus waved them back. He stared at the dead young man, his mouth slightly parted, and said nothing for a time.

Croesus exchanged a look with Harpagus. 'Master?' the slave said.

'He did it because he shamed his mother,' the king said eventually. 'Do you think Cambyses would do the same thing for me? That he would take his life, to save my honour?'

'I do not know.'

'That is a lie. He would not do it, would he?' said Cyrus. 'I miss speaking to you of things other than war. We used to, did we not? In Babylon, and before then as well. My tame philosopher. That is what Cassandane used to call you.'

Used to. Croesus saw that Harpagus had noted that. 'You flatter, master,' Croesus said. 'I'm not wise enough to have earned that name, even given in jest.'

Cyrus did not seem to hear him. 'After our war is done, we will go

29

to Pasargadae. Or back to Babylon. And we shall talk as a king and a philosopher. For the rest of our lives, perhaps, like something out of the old stories. What do you say?'

'I would like that,' Croesus said.

'Perhaps I will free you. I imagine your thinking is shackled as much as you are. I would like you to think freely with me.'

He will free me now that I am too old to run from him, Croesus thought. 'A generous offer, master, but not one that I have earned.' He ran his tongue over dry lips. 'We should leave you, master. Rest and sleep, Cyrus. Tomorrow, after the battle is won, we can go home.'

5

The army slept.

They were a city of men once more, their women and children left on the other side of the river. Some had tents, but most simply threw their blankets down on the ground, spoke for a time around dying campfires, and then let themselves drift into sleep. All feared the omen that might come in a dream, the gods whispering a man's death to him the day before it came.

The gods could not turn death aside from their favourites. They could merely give warning to those they loved. The greatest of warriors knew for decades when and how their deaths would come, and they could shape their lives around that end, fear no man in battle save the one they knew was destined to kill them. The ones the gods blessed only lightly, mere passing fancies to the divinities, knew of it just one night before.

These men lived in a world where death was commonplace; where men died in their thousands on the battlefield; where a fever could kill in a day and no one could tell you why. Yet this truth was known by all – some knew their death was coming days or hours before, some barely moments before the end. But there were few who could meet it well.

Perhaps none.

*

Sometime after midnight, many hours before dawn, Croesus woke to the sound of footsteps.

He had slept through the hundred pairs of feet that passed by his tent that night, as the sentries came and went, but this particular pair had woken him. After many years of conditioning, even his sleeping mind was able to pick out the distinct tread of a man heading straight towards him, of a guard coming to summon him to the king. He had, he supposed, had much practice.

And so, when the guard threw open the tent, Croesus was already sitting up and busy gathering his few possessions. He nodded to the guard and put a finger to his lips, and quietly, carefully, stepped over the other slaves and made his way out of the tent.

He had always slept alone when he was a king, and, at first, had been unable to sleep in a tent filled with the sounds and smells of half a dozen other men. Now the thought of being alone in the night terrified him, and he found himself quite afraid of waking without the comfortable warmth and sense of safety that their company provided. He wondered if the king had the same terror. As a boy, the stories said, Cyrus had been raised as common horse herder, and perhaps had never grown used to the lonely sleep of the king. Perhaps this was why he had fallen into the habit of summoning his slave in the middle of the night.

Sometimes Cyrus woke him for his advice in an emergency. At other times, it was to talk idly, or to share old stories. Sometimes he would be summoned to the king's side in order simply to sit in silence with him until dawn broke. Croesus often wondered if Cyrus woke anyone else in this way, though on reflection, he thought not. After all, he was the only member of the council who was an actual possession of the king.

He reached the great tent, and passed deep into it, to the chamber where the king slept, or did not sleep. A small fire burned in a tiny brazier, and by its light he could see the king, sitting upright in his blankets, staring straight ahead. He did not acknowledge his visitor.

'Where are your guards, Cyrus?'

'I sent them away.' In the darkness, Croesus could not read the king's eyes. 'I do not want anyone to hear this but you.'

'You can trust them with everything, Cyrus.'

'Not this.' Abruptly, he said: 'They say you had a true dream once, Croesus.'

'Yes.' He hesitated. 'I dreamed the death of my first-born son.'

'Did you know it? When you woke? That it was a prophecy?'

'I thought that I knew at once. I did not truly know until what I had seen came to pass.'

Cyrus said nothing, and Croesus came forward and sat on the ground beside him. 'Tell me your dream.'

'In my dream, I saw Cambyses standing over Babylon. He stood tall, like a giant or a god, towering over the city. On his back was a pair of huge black wings. Like a crow's wings, thick feathered and dripping oil. They stretched out, over the horizon in both directions. Even as large as he was in my dream, the weight of those wings should have broken his back. But he stood, tall and impossible, and he smiled at me.

'In an instant, I could see one wing dipped in the waters of the Aegean. Black oil seeped from those feathers into the sea around Phocaea. The fish floated on the surface and drowned in it. Then, in a moment, I could see the tip of the other wing. It rested, taunting me, in the main square of Pasargadae. My home. He had spread his wings over my whole empire. Then I woke.'

'Are you afraid, Cyrus?' said Croesus.

'Yes.'

Croesus thought on this. 'I have never seen you afraid,' he said.

'I have never had a dream like that before. Do you still dream, Croesus?

'I do not sleep much. I think my body knows it will die soon, and

33

wants to squeeze all the waking life it can from what time I have.'

'I do not sleep either. I suppose the happy sleep well. Not men like us.' He paused, lifted his hand and pressed his fingers against his eyelids. Perhaps some remnant of the dream was still embedded in his vision, and he sought to wipe it away. 'What do you think it means?'

'I do not know. I am not a seer.'

'What do you think I should do?'

'You should do nothing. If it is not a true dream, then it would be madness to act on it. If it is, then there is nothing you can do to stop it.'

'Perhaps it is a warning. A call for me to take action.'

'I do not think the gods have given us the power to change our fates. They decide, and there is no altering the course they have chosen. Sometimes they offer us a glimpse of our ruin, and they call that a kindness.'

'I cannot believe that. All my life I have been protected by the gods. Would they abandon me now?'

'The gods abandon us all eventually.'

'Enough. You will not speak in that way.'

'You want me to speak when you want, and to tell you what you want to hear. I think that that you have no intention of freeing me. That was just empty talk, I suppose?'

Cyrus closed his eyes and dropped his head. Croesus had never seen him look so tired. 'We should have stayed in Babylon,' the king said. 'Or we could have gone to Pasargadae. I have never even seen the palace there. It might not even exist, for all I know, except in my dreams.' Cyrus opened his eyes again and looked at his slave. 'You could not change prophecy. But perhaps I can. I am a greater king than you were, Croesus. You have forgotten that.'

'What will you do?'

Cyrus paused. 'I wish I knew how to be a better father for him. I have conquered more cities and peoples than I can remember. But

34

I do not know how to raise a son. A thing that the simplest man can do well, and I cannot master it.'

'I do not think that is true, master.'

'I am a better king than I am a father. You, I think, are a better father than you were a king. Will you promise me you will serve him as well as you have served me? That you will teach him how to be a king?'

'I am an old man, Cyrus. I will be dead long before you are.'

'Indulge a king. Promise me anyway.'

'Very well,' Croesus said. 'I can promise you that. I will serve him, and teach him, as best I can.'

'You must do something else for me.'

'Of course, master.'

'I want you to take my son,' the king said, 'and cross back over the river.'

'Tonight?' Croesus said.

'Yes. Get him away from here. Get yourself away from here too.'

Croesus felt a sudden fear, the kind of fear that he would have taken for an omen in other times. He wondered if there were aspects of the dream that Cyrus had not told him.

'I will,' he said. 'Good luck, Cyrus.'

'And to you,' the king said. Then he turned away and lay down, and curled up in his blankets like a child.

Croesus lifted a hand, almost touched the king on the shoulder. He tried to think whether or not, in all the years he had been a slave to Cyrus, they had ever exchanged a single fraternal touch. He did not think so. He wanted to offer him some simple piece of human comfort, but knew that he could not. The barrier remained between them, inviolable. Master and slave.

He leaned forward and cast a handful of sand out on to the fire. He stood and made his way from the tented chamber, back out into the night.

Cyrus stared at the wall of the tent, his eyes wide open, and made no attempt to return to sleep. He thought only of his dream.

It was an unnatural thing, to be out on the water at night, something only for skilled or foolish sailors. As the boat moved across the channel, Croesus thought of the stories of the Hellenes, of the crossing of the river of the dead, the meeting of the ferryman. He thought of drowning in darkness, then tried to turn his mind elsewhere.

Light glimmered off the shifting black water, as though the stars had fallen into the river or as if he were travelling across the night sky, the way the messengers of the gods were said to. He wondered if that was what Cambyses saw, with his faded view of the world.

The prince did not seem to share his fear of the river. He sat in the bow of the boat, leaning forward and easily keeping in balance with its shifting motions. Occasionally he dipped down to let his hand trail in the water, and Croesus fought the urge to reach forward and steady him.

'Why did he send us away?' said Cambyses. 'Have I done something wrong?'

'No, master.'

'Then why? Is it because you displeased him?'

'Now, that may be true. But the king wished for us to be safe. That is all. It is an honour for him to think of us so, don't you think?'

'It does not feel like an honour. Sneaking away in the night with a slave for company. I have disappointed him again, have I not?'

'No, master.'

'I have not deserved this. I wanted to see the battle.'

'I have seen more than enough battles, master. You will grow tired of them soon enough.'

'No. I do not think that is true,' Cambyses said. He smiled. 'I think I would like to see them for the rest of my life.'

Croesus prepared to speak again, to begin, he thought, weaning the young man away from such things. But when he looked at Cambyses's face he felt the words ebbing away. He tried to think of a dozen different ways of presenting his argument, but that face seemed to defeat them all without a single word being spoken.

The air suddenly grew lighter, and he saw the western shoreline drawing close ahead. The sun had risen behind them, and Croesus turned to face it. The Yakhsha Arta lit up under the glare, as though it had caught fire at the first touch of light. He thought he could hear the crying of the horns, the rattle of iron against bronze, the first screams, all echoing from the east. Faint, like the sounds from a memory, or a dream, but he was certain they were there.

The battle had begun.

6

Cyrus stooped on one knee. He could hear the sound of the battle being fought around him, could smell it, could even taste it. But he could not see. There was blood in his eyes. Slowly, carefully, his fingers shaking, he wiped and blinked the blood away. He lifted his head and looked around the battlefield, what little of it he could see from where he knelt. It took him only a moment to know that he was going to die.

He had long since learned that battles were not fought the way they were in stories. Fine swordplay was near useless, individual heroism a dangerous liability. For the most part, it was a matter of weight. One great mass of men pushing against another, searching for the angle of pressure that would shatter the opposing formation.

A single touch on the back of the man in front of you or to your side, connected you to the rest of the army, all the way up to those who struggled and died at the front line. With enough practice, you could read the course of the battle in that single touch, the way a rider feels the mind of his horse through the reins and against his knees.

The battle against the Massagetae had begun as a thousand battles had before. The careful, courteous advance of two armies in open ground, neither trying to gain a dishonest advantage. They drew closer, until the two front lines could see each other quite clearly, each man perhaps marking his opposite number, the warrior he would seek and kill when they closed. Then they stopped, and the barrage began.

The air had grown dark with arrows and stones and javelins. When supplies had been exhausted, the armies closed and grappled like two colossal wrestlers. Cyrus had dismounted, rested a hand on the man in front of him, and felt the changing tides of the distant battle.

Suddenly, the weight of the army had shifted. It happened impossibly fast, as though the laws of nature had been suspended, as if, for a moment, his forces had become entirely insubstantial. Faster than had ever happened before, the weight had collapsed backwards towards him.

He had had a moment to wonder if it was his fault, if his fear had spread through the army like an infection. Or perhaps, in the countless battles he had fought and won, his generalship had meant nothing. It was chance, or fate, all along. He had opened his mouth to issue an order, as if a few words of his could turn back the tide of men that was headed towards him. Then the wave of the Massagetae had broken over him, and he was lost beneath a screaming sea.

He had been submerged in the mob, with some unseen knee or hard piece of armour pressed into his chest and choking his lungs, his helmet pulled back and its strap cutting into his throat; he had thought that he would drown there. But he had fought his way out, more like a swimmer than a warrior. With no room to swing a blade, no room even to stand, he had worked his hips and shoulders against the bodies of the living and the dead, until he was born again at the edge of the mob, on his knees and without breath.

They had reached the point in battle where more men died from being trampled and crushed than from the weapons they carried, where survival depended less on skill and discipline, but simply on breathing through lungs scorched from exhaustion, standing on legs that ached to fall. You stood and lived, or fell and died.

Close to him, almost close enough to touch, were the Massagatae. They did not come forward, and he could hear them sobbing with exhaustion. If he could have found the strength to run, Cyrus could have escaped, but he did not. He did not have the strength to stand.

Tears flooded into his eyes for a moment, but he blinked them away. Someone might see him, he thought. One of the Massagetae, or one of his own men who might flee and survive the battle. They would know that Cyrus died on the ground, defeated. More than anything, he wanted to lie down. More than anything, he wanted to die against the earth, to escape into memory or dream in his last moments. But he would have to die on his feet.

With a gasping cry, he stood. He heard the horns of the Massagetae braying in victory, saw the warriors rallying themselves to stumble towards him and kill him with clumsy, exhausted hands. He lifted his useless sword high in the air, answering the call of the horns, and took a last step forward.

The Massagetae closed over him.

'Pasargadae.'

'Master?'

'That is what I will call it, Croesus. The capital of the empire. The home of Cyrus the Great.'

'Cyrus the Great?'

'That is what they call me, here in the streets of Babylon. What do you think?'

'Of the name? A little grandiose.'

'Of building a new city, Croesus.'

'I think it will be expensive.'

'Croesus of Lydia will lecture me on extravagance?'

'It would seem so.'

'Do you not think I have earned a home of my own?'

'You may do whatever you please, master.'

'Look here, on the map. There. That is where I will build it. A palace, surrounded by a great garden.'

'It is a fine vision, master.'

'It is more than a vision, I promise you.'

'You wish to live there?'

'For a time, perhaps. But I am not building it as a place to live.'

'A place to die? You are a little young to be planning your death, master.'

41

'I do not want to die at all. But when I do, I will die in a paradise. A paradise that I have made.'

'I will help you design this Pasargadae. But I hope you never see it.'

'Oh? And why is that?'

'Because it will always be perfect, then. One should never go to paradise, to see it fail.'

'You do not want to leave Babylon, do you?'

'No, master.'

'Why is that?'

'Because Babylon is my paradise.'

'And has it failed you?'

'Yes. But there is nowhere else that I wish to see.'

'I will build you a tomb here in Babylon, Croesus, if you will build me one in Pasargadae.'

'A pleasing symmetry. But why so much worry over a tomb?'

'It is how I will be remembered.'

'This is how I want to remember you. Here, in Babylon. A great king in the greatest city, dreaming of your paradise in the desert. You are a marvel, Cyrus.'

'You may keep your memory. I hope it serves you well. But a memory does not keep off the carrion birds. And it does not last for ever.'

'Neither does a tomb. But as you wish. When do we start our work?'

'Immediately. Are there any other messages from the empire?'

'A report from your scouts in the north.'

'The Massagetae have been raiding again?'

'Yes, master.'

'The nomads can wait. Let them keep their tents and horses. I have had enough of war, for now.'

'As you wish, master.'

'Come. Let us begin.'

A Garden of Paradise

I

The tomb was plainly built. Six steps led to four walls of white stone, unadorned but for a small inscription above the entrance. A simple tomb for the greatest of kings.

Looking at it, Croesus remembered what they said about Cyrus – abandoned at birth, raised by wandering cattle farmers, recognized as royalty. Who knew how much of the story was true? But if it was, Cyrus might have lived and died in a farmer's hut not much bigger than that tomb, if fate had not conspired to make him a king. Perhaps he would have been happier in that other life.

The first that Croesus had known of the defeat was some time after midday, when the first boats began to come back across the water. Panicked men came spilling out of them, speaking of disaster on the battlefield, of fighting a retreat back to water and crowding onto the boats. Croesus heard them say that was the worst time of all. Some men went mad as they waited, and threw themselves into the river to drown, choosing to die on their own terms, not willing to let fate decide.

Of all the men who they spoke to, none could say what had happened to the king. They waited until the last of the boats had crossed, but Cyrus was not with them. Harpagus was on the final boat, one arm hanging uselessly at his side – a parting gift from the

Massagetae. When Croesus saw the general, wounded and alone, he knew then that Cyrus must be dead.

The next day, a small band of cavalry crossed back over the river to search for the body of the king. The Massagetae had gone. The entire army had disappeared over the rolling plains, scattered back into tribes, their rare unity no longer needed now that the invaders had been destroyed. They had left behind a sea of Persian dead. There was not a single Massagetae left amongst them, their bodies taken away and burned or buried, whatever the nomad custom was. Looking at that battlefield, it was as though the Persian army, in a sudden act of madness, had fought only against itself.

It took them most of a day of searching to find the body of the king. The head had been cut off and left in a clay bowl filled with blood. When he heard this, Croesus remembered what the nomad messenger had said, that they would give the Persian king his fill of blood. That he would drown in it. It seemed that the nomads kept their promises.

Croesus looked around at the thousands of people who had flocked from the surrounding countryside to witness the burial of the king. He had not expected that. He had lived for so long in the closed world of the army and the court that he had forgotten the love the ordinary people had for Cyrus. The king had committed no massacres, had not forced the people he ruled to bend to his beliefs. The nations he conquered were almost unchanged by his passage. All he had demanded was tribute in gold and submission of the will. It had been an empire of peace. And yet the king had shown the world how an empire might be forged, and perhaps the generations who followed would not thank him for that. Who knew what empires would come after? What men would rule them?

A stirring of the crowd brought him back from his thoughts. The body had arrived.

Croesus watched as they carried the wrapped corpse up the steps to the entrance of the tomb. He could see the stains where some dark liquid had seeped out into the bandages, and when one of the bearers slipped, the package bent monstrously at an angle that no body could ever have managed.

We fool ourselves that we are remembered and live on in the minds of others, Croesus thought. Cyrus the king might live on for centuries, in song or in writing. Cyrus the man would be lost in one generation. He looked at the tomb, at the inscription carved above it, and it seemed an injustice that those words would outlive the man.

'What does it say?' a voice said behind him.

Croesus felt no urgency to reply. He enjoyed the sound of those words as he would let the taste of good wine linger on his tongue. There were few sounds as sweet as wine, he thought to himself. But the words of a friend from whom one has long been parted were one of them.

Croesus turned, pulled the other man close, and clasped his arms around him. He heard Isocrates laugh, then Croesus felt his friend's hands on his shoulders, gently pushing him away. 'This is a king's funeral,' said Isocrates. 'It is no place for slaves like us to be embracing.'

'Of course.' Croesus stepped back, wiping a finger across his eyes, and looked again on his friend.

He was almost as old as Croesus, but Isocrates carried his age better. He looked almost like a retired wrestler with his short legs and thick arms. His face was now creased with age, his small black eyes almost lost in skin, and he still wore his hair shaved close against the scalp, an old slaves' precaution against lice that Croesus had never been able to commit to.

'You did not answer my question,' Isocrates said. 'What does it say?'

'What?'

Isocrates tossed his head towards the tomb. 'The inscription, Croesus.'

47

Croesus looked back at the tomb, the deep letters cut into it. 'Whoever you are', he said slowly, 'and from wherever you have come, know I am Cyrus, who gave the Persians an empire. Begrudge me not, therefore, this monument, and the scant earth that covers my body.'

'Your work?'

'Yes. I helped a little with it,' said Croesus. 'Do you think they will remember him?'

'What?'

'Cyrus, I mean,' Croesus said. 'One day, another king from a distant land will come here. He will stop to water his horse at the river, and see the tomb. He will think of passing it by, but, on a curious whim, he will walk up those six steps and read the inscription. Do you think he will count it a marvel, to have come across the tomb of a great king? Or will he shake his head, and wonder what forgotten mad man lies there, claiming to be such a ruler? Will they laugh at him?'

'They will remember him.' Croesus felt a hesitant hand rest on his shoulder 'I am sorry, Croesus. I know you cared for him.'

'More than I should have done. It was one of the things you warned me against.'

'Did I say that? When?'

'"A slave loving his master is like a chair loving the man who sits in it." That is what you said to me when you were teaching me to be a slave.'

'You have a better memory than me,' Isocrates said. His eyes focused on something in the distance, behind Croesus. 'Will you love Cambyses in the same way?'

Croesus followed the other man's gaze, and saw Cambyses standing on the steps of the tomb. He was giving a speech of some kind, though Croesus was too far away to hear what was being said. The young man looked afraid, like someone playing at being a king. But we all play our parts, Croesus reminded himself. He has plenty of time to learn.

Cambyses finished his speech, and, as one, the watching crowd went to their knees and pressed their foreheads to the ground. Croesus did the same, and felt Isocrates kneel beside him. Then they stood, shaking the dirt from their clothes and wiping it from their foreheads.

'Will you love him?' Isocrates said again.

'I will try,' Croesus said. He yawned, and pinched his eyes.

'Go and rest. You will not be missed.'

'There is someone else I want to see first.'

'Oh? Who?'

'Your wife, of course. Where is she?' Croesus looked around. 'I would have thought that she would be here.'

'She is in paradise now, Croesus,' Isocrates said softly.

Croesus turned, startled. Isocrates looked back at him, blank faced for a moment. He raised an eyebrow, and smiled gently.

'The gardens, Croesus.'

Each nation has its own vision of paradise. Some say it is an infinite city, filled with the chattering souls of the dead. Others believe it to be a silent desert, where we travel ceaselessly in wordless bliss. For the Persians, it is a walled garden, filled with trees and running water.

When Cyrus had begun to plan the work at Pasargadae, he had wanted to conjure grass and trees from the pale, dry ground, to make his home in this world a paradise, a vision of the afterlife.

Croesus remembered the long hours into the night spent planning this place with the king, remembered Cyrus debating aesthetics and practicality with his architects, choosing the stone for the columns of the palace, sketching ideas for the gardens that would surround it. He should have known that this was where Maia would find her place. Many years before, he had wandered the gardens of Babylon with her, that perfect Persian garden built to appease a broken-hearted princess

49

who missed her home. Maia had looked at that place with the eye of a craftsman, mapping the layout and noting the principles of design and irrigation. Once, she had baked bread, watched over royal children, tended to the mad. Now, she was a gardener.

He wandered the orderly paths, moving under the shade of cypress and pomegranate trees, and found that a part of him did not want to find her, would be content to be searching in this place for ever. Perhaps the Persian vision of paradise included this sensation, that of searching for a friend on a warm day in a garden, listening to the running water of the canals and fountains.

He found her standing in front of a row of box trees, working on one with steady, thoughtful motions of her hands, cutting it back to some aesthetic principle that he did not understand. He watched her, without making himself known.

She had been his slave once, she and Isocrates both. He had paid her little enough attention when he had been a king – she had not been amongst the beautiful ones who caught the eye. Hard working, and plain faced, she had been just another slave of the palace. He had not thought that she would mean anything to him, back then.

After he had watched her for a time, she stood straight, her greying hair falling back over her shoulders. She moved slowly, for she was growing old too, he realized. Without turning towards him, she said: 'I know you are there.' She looked over her shoulder, and he saw that she was smiling. 'You are never as stealthy as you think you are. Even back in Sardis, I always knew when you were lurking.'

'My apologies.'

'Do not apologize.'

She knelt down and patted the grass next to her.

'I saw Isocrates,' Croesus said as he sat down. 'He said I would find you here.'

'He missed you, you know. He will not say it, but he did.'

'And you?'

She rolled her eyes. 'Sleepless nights. Weeping and wailing. That kind of thing.'

'I suppose I asked for that.'

'Of course I missed you. Does that please you?'

'It does,' he said. 'You know that they buried Cyrus today?'

'Yes, I know. It was his time, I suppose.'

'No. I do not think it was.' Croesus looked around the gardens, at the play of early evening light on the water and through the leaves. 'He should have grown old here. Just as I should have died a much younger man. Before I ruined my life.'

'Well, I am glad you did. Ruin your life, I mean.'

'You are?'

'Of course. Otherwise you would not be sitting with me now.' She laughed, but he did not join her. 'I know you counted him as a friend,' she said.

'Isocrates said the same thing. He did not seem troubled by Cyrus's death. You are not either, I think?'

She shook her head.

'One king is much the same as another to you?'

'You were different, Croesus.'

'How so?'

'You were a good king, but you never quite looked as though you belonged there. I think you belong with us.'

'I suppose you mean that kindly.'

'Of course. Kings are the worst of all people.' She paused. 'What is Cambyses like?'

'Intelligent. Anxious. Uncertain. He is still like a child. And I have forgotten what it is to teach a child.'

She said nothing, and Croesus immediately regretted what he had said. She had never been able to have children. He reached down to the ground, felt the long rushes beneath his hand, like the hair of a lover. He let the silence grow past the point of pain, until it had

51

become something healing instead.

'Are you happy, Maia?' he said, sometime later.

'Oh, I do not think of things like that. It is good to work on something that you will not live to see finished. It is a bit like raising a child, I suppose, tending my gardens.'

'Your gardens?'

'You might say that they belong to the king. But I think a garden belongs to those who look after it. I tend them, so they are mine.'

'I envy you. I wish I could say the same thing.'

'I'll teach you, if you like. You see this branch—'

He waved her into silence. 'I am a little old to start learning.'

'We must teach you other things, it seems,' she said. 'Come back here tonight.'

'Why?'

'Oh, that is a secret.'

'Cambyses will be acclaimed as king tonight. I must be there.'

'No one will miss an old slave like you. Least of all the king.'

'Very well. Where do I meet you?'

'Just come back here, after dark. You will find us easily enough.'

He stood up, one hand staying down low, ready to pluck a few rushes up to toy with on his walk back to the palace. She gave him a look of gentle rebuke, and his hand came back up empty, the fingers spread wide in apology. She turned back to her work.

He remembered, a long time ago, when he had granted Isocrates a kingly boon, a favour to his favourite slave. Isocrates had asked for a wife, for Maia. He had not understood then what lay behind the slave's desire, and he did not know now. In all the years that the three of them had been slaves together, the mystery of their marriage, whether it was lust or alliance or companionship or something else entirely, was one that he had not unravelled.

He watched her for a moment longer, then turned away, and went to lose himself in the gardens once again.

2

That night, Pasargadae was a sea of fire.

All throughout the grounds of the palace and the gardens, there was row upon row of torches, their spiked ends driven into the earth, each one standing as tall as a man. An army many hundreds strong, standing rigidly at attention and raising a flickering salute to their commander. In the sky, there was no moon to give a competing light, merely an absence. A new moon for the new king.

There was only one place that the light did not touch, a black hollow shape on the raised ground overlooking the palace: the tomb of Cyrus, watching from the shadows to see another king born into the world.

On the steps of the palace, Cambyses stood alone. Two steps beneath were the priests of the Magi, a step beneath them the body-guards, and beyond that, standing in rows a dozen deep, were the noble families of the Medes and Persians. Beyond them all, by the farthest rank of torches, Croesus watched the ceremony unfold.

It was not yet time. Croesus did not understand the ritual, but he knew that there would be no blessing until the priests of the Magi allowed it. He watched as the Magi consulted charts marked on clay tablets, looked up and waited for some co-ordination of stars above, for the spinning sky to lock into place.

They waited in silence, and there was no restlessness in the crowd, just patience, and trust in the gods. The only sounds were the uneven crackle of the torches, and the occasional, angry lowing of the great white bull who was tied to a pillar near by, the creature sounding his irritation at the crowd and the rope that held him, ignorant of how close he was to death.

Then the moment came. Far above, some ancient star reached the right position, and a priest threw his hand up in the air. As one, the crowd flinched as though struck, a wave of sharp energy passing though it, the collective will being surrendered to the new master. In spite of himself, and all the rituals he had lived to see, Croesus shivered at the power of it. He could remember, dimly, what it was to be the focus of such an event.

He heard a great bellowing cry. The bull, its throat cut, stumbled to its knees and then to the ground, the thick blood running out over the ground like slow waves. As the bull's cries faded and died away, it was replaced by the words of the priests. He listened to the Magi speaking, pronouncing what fate they had read in the stars for the new king.

He looked around, over the faces of the crowd, and saw that no one was looking at him. All eyes were on the king, and he knew that it was safe for him to slip away.

He made his way back out, moving quickly and softly like a thief. He left the palace behind, walking down the long, wide path to the gardens between the rows of torches. Flanked by so many sources of light, they cast his shadow in eight different ways at once. He imagined each shadow as some other version of himself who had taken a different path, a different life, and wondered which of them had chosen better than he had in this world.

There was light ahead. Not the controlled single points of the torches, but something larger and wilder, filtering through the leaves, along with the smell of smoke, the roar of fire.

Deep within the gardens, he saw the campfire burning. Shapes of men and women moved around it, silhouettes at first, flat like shadows cast against the wall of a cave, but it did not take long for him to pick out the broad shoulders of Isocrates, Maia's distinctive profile.

There were others there as well, men and women that Croesus did not know. Friends of Isocrates and Maia, he supposed, slaves and servants from many different nations, brought together far from their homes to serve the court of Persia. Isocrates moved amongst them, dispensing the occasional word in the ear or touch on the shoulder as if he were the patriarch of a great tribe, keeping the peace amongst his followers. That is what he should have been, Croesus thought. Isocrates would not have wanted to be a king or a general, for it was not his way to command his inferiors. But to lead his equals, that was something he could do.

When Croesus reached the edge of the light, Isocrates saw him and beckoned him forward. They all turned to face him, rose to greet him as though he were a king once again. He looked at the fire and meat and wine, and realized that it had been prepared for him, that they had saved or stolen what wine they could, and sneaked away from their duties to welcome him home.

He bowed his head, and a moment later felt arms wrap around him. He could not tell if it was Maia or Isocrates who had greeted him so. Perhaps both of them. He kept his eyes closed against his tears, and let those same arms guide him to the ground.

When he had breathed away his tears, he opened his eyes to look at the preparations going on around him. One of the men – Croesus supposed him to be one of the kitchen slaves – attended to the cooking meat. A brace of small creatures turned on a spit over the fire; birds brought down by a sling stone, or rodents snared in the garden. It was probably best, Croesus thought, that he did not know what it was. He watched it turn and brown, listened to the drops of fat hissing in the fire. The others watched with him, all silent with respect for the gift.

55

When it was ready, they cut the meat into pieces. Before they touched any for themselves, Isocrates wrapped the fat around the tiny thigh bones, small enough to be held between a thumb and two fingers, and made an offering to the gods in the way of his people. Then the meat was divided equally, wrapped in leaves and passed around the circle. Croesus ate the thin slices, and broke off chunks of flatbread when it was passed to him. He drank the wine, and wondered when he might taste it again. Perhaps never, and so each time he raised the skin to his mouth, he tried to remember everything about it. The heavy weight of it as it rested on his tongue, the slow, easing warmth that passed through him with each sip and swallow.

He waited for someone to speak. Occasionally one of them would hum or sing some small fragment of an old song or a poem, but for the most part they sat in silence.

The fire began to die down. One by one, the others began to stand up and leave, until only Maia, Isocrates and he were left. He waited for them to stand, to leave him to sit and think beside the fire alone, but they made no move to go.

Isocrates yawned, sudden and broad mouthed like a cat, and Maia laughed at him. Croesus watched as the other man rested his head on his wife's shoulder, and he felt an unfamiliar surge of longing for his own wife, decades dead and buried half a world away.

Perhaps understanding this, Maia waved a hand at him, gesturing for him to come closer to them. When he hesitated, Isocrates grunted irritably. He leaned forward, grabbed Croesus by his shoulder, and pulled him close until they sat side by side.

They lay down together, kept warm by the heat of the dying fire. Isocrates lay on his left and Maia on his right, the way a husband and wife will hold a child between them, lulling it to sleep, and he smiled at the thought. Perhaps they thought of him as a child they had raised, and could be proud of. They had taught him to be a slave, and he had lived to grow old. Slaves have no money or children, no way of measuring the value of their lives as others do. If they live, and are in favour, they have done well.

Tomorrow would be another day of service to a new king, but that did not seem to matter. He did not think he would live to see another night like this, but that seemed to matter even less. He crooked one arm beneath his head and looked up at the sky. He let himself drift, slowly, towards his dreams.

Standing on the palace steps, Cambyses could not see the faces of the people who had come to offer their allegiance, the gestures of the priests or the face of the bull as it died for him. He saw only a mass of light and shadow and shape, like some dream half forgotten.

He closed his eyes tight and opened them again, though he knew it would do no good. He could not stop himself from hoping that one day he would see the same world as everyone else, that the secret sickness that was taking his sight from him could be blinked away like tears.

But it did not matter that he could not see, and that he knew only vaguely what was required of him. Occasionally one priest or another would lean forward to whisper in his ear, to tell him what it was he had to do, what old words to speak or gestures to perform. For the most part, the ritual proceeded around him, without him. They wanted a king, that was all. They did not care what he thought, so long as he did not disturb the ritual.

Beyond those closest to him, the mass of guards and priests blended together. He tried not to look at them, for crowds had always frightened him. Because he was unable to pick individuals out, they congealed together in a sinister mass, a monster with many faces. He tried to push his fear aside, and looked for Croesus.

If he could look on that face, have him near, he felt that he could be brave. The old man had loved his father, and Cambyses had inherited that love; he'd found it second-hand, but he would use it, twist it and keep it for himself. He knew that he was not a man to whom love was given freely. He had to beg and steal it where he could, because there was something wrong with him.

If Croesus were here, then he would know what to do, what to say. Where was he? Cambyses wanted to call to him, but knew he could not. What would they think of him, a king crying out for a slave?

He thought of his father. A great king, an impossible man to follow. He looked towards where he knew his father's tomb was, the shadow on the hill. He felt his father's eyes on him, disappointed even in death. Disappointed, because he knew that Cambyses did not want to be king.

The thought had been hiding in some corner of his mind for a long time, but it was a thing that Cambyses had never been able to admit to himself until now, when it was too late. Perhaps it would have changed everything, if he had said this before. He could have passed the throne to his brother, and lived his life in peace.

Now there could be no escape. Who could imagine a king putting aside his crown? The divine succession would shatter, the ties of belief that held the empire together would come apart. No matter what he did or said, they would not let him step aside. He would be a king until he died. To say that he did not want to be king was to invite death.

He thought of the course the conspiracy would take, when they knew of his weakness. The plotting in the corners of the palace, first whispered in coded secrecy, then spoken of almost openly. His guards bribed, his courtiers turned against him. He saw the daggers and garrottes coming to find him in the night, the poison in the food, heard the tread of impostors mounting the steps to take his throne.

He would know beforehand. That would be the worst part of all: that he would know for days or weeks or months that his death was coming, that the conspiracy had advanced too far for him to stop it, that even if he were to kill one or a dozen or a hundred or a thousand, the mind of the people had turned against him; that the killing stroke would find him eventually, and all he could do was fight to delay it. He felt the panic rising in his body, like a shaking sickness, and knew that, now he was a king, he was truly alone. And he always would be.

There could be no question of trust. Not even of Croesus. He must never let anyone know he was afraid, must not even think it. He could imagine no worse thing than being condemned to death, than living knowing that others were planning your end, and he promised himself that he would never let it happen.

The priest's voice rose in one last high chant, the watching crowd raised their hands to the watching stars. It was finished, and he was a king.

Unheard over the roar of the crowd, Cambyses gave the smallest gasp, the kind of sound a man makes on first hearing of the death of another. One small breath filled with pain.

He closed his weak eyes tight for the space of three heartbeats, listening to the syncopated rhythm of his heart, tried to find some comfort there. He opened his eyes again, and looked out on a new world, one that had, from that moment, changed for ever. A world that he did not want. A world that belonged to him.

3

A king lives by ritual. It is what marks him out from other men.

The coronation was only the first of many. The next morning, in the great, high-columned audience chamber of Pasargadae, Croesus watched the presentation of the gifts. Emissaries from distant lands, members of the noble families of Persia – all came, one by one, to offer the rarest of treasures to the new king.

Croesus recognized many of the gifts, for once they had belonged to him. When he had been a king he had assembled the greatest collection of rare antiquities in the world. Since they had been taken from his treasuries two decades ago, they had passed from one man to another to buy favour or forgiveness for a slight. Now they had been brought to Cambyses, for him to distribute in turn when he needed to buy favour himself. The treasures had become symbols of the shifting allegiances that stretched across the empire, and whatever inherent beauty they had was long forgotten.

One visitor from a distant land presented an enormous emerald, and Croesus remembered every side and cut of the gem – he had handled it many times before, as he thought of embedding it into a piece of jewellery for his wife. Another brought a sword from Troy, a city fallen eight centuries earlier. Croesus recognized the handle from the time it had spent in his own treasury, but saw that the blade had been broken by a careless owner, reforged and weathered to give the illusion of age. It was a skilled forgery; Croesus was the only man who could have told the difference. Then again, perhaps the blade that he had known had simply been another imitation.

After the gifts were taken away, the throne room fell quiet. The time had come for another ritual.

The king's brother entered the chamber. As with many brothers, they had an uncanny almost-resemblance, like looking into a reflection in a fast-running stream, a mirrored distortion that never seemed to settle. Bardiya's shoulders were broader than his brother's, he stood a little shorter, but their faces could easily have been mistaken for one another.

Bardiya came forward alone, a step too close to the king, and did not bow – a small gesture of treason, a justification for what was to follow. Cambyses held out a hand, and took the sword that was passed to him. Its handle was patterned with gold, its cutting edge rounded away. An empty weapon of ritual. The king laid the blunted blade against his brother's throat, and held it there a moment. He drew it across the neck, and Bardiya dropped to one knee, bowed his head and spread his arms wide, his fingers to the sky. He held that pose for a moment – an image of utter submission, a mimicry of death. Then he looked up, and smiled at his brother.

Cambyses cast the sword aside, laughed and clapped his hands. He beckoned his brother to his feet, to come forward. They embraced, and gentle applause passed through the court. There had been a time when all brothers of a king would have to die, when the ambitions of men could not be trusted, when kingdoms were too fragile to allow even the possibility of a filial contender for the throne. Such brutal practices had fallen away, leaving merely the ghost of a ritual behind it.

Then it was time for Parmida, the king's sister, to submit to her ruler. She was no danger, no rival who would have to go through a ritual death – it was only through marriage to the wrong man that she could become a weapon laid at the king's throat. She simply came forward and offered her hand to the king. He kissed it, and looked at her with such honest affection that Croesus felt some of his fears recede. He watched as she took her place at the king's left hand, Bardiya at his right.

Croesus looked at that new king, sitting hunched on the throne and leaning forward to try to see those who came before him more clearly. He watched, like a nervous father, to see how the new king would rule. He tried, above all, not to think of Cyrus's dream.

'Let us begin,' said Cambyses.

At the very end of the day, when the courtiers were yawning openly and Croesus was fighting to keep his eyes open, one last visitor came into the audience chamber. He was not an emissary nor a general, a satrap nor a priest. He was a physician. The small, black-robed Egyptian slowly made his way up the length of the audience chamber. Clay pots clinked together at his waist, the bare essentials of his trade, and at the entrance to the audience hall, Croesus could see a small cart piled up with wicker baskets of herbs and bones and ointments. The man bowed, and greeted the king. His name was Chephren.

Later, Croesus would learn that the Egyptian had come expecting to meet Cyrus. It was the previous king who had summoned him, and in the many months it had taken him to travel from Egypt to Persia, the physician had not heard of the death of the king. Only an intervention at the last moment from an astute courtier prevented the Egyptian from making a dangerous blunder in court. They would not always be so successful. For months after, the court would receive emissaries and messengers who came responding to commands and delivering messages for Cyrus, as if his spectre haunted the throne, refusing to accept the succession.

The Egyptian introduced himself — a practised speech in which a recitation of his years of study were mixed with spells and blessings from the thousand gods of Egypt. Cambyses listened to this, in patient incomprehension, and when Chephren had finished, he said simply, 'Why have you come here?'

The man bowed again. 'Great king, your father asked me to come. I am a physician of many talents.' The Egyptian paused. 'But above all, I am an oculist. A doctor of eyes.'

A shiver passed through the king, and the court went still.

Cambyses stood up from the throne and hurried down to the floor of the audience chamber, tripping slightly on the lowest step. The king stopped in front of the Egyptian, still leaning forward slightly to give his dying eyes what advantage he could, and stared into the other man's face, the way one would examine a horse that one wanted to buy, to look at its teeth and coat and the muscles of its flanks. Cambyses judged the colour of the iris, the clear whites, the way the pupil contracted to the light and moved and tracked any motion near by. He wanted to see proof of the man's art written on his eyes.

Then the king reached out — the unsteady hand of a child afraid it will fall.

'Can you make me see?' he said. 'I am afraid to be blind.' His voice cracked slightly. 'Do not let me become blind. Will you help me?'

The Egyptian gave one long blink, his only sign of any surprise at the king's question. Then he clasped Cambyses's hand, the simple touch that he had no doubt given countless times before to the sick, the dying. 'Yes,' the oculist said. 'I will make you see.'

Cambyses smiled shyly. He turned his back and waved a hand to dismiss his guest, then sat down, and continued with the business of the court as if nothing strange had happened. The Egyptian went quietly from the throne room, and Croesus watched him go.

*

At the end of the day, as he made his way back towards the slaves' quarters, Croesus heard a pair of footsteps following him. The quick, steady tread of a man eager for company, yet too proud to run.

'What did you think?' Harpagus said, when he had caught up with the old slave.

'He did well,' Croesus said. 'He seems content to ask for help. That is good.'

'He did not call on me.'

'Harpagus—'

'It matters not. He has young men now to tell him what to do. They are the ones he wants to listen to. What young king wants old men like us to advise them? Except for you, of course. He still looks to you to tell him what to do. I cannot think why.'

'I suppose he is sentimental.'

Harpagus laughed. 'Yes. He overflows with sentiment.' He paused. 'Did you enjoy your little feast in the gardens last night?'

'You know about that,' said Croesus. 'I should have known there would be no secrets from you.'

'Oh, I do not have as many spies as I once did. They report to other men now. But I still know some things. Do not worry. You shall not be punished.'

'How kind of you.'

'It is no kindness. I need you to keep an eye on that Egyptian fraud for me.'

'Chephren? What harm can he do?'

'You saw how Cambyses fawned on him. He will have noted that well. He will do whatever it takes to become the king's favourite pet.'

'He should be careful. Royal pets do not tend to last.'

'What about you? You have lived a long life.'

There was a tone to the old general's voice that was unfamiliar. The usual barbs rounded out by something else. Perhaps even sadness.

'I wish Cyrus were still alive,' Croesus said. 'That he had lived to see this place. You do as well, I think.'

Harpagus nodded.

'I think sometimes that it is my fault,' Croesus said.

'That is not true.'

'It was my suggestion that we fight on that side of the river. I goaded him into it.'

'Did you ever know Cyrus to be goaded into anything? We would have lost wherever we fought. The gods willed it, and it was so.'

'I heard that you rallied the army and led the retreat,' Croesus said.

'Is that what they say?'

'Some would call it heroic.'

'The poets do not sing of heroics on the side of those who lost,' Harpagus said. 'And they are right not to. There is no valour in fighting a losing cause.'

'I cannot agree with that.'

'Of course not, Croesus. Still a dreamer after all these years?'

'You say I seem content,' Croesus said. 'You do not.'

'No. You are right.'

'Why?'

Harpagus looked at him, and for a moment there was a hint of the old life in his eyes. Then it was gone. 'Because I know I will die soon,' he said. And before Croesus could think of a reply, the general turned and walked away, with the slow, careful steps of an old man, his ruined arm swinging at his side.

4

What did the Egyptian do to the king? Rumours passed through the court, but no one could say for certain. All knew that the king and the oculist met twice a day, at sunrise and sunset, and no one else was allowed to be present. Some said the treatment was a spiritual one, involving sigils carved into clay tablets, demons and spirits and gods invoked in prayer, without a hand being laid on the divine body of the king. Others claimed it was robustly, ghastly physical, that honeyed needles were inserted into the jelly of the king's eye, that it was removed entirely and left dangling from a knotted cord of flesh, cut open and stitched together at the back where the scars would not show.

Croesus did not know if there was true healing or magic in what the man did, or whether the Egyptian merely believed so strongly that he could make Cambyses believe too, and heal him with that faith. Whichever it was, the king appeared to see better. His eyes troubled him less, and he began to sit back relaxed in the throne, not hunched forward like a man desperate to witness everything.

One morning, some months after the king had taken the throne, Croesus was summoned to his chamber before dawn. He assumed that he would have to wait, but no sooner had he taken his position outside, leaning down and trying to rub the stiffness from his knees, than he heard a voice calling to him from within.

66

'Come in, Croesus.'

The king's chamber had a startling, deliberate brightness. Dozens of torches gave the air a heavy, exhausting heat, and they were surrounded by polished stones to magnify the light. Croesus, by instinct, raised a hand to cover his eyes. Perhaps this was the deliberate double purpose – to part blind those who came inside, and to give the king's fading eyes as much light as possible.

Croesus saw that the chamber was decorated almost entirely in different shades of yellow. The walls were a rich gold, the table patterned with stripes of wildflower yellow, the bedding dyed a jaundiced hue. Perhaps that was the colour that Cambyses saw most clearly. The last colour he would see, if his vision went from him entirely.

Cambyses sat in a wooden chair at the centre of the chamber, his head tipped back against a cushion. The Egyptian oculist stood beside the king, preparing some liquid in a clay pot, stirring it with his fingers. His lips were moving, but Croesus could only pick out one word spoken again and again. Sekhmet, Sekhmet, Sekhmet. Some god or spirit of healing.

When his preparations were finished, the Egyptian lifted the bowl, and slowly, one drop at a time, poured a viscous black and gold liquid into the king's eyes. It sat, thick and heavy, like oil on water, brimming against his eyelids.

The liquid piled higher and higher until it was running down the king's face in slow, viscous tears. A sickly, poisonous sweetness drifted through the air, and Croesus had to fight the urge to run forward, to push the Egyptian to the ground and wipe the king's eyes clean. Cambyses endured it, his fingers scratching at the chair, and the cords on his neck standing up, straining like a ship's ropes in a tempest.

At last, the king could stand it no longer. He gave a groan of pain, and in a moment the oculist was reaching forward with a piece of white silk, cleaning the thick fluid away. He handed the king a cup of wine, resting a reassuring, intimate hand on his shoulder. 'Much better, my king. Soon you will be able to withstand it for even longer. Then my work can truly begin.'

Cambyses nodded absently, blinking the remnants of the substance from his eyes, stared at the ground and breathed deeply, like a man recovering from a trial of strength. The Egyptian bowed to him, gathered his bowls and phials and left.

'Croesus, I will need your help soon.'

'How can I serve, master?' But the king said nothing for a time. He made a gesture, and a servant parted the pale yellow curtains. Croesus looked out, and saw that under the low light of the morning sun, the dusty plains that surrounded Pasargadae shone like a sea of gold.

'Chephren tells me wonderful stories, you know,' Cambyses said. 'Of his home. Of Egypt. A place where all things are reversed – whatever we believe, they believe the opposite. Like something in a dream.'

'A remarkable place, master.' Croesus hesitated, a sudden fear picking at his mind. 'Is it your wish to go there?'

'Of course not. It is a place of the dead, and here we are in paradise. A paradise that my father made. What more could I want than that?' He paused. 'But I lie. There is something that I want.'

'What is that, master?'

'He has told me another story, as well. The king of Egypt—'

'The Pharaoh, master.'

'Quite right. His name is Amasis. And he has one daughter. Nitetis.' Cambyses smiled shyly. 'My doctor says she is the most beautiful woman in the world. I will send an emissary to the Pharaoh, and he will send his daughter to be my wife. I will bring the best of Egypt to me. Is that not wonderful?'

There was a quiet need in his voice, and Croesus thought once again of his own children. The way the world could turn on their

desires, the way they had the capacity to want, and to love, so deeply.
'Of course, master. Tell me what I can do.'

After he had been sent away, Croesus thought little of this meeting.
In the months since he had taken the throne, Cambyses had formed
many such plans, each one born in the morning, reaching fruition by
midday, only to be discarded by nightfall once the king had grown
bored with it. Wars that he would fight, great temples he would build,
innovations of science, problems of philosophy – all had fascinated
Cambyses at one time or another.

It was the ideas themselves that seemed to delight him, the magic
of possibility. Carrying them through to fulfilment held little appeal,
would be murderous to the imagination. Better to hold all of these
possibilities in the mind at once, a selection of possible worlds, than
to choose one and obliterate the rest.

The next day, as Croesus helped the king prepare his message to
the Pharaoh, he wondered how long it would take before the king
discarded the idea. The long months of messages going back and
forth would give plenty of time for the king to hesitate, to doubt, and
to let the plan fall to pieces.

Yet Cambyses persisted, more patiently and stubbornly than
Croesus had ever seen him work at any task of kingship. He overcame
the Pharaoh's diplomatic evasions and delays, offering a tempting
alliance accompanied by the implicit threat of violence. Croesus sometimes wondered what stories Chephren had told the king, what tales
he continued to tell to keep Cambyses so interested in a woman he
had never seen. But these were idle thoughts, of no real concern.
It was the nature of kings, he reminded himself, to indulge strange
fancies. What else was there to do, with no threat to fight against? And
so Croesus watched and waited as the marriage was finally agreed,
as word came that the Pharaoh's daughter had taken to her ship and

was coming at last to Pasargadae, and he did not speak a word against the plan.

The day of the wedding came, and Croesus saw that she was beautiful as the stories said. Her eyes were darkly outlined, and her skin painted in the Egyptian fashion. Cambyses stared at her, eyes gaping wide, and Croesus smiled at the sight. One would have thought he had never seen a woman before.

When it was over, when the people cried out in celebration and the drums began to beat, Croesus saw, before the king and his wife disappeared from the chamber, a first moment of intimacy pass between them. He saw Cambyses shyly reach out and take his wife's hand.

Later, Croesus would return to this moment. He would look back on it and try to remember if there had been any warning there, the sense that a mistake had been made, that disaster would follow. But in that moment, looking at Cambyses he could only feel a weary content, the way he had felt when his own son had taken a wife.

He watched Cambyses disappear with his wife, a new life about to begin.

When they came at last to his bedchamber, Cambyses let his wife go in before him. He hoped that she misread it as a kind of courtesy, rather than what it truly was.

Nitetis entered the room, her movements as confident and easy as his were hesitant. She wandered from one corner to the next, giving little touches to the fabrics and the walls, perhaps her way of marking it as a new home. He looked at the interplay of the fine muscles of her back and shoulders, and felt the ache of desire. Yet he did not move.

She stood still for a moment, almost at the centre of the room, her back to him. He felt a vain, foolish hope that she might stay that way for ever, that she would never turn around. But when she did not feel the king's hands on her back and lips on her neck as she had perhaps anticipated, Nitetis turned around and stared at him. Waiting. Expectant.

Under that gaze, Cambyses felt a slow shame binding around his heart.

He had never been with a woman. As a young prince, many had been offered to him. Time and time again, Cyrus had selected one of his most beautiful courtesans and sent her to his son. Cambyses had taken these women to his chamber or his tent, sat silently beside them for a time, then sent them away again. They, puzzled and grateful, never told anyone of this.

Had he ever been asked why he did not act as a man should, he did not know what he would have said. It was not that he longed for a man, the way he heard some did. He desired women, and yet he found they terrified him. They demanded some kind of action, an invasion that he was afraid of. More than this it was their fear of him, which they tried to hide but which he could always sense, that silenced any desire he might have felt. He wanted to be desired honestly and truly, but this, it seemed, was impossible for a prince, who saw only concubines and slaves. He had never met a woman who looked at him with longing.

He now regretted the painful brightness of his private chamber, that left no shadow for retreat. He should have taken her to a labyrinth for their wedding night, where they could have chased each other until dawn without once meeting, always divided by a stone wall, an impossible sequence of turns. But there was to be no hiding from this.

He had accomplished so much as a king through pretence, acting the part that was given to him and hoping that none would expose his fraud. He would stay one step ahead of them all for the rest of his life, and never let them know how afraid he was. But this was not something he could overcome through trickery or false confidence. The simplest of acts, and he did not know what to do, could not act

71

as a man should. They shared no language, and even if they had, how could he possibly explain this aberration? She would laugh at him if she knew. He felt the tears come, and bowed his head in shame.

He felt gentle hands on his shoulders. They moved to his chin, tipping his head up. He shook his head, his eyes still closed. Then, for the very first time, he felt a woman's lips against his.

He stood still, then found the courage to answer her kiss. He found that he understood, that the knowledge of this waited in his body, had been waiting a long time. He felt that this was something that he could learn. That he was not broken. That he might come to understand what it was to love.

He opened his eyes, and looked at her face. Before, he had not come close enough to truly see her. Now he saw that she was as beautiful as they had all said.

She smiled at him, and took his hand in hers. Another man would have wondered at her confidence, her knowledge of an art that should have been forbidden to her. Cambyses never thought to question it. He was only grateful that, at last, this part of his life could begin.

He closed his eyes again, and let her take him to the bed.

5

'Croesus.'

A woman's voice that he did not know called to him from behind. He wondered at first if it was the king's wife, for he had yet to hear the Egyptian speak. But when he turned to see who had followed him in the corridors of the palace, it was the king's sister, Parmida, her servants trailing her like the wake of a ship.

He began to bow, but she lifted her palms, gesturing for him to stay upright. 'There is no need for such ceremony,' she said.

'Many thanks, my lady. You are kind to an old man, and his aching limbs.'

'Oh, I do not think that is true. You seem to be strong enough. I think you may outlive us all.'

'You are kind to say so. What may I do for you?'

She hesitated, looking up and down the corridor.

'Perhaps you would extend your kindness further,' Croesus said, 'and permit me to sit down somewhere? That is, if you can forgive a slave for asking such a favour.'

'Yes,' she said, 'of course,' and her eyes thanked him.

She led him to a private chamber, thick with throws and cushioned seats, where they would be overheard by none but her personal slaves.

He knew that she need have no fear of them. They had no ears to hear unless she willed it.

She turned back to him, and her smile had gone. 'Will you dine with us, tonight?' she said. 'At the king's table?'

'I will do whatever you command.'

'It is not my command. It is my wish.'

'I obey those too, my lady. Though rather more gladly.'

At this, she seemed to relax a little. She looked away, through the stone pillars and out towards the gardens, lost in her own thoughts for a time.

'Is my brother a good king?' she said.

Croesus thought on this for a time. He wondered if there was anyone else to whom she could have asked such a question. Any other man of the court would have passed her some platitude, any younger slave would know better than to answer at all. This is what I am to these people, he thought. Someone to whom they can speak without fear, like an ailing grandfather whose mind is starting to drift away, or a wandering holy fool.

'I do not know that I can answer that,' he said.

'I think, sometimes, that . . .' She trailed off. Even the king's sister had to be careful not to speak treason.

'Do not be afraid,' Croesus said. 'Your father built a great empire from nothing. Now we must merely tend to it.' He spread his hands wide and gestured outside. 'Like a garden.'

'Yes. You are right, of course. You will help him?'

'I promised your father that I would help him. We will both help him.'

'I hope so.'

In spite of her words, she still seemed afraid. This was what Pasargadae has become, Croesus thought to himself. A palace filled with frightened children.

'You seem sad, my lady.'

74

'I miss my father,' she said simply. 'My mother too.'

Croesus said nothing. He remembered thinking that he would go mad with the grief when his own mother and father had died. Now he could not even remember what it had been like to live with such certainty of love.

'It passes,' he said eventually, 'though I suppose it is little comfort for me to say it now. You will build your own family soon, your own life. And the pain will pass.'

'I think that you are wise, as people say.'

'They still say that? Well, I suppose that all old men are wise in one way or another. We try our best to remain foolish, but I suppose some knowledge grows over time. Like skin healing over a stubborn wound. I am glad to be of use.'

'Thank you, Croesus.' And, to his great surprise, she reached out and took his hands in hers. 'I will see you tonight.' Then she stood, and was gone in a moment.

What happened after that meeting, whether he spent the day running errands at the king's service, waiting patiently to be called upon, or dozing at leisure in some quiet corner of the palace, he could not afterwards remember. He would have thought, would have hoped, that he might recall how it had passed, that last day of peace. Instead he let it slip away, unnoticed and unremarkable, until the evening came.

There was no light in the king's dining chamber. No windows to grant the setting sun admission, only a pair of tiny braziers as a bare concession to those, unlike the king, who still lived through sight. From time to time, someone's words or breath or motion would dismiss the light of one of these little fires. A stillness would descend, none wanting to eliminate the last source of light, none feeling they could act to repair the flame. At last, the long-fingered hand of the king would emerge from the darkness, take a burning taper from one brazier and relight the other, and all could move and speak a little more easily again. Croesus did not know what desire of the king led him to seek blinding light in his private chambers, and darkness for when he dined. But he knew better than to question such a whim.

At the entrance, Croesus closed his eyes, and tried to hear as the king would hear, to know who was gathered around the table that night solely through the interplay of voices. Above the rattle of bowls and silver cups, he could hear the sharp, abrupt tone of the king's voice, the softer echo of his brother Bardiya's. Then two voices together, one after the other: the king's wife Nitetis, speaking in her native tongue, and the translator who spoke half a beat behind her. Once or twice he thought he could hear Harpagus speaking, but he could not be certain. There were others in the darkness whose voices he did not know well enough to place.

He entered, stepping into a small patch of light by the doorway, and bowed. He heard the voices fall silent.

The king leaned forward into the sparse light. 'A slave at the king's table?' he said.

'It is my request,' Croesus heard Parmida say, and was glad to know that she was there.

'If it is your request then it must be done. Sit, Croesus. Sit with us.'

He felt his way with the backs of his hands, the edges of his feet, not willing to risk touching his betters with his fingers or his palms. After only a moment of this hesitant fumbling, he felt a servant's hand close around his shoulders and lead him to his place. His guide moved so confidently that Croesus imagined that he must have lived his entire life in darkness. Perhaps they raised slaves for this very purpose, born in some blackened chamber, raised in shadows, serving at a midnight table until he found his way, stumbling and old, into a dark grave, never once permitted the dangerous luxury of light.

At first, Croesus sat quite still, listening to the others talk. They spoke in ebbs and flows, for there were many who sought the cover of other conversations to speak a little more freely. There would be near silence for a time, then a great flood of words, everyone talking over each other. After a time, one conversation would pause and halt, then another, and then all the rest, exposed by the quiet, would recede back into silence. Only Cambyses spoke when and how he willed it, and it was in one of these sudden silences that Croesus could hear the king being pressed by his brother on some point of governance.

'You say that we must send grain to the Ionians?' he heard the king say.

'There is no "must" for you, my king. But I suggest that you do. Their harvests have been ruined by the floods,' Bardiya replied. 'We should act now, if we are to assist them.'

'Even so . . . I think perhaps I will not.' The king's voice had the beginnings of finality. 'I am not so fond of charity.'

A pause. 'They will starve, Cambyses,' Bardiya said softly.

'They will starve?'

'Yes, my lord.'

There was a stillness. Cambyses leaned forward into the light again, trying to imagine this, to conceive of a world where one could die for want of food. A world so very different from his own.

The king let his blank gaze rest upon the table in front of him, as if in the whorls and cracks of the wood he could imagine a land of flooded fields and rotten crops, could see starving children looking to their mothers in silence, too weak to cry out for them. Then the king gave a little shrug. When he spoke again, Croesus knew that though he had tried, his imagination had failed him. This idea was beyond him.

'Very well,' the king said. 'If you say that it should be done, then let it be done.'

'Your people will be thankful.'

'I do not act for them. I do it for you,' Cambyses said with a simple honesty that would brook no argument. He sat back in the darkness, and Croesus heard a rustle of cloth, the sound of hands clasping. 'This family means all to me. Parmida, Bardiya. And now Nitetis.' He paused, and Croesus heard the translator speak this words in the Egyptian tongue. Silence followed his words, and Cambyses laughed. 'I have embarrassed you, perhaps,' he said. 'Come, let us eat.'

The meal came, those same confident hands bringing strong wine, and strange meats that he could not identify. Croesus could not help remembering the stories he had heard, of men being fed their children under the cover of darkness, in the most brutal, blasphemous act of revenge. He had no relations left, but the thought would not leave him, and he found he had little appetite.

'We were speaking of the peace of the empire, before you came, Croesus,' the king said.

'There is no trouble on our borders?'

'No. All is quiet.'

'That is well. A tribute to your fine rule, master.'

'Perhaps.' The king leaned back in his chair, into the shadows, and Croesus heard him sigh. 'I sometimes wish for more to do.'

'You have lands enough, don't you think?'

'No.' The word came out of the darkness flatly. 'There must always be more. Is that not what makes a people great? What makes a king great? My father, what made him great?'

Silence fell again. Cambyses took up one of the braziers, and held it close to his face, looked at each of the people at the table in turn. None could hold his gaze. He reached out and took his wife's hand, kneaded it with an insistent, possessive kind of affection.

'Croesus.'

'Yes, master?'

'My father. He liked to tell a story about you. I want you to tell it to me yourself.'

78

'I am not much of a storyteller, master.'

'I do not believe it. How many years have you lived?'

'I have lived for almost seventy years, master.'

The king laughed. 'I did not know that men could grow so old. I thought that only trees and rocks and seas could live such a span. There is some touch of the gods on you, some blessing. Or perhaps a curse, do you think?'

'I do not know, master.'

'You must have plenty to talk about. Tell this story.'

'Of your father?'

'No, I do not wish to hear of him. Tell me of Solon.'

Croesus felt a cold touch on his heart, the touch that the gods are supposed to give in warning or prophecy, as he thought of that Athenian philosopher. It had been almost half a life ago that he had spoken with Solon. It was a different man who had lived then, with a face that resembled his and a name that they shared, but little else in common. He had forgotten most of that life. But this story was something that he could not forget.

'Your father spoke to you of Solon?'

'I was raised on that story. He gave it to me at night, as though giving me some treasure of the mind. A gift, though I never understood why he placed such value on it, why he told it to me again and again. He wanted to teach me something, but I never understood the lesson. Perhaps if you tell it to me, I may understand it better.'

Croesus looked around, as if looking for help. But all the others at the table withdrew silently into the shadows and waited for him to begin.

'There is little to tell,' he said. 'When I was a king—'

'As wealthy and powerful as me?'

'Of course not, master.' More so, he thought to himself. 'None who have come before can compare to you, but I was well regarded in my own time. A philosopher came to my court. Accounted a wise man, so

I had been told. He was certainly an old man. Perhaps even as old as I am now.' Croesus paused. He had not thought of this before.

'Well?'

'We spoke for a time, and I asked him who was the happiest man he had ever met. He did not say me.' Croesus let his gaze drift to the fire closest to him, his eyes following its wandering, flickering flames. He spoke again. 'He told me that no man was happy until he was dead. That a whole life is what matters, not the contentment of a moment. That when you see a man die, and know what he has done with all his time, that is the time to decide whether he lived well or not, whether one could call him happy. I thought I was happy, thought him a fool, and sent him away. You know yourself what happened to me next.' Croesus paused. 'I think now that he meant happiness does not exist.'

There was silence when he stopped. Croesus, still lost in memory, did not attend to the quality of this silence. There are many kinds of wordlessness that can follow the telling of a story. That of respect, or of confusion. Or of fear. At last, when the silence did not pass, Croesus lifted his eyes and looked at the king. He understood then why the others did not speak.

Cambyses was hunched forward like a man in pain, so that his face hovered over the two braziers, illuminated by the fire. His palms were flat upon the table, his weak eyes half closed. His teeth were bared, and the look on his face was that of a man at some great and terrible act of labour, the effort of thought physically rendered.

For a moment, Croesus thought that he might be on the brink of some kind of understanding. A moment when an imagined world opened before him, where he could see some idea that was beyond himself. Then the world closed shut. The grimace went from his face, and the king relaxed, sank back into his chair. Not with a satisfied air, but with the weary, resigned posture of a man who has fought and been defeated.

'No,' the king said, the sound of his voice almost like regret. 'I still do not understand. I do not think it means anything.'

'A foolish story, master. Pay it no mind.'

Cambyses looked at him, and in those weak eyes Croesus saw something that he had never seen there before. Distrust. The way a man will look on another whom he suspects is cheating him, although he cannot prove it. He felt that he should speak, should find some way of countering the suspicion with a flattering word, but, caught in that gaze, found that he could not.

A new shadow entered the room, standing in the entrance and giving a soft clap of his hands to make himself known. The king freed Croesus from his gaze to address the newcomer.

'What do you want?'

'A visitor has come, and requests an urgent audience with you. A Hellene, named Phanes.'

Cambyses shook his head. 'Who is this man?'

'I have heard of him.' It was Harpagus who spoke. 'A mercenary general, now in service to the Egyptian Pharaoh.'

'And? What message does he bring from Egypt?'

'He requests a meeting with you in private.'

'He seeks to interrupt me now? Take his message and get out.'

'He says that he has urgent words for you, and you alone. Vital to your honour, and your safety. He says you may have him put to death if, after he has spoken, you consider his words of no importance.'

The king said nothing for a time. Croesus wondered which word it was that had caught his attention – honour, or safety. 'We shall see about that,' Cambyses said at last. 'But, very well.' He shoved his plate forward. 'I have no appetite left.' He waved a hand absently, the gesture encompassing the whole table. 'Leave me. All of you.'

Croesus rose, and immediately felt hands on his back, those same careful servants coming forward out of the darkness to guide the guests away. Under the cover of scraping chairs and moving feet,

Croesus permitted himself a sigh of relief, heard it echoed by many of the others as they went. He was grateful for the chance to slip away.

He saw almost none of the others as they left the dark chamber, guided by the servants. But, passing into light for a moment, he saw Nitetis hurry past him, her face pale, her eyes alive with fear, before she disappeared into the darkness and out into the palace. So brief had been the sight, so strange and powerful the fear on her face, that he assumed he had imagined it.

6

Cambyses sat quite still, in that too-bright chamber that was his private room. He thought about what Phanes had told him. He wished he were still in the dining chamber, where a retreat into darkness would have been possible, where his foolishness would not be so exposed. In his mind, he turned the words over, first one way, and then another, looking for some way out. There was none.

He looked up at Phanes, the hard-faced general who stood before him, seeking some sign of deception. Cambyses did not think he had many talents, but he had always been able to see through a lie. Perhaps in his heart, Cambyses thought, he had always known it to be true.

'You may leave,' Cambyses said. He paused. 'I wish you had not told me what you have. But I suppose I must thank you for it. You will be well rewarded.'

If the king had seen the barest hint of a smile on the general's face, he would have had him put to death that instant. Perhaps he would not have been able to wait for the executioner, and would have taken the man's life with his own hands. But Phanes gave no such sign. Cambyses knew he would have to watch for that mockery, once the news had spread. He would spend his whole life looking for that trace of a smile, the hand that covered the beginnings of laughter.

Phanes bowed and left, and once he had gone, Cambyses allowed himself to cry.

After a time, when the hollowing sobs had eased a little, he told his bodyguards to leave him. He did so without raising his head – one hand still pressed to his eyes, the other pointing, stabbing at the door with two fingers.

The half dozen men glanced at one another. It was dangerous to leave Cambyses in such distress. They knew the suicide of a king would always be disbelieved, for such a death did not make sense. How could a king ever wish to die? What sadness could such a man of wealth and power possibly know? They would be blamed as assassins and put to death by whoever claimed the throne. Such things had happened many times before, and so they looked at their king, trying to find in him some desperate trace of the suicide. Then they looked to each other again, and in a conference of gazes reached some silent, mutual conclusion. They filed slowly from the room.

Cambyses crossed his arms and grasped his own shoulders, embracing himself. He began to rock gently back and forth, as though he were parent and weeping child all in one, and hoped to somehow lull himself to sleep.

There was no shame so complete as that of a king, he thought. An ordinary man may be tricked and fooled a hundred times in his life, make a thousand mistakes that he cannot repair, and yet none remember, and he may go to his death forgotten. But the foolishness of a king, that lasted for ever. For as long as they spoke his name, they would remember this humiliation.

He reached up his hands and extended his fingers towards his face. After a moment's hesitation, he moved them closer still, pushed the points of the nails past the film of tears to rest on the surface of his eyes. He could feel every nick of the nails acutely, felt the unevenly cut edge of his left forefinger almost catching on the jelly of the eye. He sat quite still for a time, enjoying the closeness of it. A few pounds of pressure, a moment of pain, and his ruined eyes would be taken from him. He would no longer have to look on the world that hated him.

But no, he thought. Not yet. There was something else that he would do first.

In another part of the palace, Harpagus sat awake at his table.

The hour was late, but he had no intention of retiring to bed. He slept little, for dreams were no comfort to him. In them, he saw Cyrus disappearing into the Massagetae hoards, heard the screams of a son and wife forty years dead. So instead of sleep, he lit a fire, sat at his table, and read and wrote the night away.

He had lived his life amidst these papers. It was an indulgence in a world where to write was the rare mark of a learned man, and to have paper enough to write on at leisure the mark of a wealthy one. When he had entered the service of Cyrus, the Persian king had offered him a world of riches, the finest satrapies to rule, whatever reward he wanted. He had chosen paper, ink, a good horse and a good sword. In his years as a general to the Persian kings he had sought to reduce the world to paper and wax, a world that he could understand and control. Or that is what he had once believed. Now, he felt control slipping away from him. No matter how hard he worked, there was always more to do. His mind was growing old, or else the world had grown more complex. There must have been a time when he could have held all of it in paper, when it could be captured entirely. When a man could know everything that could be known. That time had passed, though, perhaps many years before. No one could ever understand the world now. No one ever would again.

His senses were not what they once had been, and it was some time before he noticed that someone had entered the chamber silently, the way the gods of the Hellenes were said to carve instant forms from the shadows and air. He looked up, and saw a young man of the court whom he recognized but could not name. One of the many eager young men who had replaced him at the side of the Persian king.

'Why are you here?' Harpagus said.

'The king would like to speak to you.'

There was silence. Harpagus stared at his visitor, and that careful, blank face looked back at him.

'I see.' Harpagus felt his hands begin to shake, and put them on his lap beneath the table to hide them. 'I do not think speaking is what he has in mind. Am I right?'

The other man did not reply.

'What is your name?' Harpagus said.

'Prexaspes.'

'Prexaspes. I know why you have come.'

'You have had word?'

'No. You have no traitors selling secrets. You have done your work well, and caught me with no warning.' Harpagus looked away. 'But I knew that, sooner or later, it would come to this. I suppose that I am surprised it took him this long.'

Outside the chamber he heard the familiar sound that had followed him all his life, the martial sound of metal against leather. 'You could have come alone,' Harpagus said. 'Are you so afraid of an old man?'

'Everyone is afraid of Harpagus. The terrible general, the scourge of Ionia.'

'Do you mock me?'

'No. You were a great man, in your day.'

'In my day I was a killer of men. That is how they will remember me, is it not?'

'Yes.'

'It is too late to regret that.' Harpagus paused for a moment. 'I have done nothing.'

'Are you begging for your life?'

'Hardly. I thought you might be curious, that is all. It is not something that you forget, when you kill an innocent man.'

'It does not matter. He believes you to be guilty. Eventually, you will tell him what he wants to hear.'

'Yes. I suppose I will.' With the admission, he felt his hands stop shaking, and he knew that he was not afraid any more.

He placed his hands on top of the table, felt the parchment like leaves beneath his fingers. A world was here in the abstract, in letters and numbers, but he wished he could make it come to life before him, like some magician from the old stories. To see mountains, and feel the sea washing over him. To walk through the streets of Ecbatana one last time. There was so much else that he should have done, he thought. I have wasted my life.

He looked up at Prexaspes. 'He will come for you one of these days, you know. That is the fate of men like you and me. We do the worst of things for our kings. One day they look on us with fear, remembering what we have done in their name. Then they cast us aside.'

'Perhaps.' Prexaspes shrugged. 'But I will live for a time as a great man.'

'Take care of your family, will you? A king took mine from me, many years ago. He will take yours from you, if you anger him.'

'I will keep them safe,' Prexaspes said. He glanced at where a sword hung on the wall. 'Perhaps I should leave you alone for a moment,' he said.

Harpagus looked at the sword as well, the blade hacked and notched from countless battles fought for the Persian kings, its point and edge still keen. 'No. I thank you for the courtesy. But no.'

'You should. It will be . . .' Prexaspes hesitated, and fell silent.

Harpagus felt his mouth twitch at the other man's hesitance, the barest trace of a smile. 'You will need a harder heart than that, for the work you have ahead.'

87

'I am sure I will learn.' Prexaspes lifted his chin, looked proudly at the other man. 'You should accept my offer. It will not be a good death, that the king will give you.'

'Yes, I know. But I would like to know how I can meet that death. I do not suppose I will meet it well. I have yet to see a man who can. But I would like to try. Perhaps that will be enough.'

'As you wish.' Prexaspes gestured towards the chamber door, like a man inviting a guest to his home. 'Shall we go? Are you ready?'

Harpagus said nothing for a while. Then: 'Will you let me write one letter?'

'Of course. Take all the time you need.' He paused, then said, 'Who is it to?'

'Croesus, of course,' Harpagus said. Then, paying no more mind to his executioner, he bent down over his sea of papers and found an unmarked sheet of Egyptian papyrus.

He wrote the letter slowly, carefully. He did not rush, and he did not hesitate as he filled the paper with his small, crabbed hand. When he had finished he looked it over, satisfied that every thought he wanted to share had been marked down in ink, that there was nothing that remained unsaid. Then he picked it up from the table and held it out over the fire. The flames caught a corner, and in a moment had burned it to nothing. He blew the ash off his hand, and stood.

With the stiff motions of an old man, holding his crippled arm close against his body like a man cradling a child, he followed Prexaspes and silently left the room.

Croesus blinked against the darkness. The stone wall was cold against his back, and at first he thought this was what had woken him. He shared a corner of the room with Isocrates; a little luxury in the communal world of the slaves, a blanket draped between two columns

88

giving the illusion of private ownership. If he rolled the wrong way in the night, he would wake shivering against the stone.

This time, he had not emerged from his dreams by chance. He felt a hand against his shoulder once more. His eyes adjusted, and he saw Isocrates kneeling beside him.

'What is it?' Croesus said. 'Does the king want me?'

'No.'

'Is something wrong?'

There was a pause in the darkness. 'I wanted to say goodbye.'

'What?'

Isocrates looked down at the ground. 'One of the others overheard the guards talking.'

'What have you heard?'

Again, Isocrates said nothing for a time. Then: 'There is going to be an execution tomorrow. Cambyses has ordered it.'

'Who?'

'Servants and slaves.'

'How many?'

'All of us, Croesus.' Isocrates looked back at him. 'All of us except you.'

Croesus remembered when he himself had been the condemned man. That unnatural creature whose mind and flesh cried out for life, who would think and hope until the final moment. He looked at his friend, and thought: a dead man is speaking.

'Why?' Croesus said at last.

'There is no why. You know that.' Isocrates hesitated. 'I thought that you might have been told.'

'I know nothing.'

Isocrates looked away again, his eyes dull. 'I would like to know why, at least.'

'Do not talk like that. You must run.'

'Where would I go?'

89

Croesus closed his eyes, hoping to shut out the world he saw through them, as one can in a dream. But when he opened them again, Isocrates was still kneeling at his side, the look of defeat on his face like a death mask. From the rest of the room, as if in confirmation, he could hear the word being passed from one to another. He heard some men praying, others crying, others still issuing whispered denials, refusing to believe what every man knew to be true. A chamber filled with the condemned, with nothing to do but to wait for the dawn, and the death that would come with it.

'What are you going to do?' Croesus said.

'I will try and get to the women's quarters, to see Maia.'

'If they catch you, they will . . .' Croesus trailed off.

'Croesus, I—'

Croesus stood and waved him into silence.

'Wait for me here.'

'Croesus—'

'Wait here, I said. You have the rest of the night to get yourself killed. Give me a little time. Then you can do what you want.'

'I did not wake you for this, Croesus.'

'I know. Just wait.'

The other man nodded, tipped his head back against the wall, crossed his arms over his knees, and waited. Perhaps he would use the coldness of the stone to keep himself awake, not wanting to waste what few hours he had left in sleep.

Croesus turned away, picked his way through the hundred weeping, praying men, and pounded on the door to their chamber.

'I wish to see the king.'

When he entered, Croesus at first thought he had been misguided, that through conspiracy or mistake the guard had taken him to some other, forgotten corner of the palace grounds.

The king's private chamber was no longer a place of light. The torches had been taken down, the gaps in the walls covered with black cloth, so that not even the soft light of the moon and stars was permitted entry. Croesus could not find the king in the shadows, but knew that he was there. The sweet smell of wine was in the air, and something moved within the room unseen, like some creature of myth, hiding in darkness, hating itself.

'Why have you come here, Croesus?' The king's voice was clear.

'Forgive me for disturbing you, master.'

'Why have you come?'

'I have heard . . .'

'Yes, Croesus?'

Croesus stood silent for a moment longer, clasping and unclasping his hands. 'Are the slaves to die?' he said. 'The servants too?'

'Yes.' A pause. 'I am sorry for it.' The king's voice broke, and stifled sobs escaped the shadows.

Eventually, the voice recovered its strength, and spoke again. 'But it is necessary. You agree, don't you? It must be done.'

'Master. Please tell me. What is wrong?'

A stamping sound, as the king stood, and strode out of the darkness. He moved so quickly that Croesus saw his grieving face for only a moment, before the world rang into half silence, upended, and Croesus lay on the ground, one hand to his bleeding ear, the other held up to ward off another blow.

'You mock me! I know you do! You must have known!'

Croesus pressed his face to the floor, felt his hands shaking like a fever-struck man. 'I know nothing.'

A hand rolled him over roughly, and Cambyses's face was but a few inches from his own. The king's eyes hunted over Croesus's face, as if he were looking for a lie hiding in a treacherous fold of skin. Then Cambyses stood, a little of the tension ebbing from his body, like a bowstring half untensed, the arrow still nocked.

'What you say is true,' Cambyses said. 'You would not have come and played the fool. You would not dare to do that, would you? You old coward.'

Croesus rolled over onto his knees. He did not yet dare to stand. 'What has happened? Tell me. Please. So that I may help you.'

Cambyses walked back to his throne and leaned against it, one hand on each of its arms, his arched back facing Croesus.

'My wife is not . . .' Cambyses broke into sobs, and could not finish. It did not matter. In that moment, Croesus knew it all.

He imagined the Pharaoh receiving those endless emissaries, demanding a daughter that he could not bear to be parted from. Perhaps his spies had told him something of Cambyses; that he was strange, unstable; that he was not to be trusted as a husband. Impossible to refuse the king of Persia, unthinkable to agree to his request. And then the Pharaoh had thought of another way out. An impostor.

'Who is she?' Croesus said.

'A whore, dressed as a princess. And I believed her.' Cambyses leaned forward, put his head against the back of the throne and cried again.

Croesus got to his feet, and felt his arms, in a father's old instinct, stretch out towards the king. He took a step forward.

Cambyses glanced over his shoulder. 'Look at the ground! Don't look at me! Don't touch me.'

Croesus did as he was told. 'How do you know this, master?'

'Phanes told me. That Hellene. Then she confessed everything to me. Begged me to spare her life.'

There was silence. Croesus watched the kings hands tighten and loosen on the arms of his throne. From time to time, Cambyses would shake his head, mutter to himself. Or he would give a laugh like a bark, a sudden sob, tears that ended as abruptly as they began. He seemed to forget that Croesus was there, the old man hunched up, his ear still ringing from where he had been struck.

92

'What will you do, master?'

'Others must have known. The slaves, the servants. Some of the nobles too. Prexaspes has been helping me. We'll have their names soon enough. But I know that you would not betray me. I believe that.'

'Thank you,' Croesus whispered. He did not know what else to say.

'I did not believe it at first. But Harpagus told me you were innocent.'

'Harpagus?'

'Yes. I know that he must be involved. He lived when my father died. That makes him a traitor in any case.'

'Where is he? May I speak to him?'

'You wish to see him?'

'Yes, master.'

The king said nothing at first. Then: 'I wish that you had not said that.'

Cambyses clapped his hands at his bodyguards. When Croesus saw two men go from the room rather than one, he knew then what was to come. They did not need two men to escort Harpagus. They needed two men to carry him.

When they returned, dragging a heavy weight with them across the stone floor, he was glad of the darkness in the king's chambers. What the guards brought in and placed on the ground at the king's feet resembled a piece of butchered flesh more than a man, and Croesus could not stand to look at him for more than a moment. Even in that half glimpse in the darkness, Croesus could see the white of the skull where the scalp had been peeled back, the reddish hollows where the ears had been cut away.

The mutilated thing on the ground began to move. Harpagus breathed, a rattling, half choked sound, and pushed himself up from the ground with fingerless hands. He knelt on legs that could not

93

stand and turned his head around the darkened chamber. At first Croesus thought the general was looking for someone who might help him to live, or to die. But when the general's face turned at last towards Croesus, the old slave saw that Harpagus acted on empty instinct. He could see nothing, and never would again.

'Harpagus,' the king said.

The blinded face turned to Cambyses. 'My king,' Harpagus said, and his voice was clear and distinct. They had cut away and broken so much of the man that it seemed impossible that he might still speak with such clarity. But his torturers had not touched his lips, his tongue or his teeth. They had reduced him to a thing that could do nothing but breathe and suffer, confess and denounce.

'It is true, what you have said? Of how you conspired against my father? Against me?'

The eyeless head nodded, defeated.

'And Croesus? Did he betray me, as you did? As the others did?'

A low moan broke from Harpagus, and Croesus was certain that now, at last, he would give the denunciation that would end this pain.

'No,' Harpagus said.

'We must be certain. We will have to question you again.'

'Do what you want. But that is the truth. I will not say otherwise.'

'You see, Croesus?' the king said, turning away from the ruined man. 'This is how I know I may trust you.'

Croesus looked at Harpagus, and did not reply. What act of stubbornness or loyalty or love had kept Harpagus from giving Croesus's name? His mind would have tricked him by now; broken by pain, it would have made him believe that Croesus had committed some unforgivable act of treason, that he was only speaking the truth to give the old slave up. But he would not. And Croesus would never know why.

'Croesus? You wish to speak to him?'

'No, master.'

'No? Then we have wasted our time.' Cambyses raised his hands, ready to clap, to send Harpagus away and begin the torture again.

'Wait,' Croesus said. He swallowed, his throat dry. 'Let me kill him for you, master. You would honour me.'

'I did not think that was your way, Croesus.' The king paused for a moment, weighing the decision, a man's life at his whim. Then, he said, 'As you wish.'

Croesus hesitated. 'May I have a blade, master?'

'A blade? What business has a slave with a blade?'

'Master?'

'Do what you want with him. But you shall have no assistance from me.'

Croesus felt the bile rising, and swallowed hard to keep it down, and felt a coward's longing to take back what he had said. He stepped forward until Harpagus was at his feet, until he was close enough hear the soft, persistent gasps of a man for whom even to breathe is pain. Croesus gripped the back of the kneeling man's head, held it close against his body. He could go no further. He had never killed a man. He did not know what to do.

He felt the man at his feet shift slightly. Looking down, he watched as Harpagus lifted what remained of one hand high up on his throat, marking the place. Then the stump moved to Croesus's hands, and guided them to that place. Harpagus said a word, so softly that Croesus could not quite hear it at first.

Harpagus spoke again. 'Please,' he whispered. 'Please.'

His thumbs went into the throat, his hands clasped tight around the neck, and Harpagus, who a moment before had seemed almost dead, burst into sudden, terrible life.

The ruined hand beat against Croesus's face and chest, shattered legs shook and jerked and fought to stand, the body fighting against a mind that wanted only to die. Croesus found a hate for that stubborn instinct of life, fighting for itself even when only suffering

95

remained for it. He went to his knees, forced Harpagus against the ground, and knew a feeling more powerful than love or mercy or disgust. More than anything else that he had ever wanted, he wanted this moment to end.

He lifted Harpagus's head and brought it down against the ground, again and again. He beat his friend's head open against the stone.

Even when, at last, Harpagus lay still, Croesus kept his thumbs pressed against the throat for a long time, for fear that he might be mistaken, that he might release his grip, only to hear the man gasp and rattle his way back into life. He knew he would not find the courage a second time.

When there could be no more doubt, he stood, his legs strong and steady. He found Cambyses regarding him, the king's head drawn back, his mouth slightly parted; stilled and muted by what he had witnessed. I have never killed a man, Croesus thought, and he has never seen one die. Croesus met the king's gaze blankly, and promised himself that, no matter what happened, he would not look away first.

The king's head dropped. 'Give him water,' Cambyses said.

Croesus felt a bowl of water being pressed into his hands. He took it, but made no move to drink. He knew he would retch if he tried to swallow anything.

'Your hands, Croesus.'

He stared down dumbly, and saw that there was blood on his hands. He poured the water carefully, and washed the blood away. He lifted his hands to his face, found a speckled spray on his cheeks, and wiped that away too.

'Will you grant me a boon,' said Croesus, 'for the service I have done you?'

'Whatever you ask, Croesus.'

'There are two other slaves who knew nothing of this conspiracy. I know this to be true. They are loyal, and they love you. Will you spare them?'

'Two.' Cambyses said nothing for a time. Then: 'I suppose that I may spare two. Give me their names.'

'Isocrates. And Maia.'

The king paused again. 'I did not know you could do something like this,' Cambyses said, staring at the broken body on the floor. 'You did it for love of me, I think?'

'Yes, master. For love of you.'

The king nodded slowly. 'I will let them live, if you say they may be trusted. But only those two.'

I am glad I never killed a man before this, Croesus thought. What a fool Cambyses was to let an old man know this power. 'What will we do now?' he said.

'You grow senile, I suppose.' Cambyses sat heavily in his throne, cradled his head in his hands. 'We will go to Egypt, of course. I do not want to. But there is no other way to answer this shame. Is there, Croesus?'

'Perhaps . . .' Croesus fell silent. The king's words had sounded like a genuine question, yet even in the darkness Croesus could see a watchful glitter in the king's eyes. The question was a trap. Cambyses was learning to set them – Croesus would have to learn, and learn quickly, to avoid them. 'No, master.'

'My father conquered many nations, but none as great as Egypt. If I conquer Egypt, will that make me a greater king than my father?'

Croesus saw that the truth would not help him. 'Yes,' he said.

'Thank you. I will spare your friends. And you. But no other. Now, leave me.'

The slaves fell silent when Croesus returned to the chamber. A hundred sets of eyes turned towards him, all filled with hope that the chosen man, the favourite of the king, might have won them their lives. He dropped his head, unable to meet those eyes of the dead. A low moan passed through them. They understood what it must mean.

Isocrates had not moved at all, or so it seemed; he sat back on his haunches, his head against the wall. Only his eyes moved as Croesus approached, and Croesus saw the briefest flicker of pain or fear in them. Then it passed.

'You tried,' Isocrates said quietly. 'I thank you for it.'

Croesus sat beside him, and said nothing for a time.

'You are safe,' he said, after a time.

'What do you mean?'

'The king will spare your life.'

A pause.

'And Maia?'

'Yes.'

'The others?'

Croesus closed his eyes. He was so tired. It took him a long time to find the courage to look at his friend.

'I thought you had learned to be one of us,' Isocrates said. 'But I see that you are still a king. Still willing to choose who is to live and who is to die.'

'You do not know what I have done for you.'

Croesus saw the other man's eyes looking over him, searching for an answer. Where they found the blood, on his hands or face or knees, Croesus did not know, but he saw then that Isocrates understood.

'Is this the end of the killing?' Isocrates said.

'No. The beginning of it.'

'Then will you do what you must?'

Croesus did not reply. He lay down, and rolled to face the wall, and thought of the promise he had made to Cyrus. To teach Cambyses, to protect him, to make him a great king. Now, he thought of how he must break that promise.

He heard Isocrates stand and go to the others, to give them the words that Croesus did not have the courage to speak.

Croesus let exhaustion take him. He fell asleep to the sound of the other men weeping.

When he woke, there was silence. The slaves had gone.

'You. Stop.'

'How may I serve you, my prince?'

'What is your name?'

'Croesus, my prince.'

'Of course. My father has so many slaves here in Babylon. Who can remember them all? But I suppose that I should remember you. You are not like the others.'

'I am of no consequence.'

'That is not true. I remember seeing you when I was a boy. You had a kind face, then.'

'Not an unkind one now, I hope.'

'What? I cannot see. Come closer.'

'My prince, there is no need to—'

'Be quiet. Yes. It is still kind.'

'I am glad, my prince.'

'Did you know that sometimes my father would strike me? When I displeased him.'

'I—'

'And when we came to Babylon, he let a priest beat me. A ritual, he said. An honour.'

'I am sorry that you have suffered.'

'When he struck me as a boy, I thought of you. That kind face. I wondered what it would be like to have you as a father.'

'You have a much greater man as a father than me.'

'My father has many wives. I perhaps will have many fathers.'

'It would be a poor prince indeed who had a slave for a father.'

'It pleases me to think of you that way.'

'I am pleased to be thought of at all. I have no sons left to me.'

'Is that so terrible?'

'To be an old man who has lost his children . . . I suppose there must be worse fates. But I cannot think of them, my prince.'

'If your children are gone, they cannot disappoint you. You do not have to see them fail. That is what my father thinks of me.'

'You will be a great king, my prince.'

'Perhaps.'

'Forgive me. I must go to the king. He has asked for me.'

'My father meets with his generals today, does he not?'

'Yes.'

'Will there be another war?'

'There will always be another war.'

A Silent Desert

I

The desert of Sinai.

This land should have been empty of life, an airy tomb filled with the bones of the dead. Yet, here and there, when the winds were still, the sand was marked with the tracks of camels where some caravan of the desert people had passed. It was a place where life had to stay in constant motion, and to stay still was to die.

A lone traveller, or a dozen men – these could cross the desert, with a good guide and good fortune. Digging out the hidden plants of the desert and draining the moisture from them, taking some mouthfuls of dirty water from a *wadi* to buy another few hours of life beneath the burning sun. At the end of the desert journey, the traveller's skin would be blistered from his body, his tongue bulging from his mouth with thirst, his eyes swollen shut from the cutting wind, but a man could come to the other side with his life. No army could make the crossing, or so it had always been said.

The Sinai had stood impenetrable for centuries, letting in only the explorer, the merchant's caravan, the desert nomads, and repelling all invaders with natural force, the sun the solitary watchtower and the vultures the only guards. Here, at least, cities and civilization were rejected, the farmer and the soldier refused passage.

Yet now an army marched across it, filling this place of silence with a quantity of sound and motion that had been unheard and unseen in it since the world was born. Perhaps, from a distance, the army would appear as a shimmering on the horizon, an indistinct phantom born of thirsty eyes. Perhaps this sea of men might be seen as a sea of a different kind, and some lost nomad, his waterskin empty and familiar *wadis* dried up, would come running towards them, his arms spread open, hurrying towards his death. To find a sea of water in the desert was still more likely than to find an army here.

It was the king of Palestine who had given them the key to the desert. Cambyses had gathered his troops in Pasargadae, promised them a miracle, and begun the long march to the south and west. They moved on, through Syria and Phoenicia, stopping only to take tributes along the way, greeted by fawning ambassadors and nervous pontiffs eager to win favour with the new king. In Phoenicia they assumed they would stop, gather ships and take to the sea, for that was the only way to enter Egypt from the east. The men spoke fearfully of it, for meeting the long ships of the Egyptians in waters their enemies knew so well seemed a fool's death.

Yet they left Phoenicia on foot, marching on until they reached the edge of the Sinai. They waited there for three days, staring out at the uncrossable expanse, waiting for the miracle their king had promised them. On the morning of the fourth day, thirty men came out of the desert. Their leader beckoned to the Persians without speaking, then turned their camels back the way they had come. A shudder of fear seemed to pass through the army, as if it were one man being beckoned to the executioner's ground. But the will of the king ruled over it, and the soldiers stepped hesitantly onto the boundless sand.

That first day, just as they were on the verge of collapse, they came upon stones marking the ground. They dug with their daggers, helmets and bare hands until they found treasure – a fortune of water, wrapped in dark leather and buried in the the desert. It was a gift from the king of Palestine, hidden by the nomads, bought with the gold of the Persian kings. When they dug it up, the water was almost boiling and tasted of the hot leather it had been kept in, but it was more delicious to them than the sweetest wine of the Cyclades.

They erected canopies at noon to escape the midday sun, slept in shivering heaps at night to fight off the cold, waiting for the dawn. Then they woke and marched, looking out for the stones that marked the water, until they were at the very centre of the desert, the halfway point of the journey, when there truly was no turning back. They would make the crossing or they would die in that place.

When he stared at that army in the centre of the Sinai, Croesus thought of how unnatural it was. An army in a desert. A great gathering of men dedicated to destruction, passing through a land where there was nothing to destroy. Was there anything more futile? Perhaps only if there were another army gathered here to fight over the worthless desert, men killing men for a prize that existed only in the minds of their kings.

Shortly before midday the word came back, passed from one man to another, summoning Croesus to the king's side. The slave turned his steed out of line, and made his way up the column of men. He drew close to the centre of the army, and saw, as he had seen so many times before in the month-long march, three riders together, Cambyses and his two companions. On the king's left hand was Prexaspes. There were few who could have named him a month before, when he was just another anonymous young nobleman, circling the king and seeking favour. All knew his name now.

At first, there had been no title for the work that Prexaspes did, and there were many who nervously fell silent when introducing the man, uncertain of what to call him. The King's Eye – this was the euphemistic title that had come to be accepted at last, though Croesus thought he better resembled some other part of the king. A muted throat, perhaps, that swallowed and consumed, but did not speak.

Prexaspes rarely left the king's side. He said little, and was quietly attentive, like an eager student at lessons. Occasionally the king would mention a name to him, and Prexaspes would repeat it to himself several times, marking it for remembrance. Whether it was a man marked for reward or death, Croesus never knew.

On the other side was Phanes. A Hellene, he held an uncanny resemblance to Isocrates, as if he were some other version of the slave from another life, dedicated to war. Whenever he saw the general, Croesus wondered what terrible force of ambition had brought him halfway across the world to leave the service of the Pharaoh and serve Cambyses. Unlike Prexaspes, Phanes spoke constantly. Not to flatter, but because the king was in constant need of reassurance. Many times a day, Phanes would repeat words that he had said many times before, about the weaknesses of the Egyptian army, the strength of the Persians, the ways in which they would subdue the great nation, repeating these words again and again until they took on the quality of prayer.

If these two new favourites of the king had any kind of rivalry, it was not on open display. They had neatly divided a world between them, though Croesus wondered how long that could last. When Phanes would look at the secret world that Prexaspes ruled, and Prexaspes look at the force of the army, each would surely feel a craving for another kind of power.

He rode to them, and offered the king a bow from the saddle.

'Master. You asked for me?'

'Did I?'

'Yes, master.'

Cambyses pinched the sweat from his eyes. 'Did I do this, Prexaspes?'

A pause. 'I do not recall, my lord.'

'Phanes?'

'Yes,' Phanes said, and glanced at Prexaspes. 'Though you did not give your reasons.'

'Well. No matter. I am sure I will remember.'

Croesus bowed again. 'I will leave you, master.'

'No, no. Stay, Croesus. We were speaking of what we will do when the war is finished. Phanes?'

'With your permission, my lord, I will take my sons, and we will go home.'

'The Pharaoh would not let you go?'

'No. Amasis would not permit it. My sons will see their home again. I will see it again.'

'A very fine ambition. Do you not think, Croesus?'

'Yes, master.'

'Prexaspes?'

'I wish only to serve you as best I can, my lord.'

'Oh. How dull. You must think of something better. Or I may give you a task you will not like.'

'Yes, my lord.'

'And you, Croesus? What will you do? Die, I suppose, after the war.'

'Or during, master.'

Cambyses laughed, a little too loudly. 'Perhaps you are right. What else is there for an old man like you to do but die?'

'And what will you do, master?' Croesus said.

Cambyses said nothing, and Croesus saw, out of the corner of his eye, both his advisors tense. What fool asked a question of the king? To the king belonged all questions, to his advisors every answer. To go against that seemed almost a violation of a natural law.

But Cambyses seemed amused.

'I had not thought of that,' he said. 'A good question.' He thought for a time, his eyes wandering over Croesus, as if searching for the answer there. 'Follow me, Croesus. Away from the line.' Phanes and Prexaspes both made ready to follow, but Cambyses waved a dismissive hand at them. 'No. You both stay here.'

Croesus tried not to look at them. He did not think that he would like what he saw there. He urged the mule forward, and followed the king away from the marching soldiers. Behind him, he heard the word to halt, for it was coming towards midday. He glanced back over his shoulder and saw the men hurriedly setting up their shelters of cloth to huddle beneath, with the same sense of urgency as if they had been setting their spears against a cavalry charge.

Cambyses seemed to feel no need to take cover in this way. Often, Croesus had seen him wandering idly, like a man walking beside the sea, whilst his men cowered in hiding from the sun. He did not seem to feel the heat. He stared out into the desert, a little smile playing across his lips.

'A wife,' Cambyses said abruptly. 'And children.'

'Master?'

'That is what I should do. After this war. What do you think?'

'It is what most men desire. An honest ambition.'

'So it is said. Yet I think it is not for me.' He paused. 'Perhaps I will return to this place.'

'You like it here, master?'

'It is beautiful, is it not? I would stay here for ever, if I could.'

Croesus assumed at first that it was some kind of strange joke. But he glanced at Cambyses to read his mood and found him looking out with a shy smile, and Croesus knew that the king meant what he had said.

'I could live with these desert people,' Cambyses continued. 'Who needs eyes to see here, where there is nothing? Who will speak of my shame here? These tribesmen know nothing of such things. To live a life without shame and judgement. Would that not be beautiful? I will avenge my dishonour in Egypt, but there will be more shame to come. Unless I come back here.' He paused, and looked suddenly afraid. 'Would you come with me, Croesus? I would be frightened to come back on my own. Will you promise me that?'

In his mind, Croesus thought of the journey they would make. They would take another slave who spoke the language, camels and gold to buy their way into one of the wandering tribes. They would learn the ways of the desert tribes, live in this impossible place, and die there too. Of all the ends he had thought of for himself, this was not one he had ever imagined. He wondered what they did with their dead; whether they interred them in caves, or if they burned them out on the sands, as if they were giving their dead back to the endless sun they lived under. If that was the end he came to, the one that was meant for him, he wondered if he would die happy. If the king might die happy.

'Yes,' Croesus said at last. 'I will come back with you.'

'Thank you,' Cambyses said. His eyes shone. Bright. Then too brightly.

He stooped, the colour leached from his face. Like a bull struck dead, his mouth fell open, his tongue lolling from between his teeth, then he slid from his horse and fell to the burning ground.

2

The army moved on, for what else could they do? To stay still was to die, to retreat was to die.

They laid the king in a covered cart, his fever worsening each day. None in the army were told of the king's sickness, yet all knew. Rumours spread, and there were some, terrified by the omen of a fallen king, who disappeared into the desert at night. They went to their deaths, for without guide or water they would not last a day on the burning sands. But if to run into the desert were an act of madness, to stay with the army seemed a double madness, when the gods had struck down the highest amongst them.

At night in the king's tent, Croesus sat at his side and waited. Often, it was only he, the physicians, and one of the ten thousand Immortals who remained in the tent with Cambyses. Prexaspes and Phanes came to see the king each day, for neither wished to appear disloyal. But they looked at the king with fear, and they left as quickly as they could. In life, the king was ever surrounded by those seeking to draw favour from him. In death, he would always be alone.

It was during the third night of the fever that the crisis came, and Cambyses began the last fight for his life. When it began the physicians left, filing silently from the tent as if by some prearranged signal, for none wished to risk being at the king's side at the moment of death.

As the last of them walked out into the night, Croesus gave him a message, and a handful of coins to ensure its delivery. He sat back down beside the king and held his hand, like a desert stone between his palms, warm and unyielding. He waited, drifting away into a half sleep, and did not know how much time passed, with the king's burning hand held in his own. When he came to himself, he found that Isocrates stood over him.

'Is he dying?' said Isocrates.

'I do not know. Do you know anything of this sickness?'

'It could be many different things.' Isocrates glanced at the guard who stood at the entrance of the tent. Then he knelt, and examined the king for a time, rolling open his eyes, putting his lips to the man's forehead to feel the heat of his skin. He stood once more, and when he spoke again, it was with regret. 'I think that he will live, if he survives the night. The fever is close to breaking.'

Croesus saw motion from the corner of his eye. The guard had been looking out of the tent for some time, apparently measuring the passage of time by the height of the moon in the sky. He now made as if to go, lifting his spear and opening the flap of the tent.

'Why do you leave?' Croesus said.

'My replacement is late. He will be here soon.'

'You will abandon your king?'

'You would do well to hold your tongue. You are still a slave. Do not think to threaten a free man.' And without another word, the guard walked away.

They watched him go, and turned to face each other.

'We do not have much time,' said Isocrates. He paused, and let his gaze drift down to the sleeping king. 'I will do it, if you will stand watch. It will not take long.'

There was a long silence.

'I did not ask you here for that,' said Croesus.

'The guard leaving? That was not your doing?'

'No.'

'I do not understand.'

Croesus reached out, his robe folded up over his palm, and wiped the sweat from Cambyses's face. 'How many has he killed so far, do you think?' Croesus said.

'Hundreds. The slaves and servants. Many nobles as well. Harpagus. Or had you forgotten him?'

'How many did I kill when I was a king? One war after another. Thousands, or tens of thousands. Would you have killed me, given the chance?'

'Perhaps I should have done,' said Isocrates. 'We do not have time for this.'

'I made a promise to Cyrus,' Croesus said. 'He had a dream. A great empire. Ruled by generations of his children. Ruled for peace. One last great war, and then an end to wars. That is what he wanted for his son. For all of us.'

'A fool's dream. Only an old king like you could have believed such vanity.'

'You did not say such things to me. When you were my slave, and I sought to build an empire of my own.'

'No. I wish that I had.'

Slowly, Croesus leaned forward, put his face in his hands. 'Cambyses made a promise to me. Before the fever took him. That after this war, we will go to the desert together. That he will give up the throne.'

'You cannot believe him.'

'I have to. The war with Egypt will happen whether he lives or dies. But I will take him away, afterwards. I cannot make him a good king. But I can save him. I can keep my promise, in part at least.'

For a moment, Croesus thought he saw the other man's body go tense. Then they both heard the heavy tread of the guard approaching, and knew the moment had passed. It was too late.

'I forgave you for the death of the others,' Isocrates said softly. 'I do not know if I can forgive this.'

'We cannot change what will happen.'

'I suppose you must let yourself believe that. For the rest of your life, you will wish you had found the courage to do this.'

'If you truly believed that, then you would have done it without my help. You think I could stop you?'

He could not remember ever seeing pain on Isocrates's face before, but he saw it there now. 'You do not understand me at all, do you, Croesus? Do not come looking for me any more. Or for my wife, to beg for our help.' He nodded to the sleeping king. 'You have chosen your place. At his side.'

'I do not want to choose.'

'You already have.' And he left.

Croesus did not sleep that night. He stayed kneeling on the ground, like a penitent at prayer, and waited to see if the king would live or die.

He watched the king's eyes moving beneath his closed eyelids, frantic dartings beneath the skin, and wondered what fever dreams were passing through his mind, what things he saw, what pieces of the mind were being destroyed by the fire that raged there.

Sometime during that prelude to dawn when the sky begins to lighten but before the sun is seen, Cambyses woke. Croesus did not notice at first, for the king lay quite still, his eyes staring straight ahead, barely open. Then the king turned his head a fraction and he faced Croesus.

His face was still and unchanged. His eyes burned with madness.

3

A little out of bowshot, the Egyptian army stood before the Persian force.

There were only the occasional sounds to suggest that the army before them was anything but a mirage; the wooden clatter of spear shafts against each other, the metallic sound of a man shifting in his cuirass, the nervous whicker of a horse that could sense the imminence of its death. In a few moments, the killing would start. In a few hours, Croesus knew, most of those Egyptians would be dead.

He thought of how many times he had seen a doomed army like this one. All of them the same. The outcome had been determined beforehand. The Egyptians would be slaughtered by the tens of thousands. All who stood there knew this, had known it for days beforehand, as the two armies marched and manoeuvred into position, as their generals gave their speeches and the priests sacrificed and cast their auguries. The battle itself was a formality, the bloody proof to a martial theorem that needed no testing.

Phanes had told them everything. He offered up every detail of the Egyptian forces, the habits of the generals, which regiments would fight to the last and which would be the first to surrender, the battle-field that the Egyptians would try to use and the one that the Persians could force their opponents to take. It was as cruel and intimate as a lover's betrayal.

Prexaspes, Phanes, and Cambyses. The three were united again, as before. Phanes continued to talk incessantly, and was now able to point out where his predictions had come true – the disposition of the Egyptian army was proof positive of his knowledge. Prexaspes still said nothing – he was just a little more watchful than before, as they all were, trying to discern how the king had changed.

When anyone mentioned the fever, Cambyses seemed puzzled, confused as to why this was being spoken of, as if it were something that had happened to some other man. Croesus could not help but wonder what pieces of the king's mind had been taken from him by the pitiless glare of the sun.

Phanes was about to give the command to advance, to begin the inevitable slaughter, when on the battlefield Croesus saw movement from the Egyptian ranks. A regiment of men advanced in front of the army, the sun glittering on their bronze armour. They were the Hellene mercenaries who had remained loyal to Egypt, even after Phanes defected. They stood on the desert plain between the two armies, and brought forward half a dozen prisoners with them. Croesus had only to look at Phanes to know who the men were.

One by one, the prisoners stepped forward. In shaking voices, they denounced their father as a traitor, the Persians as cruel aggressors cursed by the gods, themselves as collaborators. Occasionally one would stumble over the words he had memorized, only to be quietly reminded by the soldier next to him. The last, the youngest, broke down in tears, unable to finish, and was beaten to the ground for his failure.

When the confessions had ended, the Hellenes knocked the men down, wrapped their fingers into hair, and raised their knives high, for Phanes to see. They leaned forward, and began to cut.

Croesus closed his eyes and looked away, but he could still hear

117

them, sounding like men screaming underwater. It went on for longer than he thought was possible, and it was only when he was sure it was over that he looked back. There, he saw the worst sight of all.

Phanes's sons lay on the ground, the sand blackening beneath them. Beside each of the bodies, a man had stepped forward with a bowl to catch the blood as it fell. Croesus watched as they passed the bowls around between all of the Hellenes. They each drank in turn, the hot blood flowing from their mouths and staining their beards a reddish black. Then, as one, they gave a single cry, the first note of the paean echoing out over the battlefield like the scream of some angry, dying god. They stepped back into line, and the two armies returned to silence.

Croesus stared straight ahead. He did not want to look at Phanes, or Cambyses. He feared what he would see on both their faces – the grief of one, the indifference of the other.

'You will have more sons, Phanes,' he heard Cambyses say, after a time, 'and a kingdom of your own to raise them in.'

Croesus could hear Phanes weeping. The ugly sound of a man un-used to tears, who had never imagined he would have use of them again.

'Come,' Cambyses said. 'Let us begin.' He signalled to the soldier beside him. The drums rang out to signal the Persian advance, and the doomed Egyptians surged forward to meet them.

It took only a moment to see what would happen. The Egyptians stood their ground as best they could, and one who had never seen a battle before might have thought the two sides evenly matched. But, after only a short time, Croesus saw where the Egyptian flanks were already beginning to draw back. Just a little, but he knew it would be enough.

From the edge of the battlefield, over the course of an hour, he watched as the Persian line reached around on both sides, like ten thousand creeping fingers. First, they drove the Egyptian army into an uneven line, then they began to fold it into a curve, a horseshoe, the way a man might break a branch in two, bending both ends against one another. They were driving it into a circle from which there could be no escape.

At last, the circle was closed.

As the Egyptians fought and died in their thousands, Croesus watched and tried to think only of the desert, a purifying place of heat and emptiness, where all this would be forgotten. Where he and the king might learn to forget together.

When the killing was over, the king gathered his councillors to him again, among them Chephren, appearing unmoved by the slaughter of his countrymen, and Prexaspes, untouched by the battle, for his wars were fought entirely within palace walls. They came to the king, but one amongst them was missing.

They waited in silence for a time, to see if Phanes would come to them from the field of the slain, perhaps bearing a wound that would explain his delay. Then they waited for others to find the man, though none doubted by then what must have happened. At last, a messenger came from the field, to tell them what they already knew.

The soldiers cleared a path through the sea of the dead so that the king's horse would have no chance to trip and throw him; a corridor of reddened sand, flanked by five thousand dead on each side. Looking down, Croesus saw how most of them had died without a wound on them, run down or crushed to death without having given or received a blow. That, he thought, was something that none of the stories of war told you.

They found Phanes with his sons, the bright new blood laid over the old blood in the ground, the dagger still gripped tight in his hand, his throat opened like a sacrifice on the altar.

Croesus remembered how the Hellenes believed the spirits of the dead are restlessly thirsty, that they wander through the afterlife like dying men in a silent desert, that only the blood of the living can satisfy this thirst. Perhaps that is what Phanes wished to buy with his life – one last gift from a father to his sons, to ease their suffering in the next world with a gift of blood.

'Why did he do it?' Cambyses said at last.

'Master?'

'I would have given him a kingdom. Why did he do it?'

'They took his children, master.'

'Yes, that is true,' said the king. 'So that is the worst thing, Croesus?'

'Master?'

'To lose your children.'

'Yes. Yes it is.'

'The worst thing I could do to someone?'

Croesus hesitated, caught. 'Yes.'

'I am glad I have no sons. And I am glad that I know this.'

'Why, master?'

Cambyses tilted his head towards Prexaspes. 'The Pharaoh is dead. Or so Prexaspes tells me.'

'Amasis died in battle?'

'No,' said Prexaspes. 'He died of a sickness.'

'Before he even knew that we were coming,' said Cambyses. 'If he had only known that we were going to destroy him. He died believing that he had won, that his trick had worked. But it does not matter. Chephren tells me that he has a son.'

'Psamtek,' the oculist said.

'I will have my revenge on his son, Psamtek. On the sons of his son. You have given me that, Croesus. Thank you.'

The king had a strange expression on his face, and Croesus thought at first that it was some sign of doubt, or of mercy. Then he realized the truth of it. The king was trying not to smile.

'What will you do, master?'

'Oh, nothing much.' He looked at Croesus, and let the smile fully emerge. 'When we have taken Memphis, I will have a parade. That is all.'

4

On the outskirts of Memphis, there was a short stone tower, open topped. It had been built for the Pharaohs to sit and watch the great displays of power. A victorious army returning to the capital, a procession in supplication to the thousand gods of Egypt, a burial train for a nobleman, the arrival of the harvest from the banks of the Nile.

Now, Cambyses sat on the shaded wooden throne that had once been reserved for the Egyptian ruler, his face painted in a mocking imitation of the style of the Pharaohs. Croesus sat to his left, and Psamtek, Pharaoh for only six months, was bound to a chair on his right. This son of Amasis was a little less than forty years old. Younger than I was when I lost my kingdom, Croesus thought.

They sat in silence for a long time. Then distantly, but growing closer, Croesus could hear the drums. The approach of the parade.

The women came first, the wives and daughters of the Egyptian noblemen. Most were little more than girls, and many were children, all of them dressed in the filthy rags of slaves, each one struggling to carry an urn of water from which they were forbidden to drink.

Fringing the group, laughing and dancing, were the prostitutes of Memphis. They were the worst of the city's whores; their faces gouged with disease, their hair crawling with lice. They were dressed in silk and linen and gold, all the finery of the nobility gifted to them, queens for a day. They flirted with the soldiers, and spat and clawed at the women who now wore their rags. And at the front of this procession of whores and noblewomen, her face marked out with a stripe of excrement, was Amasis's only daughter, the one he had hoped to save from marrying Cambyses, now given as a common whore to the Persian army.

On seeing her, Cambyses laughed. 'She's an ugly girl, is she not?' he said to the Egyptian king. 'There was no need for all this trouble. If your father had sent her to me, I would have sent her back.' Psamtek did not reply. His face had not changed at all, even as his sister and daughters marched by, shamed and violated. Cambyses turned back to the procession. 'Look, Psamtek,' he said, pointing at the next group to arrive. 'Here come your boys.'

Two thousand men walked barefoot on the hot stones, twenty columns of a hundred, marching to the beat of the drums. They carried metal bits in their teeth and wore bridles on their heads. Each one was roped by the mouth to the man behind, the taut hemp cutting furrows in the flesh of their necks. They were the sons and brothers and cousins of the Egyptian nobility. Their execution ground lay a short distance ahead of them, in full view of the stone tower. There, a regiment of Persian soldiers leaned in boredom against their spears, waiting for the killing to begin.

To his horror, Croesus saw that the men of the column struggled and fought against each other. Some walked forward quickly, going eagerly to their deaths, wanting nothing more than an end to pain and shame. Others moved as slowly as they could in spite of their suffering, trying to snatch some last sensation from the world, some treasured memory from their minds, before both sense and memory were taken from them for ever. Each pace the column took was a wretched tug of war between the slow and the quick.

Still, Psamtek did not cry; even when his sons walked past, marching to the killing field, his face remained quite still. Cambyses frowned, disappointed. He had nothing more to show the Egyptian. He opened his mouth to speak, to find some goad that might finally break his prisoner, but before he could say anything more, a new sound interrupted him. Another group was approaching, trailing after the men and women, streaming in from the city.

They were beggars. The deformed, the mad, the blind and the deaf. Hundreds of them moving in a ragged mob, those who could not walk leaning against those who could not see, those who could not see listening to the barked, contradictory directions of the mad to find their way. Codependent, more like some vast, misshapen entity than a crowd of individuals, they made their way towards the tower, a besieging army of the destitute.

They cared nothing for the war between the Egyptians and the Persians, too sickly to be press-ganged into the fight, too poor to have anything to lose in defeat. Most had not even been aware that the war was being fought, lost as they were in the battles of their own private madness, or in the more immediate conflicts in the streets of Memphis, their own struggles against hunger and disease. But a festival was something they did understand; a place where money and food would be given freely, where even the cruel would forget their cruelty for a day. They had heard the distant drums and marching feet and seen the soldiers round up the prostitutes, a sure sign that a festival was about to begin. They roused themselves from the doorways of temples, the rooftops of abandoned buildings, the ditches outside the city walls, the broken-open tombs of the dead that served as their resting places. They woke and gathered and marched to the stone tower, puzzling when they arrived that the only men there were the soldiers and the condemned. Still they came forward, hoping for bread or coin enough to last another day.

Psamtek stared out into crowd of beggars, his face suddenly deformed with grief. At first, Croesus thought he had finally been broken by the sounds of execution. The marching columns had reached the killing ground, and somewhere amongst them Psamtek's sons were dying. But as Croesus followed his gaze, he saw that the Pharaoh was looking at one man in particular from the crowd.

The beggar returned the Egyptian king's stare, and broke from the mob. An old man, older even than Croesus, who walked with the deliberate, unsteady steps that children and the elderly share. He came towards the tower, his eyes bright with hope. He seemed not to understand that Psamtek was no longer a man who could dispense favours, that the Pharaoh could no longer even help himself.

Psamtek sobbed once, clapped both hands over his mouth. He did not cover his eyes, perhaps hoping that the beggar would be revealed as an illusion, the way dreams crumble under the sight of the waking mind. The old man did not disappear, hobbling closer and closer, both palms held up in supplication.

'Who is that man?' Cambyses asked.

The Egyptian let his hands fall from his mouth. 'A friend of mine,' he said in a monotone. 'He was wealthy once, and happy. Now he is a beggar.'

'I do not understand.'

Psamtek looked at the king. 'My own suffering is beyond tears. But my friend, reduced to a beggar in his old age, all hope taken from him. I can cry for that.'

Croesus looked down again at the old beggar. He came forward to the tower, his hesitant, hopeful palms extended, and the guards around the tower watched him approach. Once he had come close enough, crossing some invisible, arbitrary line, one of them stepped forward and pushed the beggar back. Undeterred, the beggar circled round and tried again. This time, the guard kicked him to the ground and barked a curse at him. The beggar tried one last time to break through. Another guard swung up the butt of his spear, and the beggar fell, blood pouring from his nose. Without uttering a cry or complaint, the beggar picked himself up, and tottered back to rejoin his companions.

Croesus stared at the king, who looked back and forth from Psamtek to the beggar, a confused, satisfied smile on his face. He remembered the king as a boy, always serious; for him, even games seemed to have so much at stake. Cambyses had hated to be scolded, always appearing on the verge of some terrible humiliation that would wound him for days and weeks. But he always had, like all children, the aching need to be loved. It had emanated from every part of him. Now that had gone. The king had given up all hope of such things, and replaced it with something else.

Croesus faced the parade once more, closed his eyes and listened to the screams of dying men. What a thing it was, to be an old man and to see such things, to have no hope of living long enough to forget them. There was always hope for the young, that the world would heal and be reshaped as the decades pass, if only you could survive to see it. An old man looks on the broken world that surrounds him, and knows he will die there.

Croesus found he was crying. He did not know when or how he had started, but now the traitor tears spilled from his eyes like a confession. He turned his head from the king, but it was no use. Cambyses had already noticed.

'Stop crying, Croesus.'

Croesus nodded, but the tears continued to fall. 'I am sorry,' he said.

'Stop!'

'I cannot.'

The king hissed. What order he wanted to give, Croesus did not know. A command of punishment, banishment, execution. But before Cambyses had the chance to speak, the king saw that Psamtek had stopped crying and was looking at him. The Persian courtiers observed him. Even his guards were watching him in silent judgement. Under their eyes, Cambyses hesitated.

'Even I can be forgiving, Psamtek,' he said slowly, trying to find

125

the words, like an actor recalling a long-forgotten part. He glanced at Croesus, as if the slave were a prompt. 'You shall enter my service, Psamtek. The way Croesus has.' He glanced at those around him, and found them expecting more. 'Your sons will be spared as well,' he said. Beside him, Prexaspes shook his head. 'Ah,' Cambyses said. 'It seems we are too late for that.'

Croesus stared out to the execution ground. Half of the two thousand had been killed already, and the others marched patiently forward into the thrusting spears, stumbling over the corpses of the dead to find their own private place to die. The Pharaoh's sons, at the head of the column, would have been amongst the first to be killed. They had missed their reprieve by a matter of minutes.

'Never mind,' Cambyses said. He leaned forward and placed a brotherly hand on Psamtek's shoulder. 'Let us go and see your father.'

When they broke open the tomb, Croesus braced himself to smell, once again, the stench of the dead. But when the trapped air of the burial chamber flowed out over them, there was only a soft, alien combination of odours. The sickly scent of dry spices, a hot smell a little like leather.

The soldiers removed the remaining stones that sealed the chamber, and began to loot the treasures that had been buried with Amasis. There was no time to differentiate between priceless relics and worthless clay totems or embalmed animals. Everything went into the soldiers' sacks, to be categorized later. The most valuable would be sold or traded in the markets, the gaudy and worthless would be given as gifts to lovers, the religious relics would be discarded entirely. Cambyses let them do as they pleased. It was the soldiers' reward for their part in the blasphemy. He ignored all of the relics, walked forward to the sarcophagus, and gave an order to his bodyguards. With bronze levers, they prised the lid off.

A man lay sleeping there. For a moment, Croesus wondered if the Egyptians had enacted some strange conjuring trick, some unfathomable joke, by placing a sleeping man in the tomb of Amasis and hiding the old Pharaoh's body elsewhere. Then he looked closer, and saw that the skin was stiff and dry, that what he had mistaken for the colour of life were dry whorls of paint. Croesus had heard of the skill of the Egyptian embalmers, of corpses that could survive a thousand years without a single sign of decay. This was the first time he had seen their work for himself.

He saw that Cambyses was smiling. Perhaps it pleased the king that the body still had the illusion of life. That it still resembled a living thing, on which he could extract his revenge. A living thing that would feel pain.

The king turned and gestured. The torturers came forward.

The three of them laid out their tools, uncoiled their whips, struck fire from flint and tinder and began to heat the stones and boil pans of water, motions as practised and ordinary to them as a merchant laying out his wares. If they found the task they had been given strange, they showed no sign of it. They understood the relationship between pain and truth. Inflict enough pain, and a truth would emerge. What truth could be extracted from a corpse was not their concern. If they inflicted enough pain, even on a body that could not feel it, eventually Cambyses would be satisfied.

'Begin.'

They started with the whips, and soon the small chamber echoed with the dull thud of leather against dead flesh. They whipped his genitals, the soles of his feet, his mouth and his eyes. After a time, the torturers traded their plain leather whips for those with spikes and barbed pieces of iron and let the strokes fall harder and more heavily, but the skin would not part beneath their blows.

They took their pliers and pulled out his fingernails. They tore out his hair, in single strands and great clumps. They held the corpse's nose and poured torrents of boiling water down his throat. They took half a dozen foot-long iron spikes and pierced the corpse with them, tapping them in gently with hammers, placing them carefully to miss the vital organs that were no longer there, sheering through nerves that could no longer feel pain. Finally, they took their tongs and picked up the stones that were now red with heat. They inserted the stones into his anus, under his armpits, upon his testicles and his palms. One of them broke the corpse's jaw and prised it open, and put another coal into his mouth.

Cambyses watched in silence at first, his fists slowly clenching and unclenching. Occasionally he would mutter something to himself that Croesus could not hear. Then as the torture continued, he spoke more often, and louder.

He began with curses on Amasis, on the man's family and on his country, repeated again and again like a sorcerer's incantations. Soon he was speaking so rapidly that Croesus could barely make out what he was saying. He could hear only names – the names of the people that Cambyses hated. Sometimes, Croesus could hear Cambyses screaming his own name. Sometimes he shouted his father's name.

He leaned forward and screamed into the dead man's ears, while the torturers continued around him, leaning over and under him, waiting patiently for him to move so they could access certain parts to work upon.

After the stones had been placed, he pushed the torturers aside impatiently. He climbed onto the sarcophagus and straddled the corpse, began hitting it with open-handed blows to the face and neck. Stiff with death, the entire body moved as one under his strokes, the feet jerking as the head was struck. He stepped down and pulled out his sword and began to cut into the dead man. Bloodless wounds opened, but the body would not come to pieces. The embalming had made the tendons and joints like stone, and try as he might, the king could not destroy the corpse.

At last, Cambyses stopped, panting and exhausted. He looked again at his torturers.

'Burn it,' he said. 'Give him the Second Death.'

The Second Death – Croesus did not know what Cambyses meant by this, but the king spoke with confidence. It must have been some fragment of Egyptian lore he had learned, some custom that he meant to use against the dead man.

The torturers hesitated. To the Persians, Croesus remembered, fire was a face of a god. It was an impious thing to give a dead man to the fire. But looking at the king, they saw there would be no question of disobeying. Slowly, reluctantly, they piled the kindling in the sarcophagus. They gave the body to that god of fire.

Psamtek had said nothing during the torture of the corpse. But now, as the body burned, Croesus saw his eyes tighten; it must have been a sacrilege to the Egyptians as well.

As the dead man burned, Cambyses seemed to remember Psamtek. He walked towards the Egyptian, and embraced him. The Egyptian did not flinch from this. His face broke into a smile, and it was as though, at that very moment, Croesus could see his mind breaking.

'Now I know you will be loyal to me,' Cambyses said. 'My father took everything from Croesus before. And look, here he stands. My most loyal slave. You have nothing but me now.'

Psamtek stared at Cambyses. Then he knelt, and kissed the king's hands. 'I am yours for ever,' he said.

5

'Tell me everything,' she said. And so he did.

After the parade and the desecration of the corpse, the king's retinue returned to the palace at Memphis. Built on a hill, this sprawling white stone complex looked out on the city and the Nile, the pyramids of the necropolis, the black earth on the banks of the river and the red desert sands beyond.

Cambyses wandered the halls of this palace with Psamtek as his guide, telling him what treasures to take and what relics to destroy, erasing an ancient line of kingship and replacing it with the new. In all the chaos of the looting, none had noticed Croesus quietly slip away.

He could not run any more, but he managed a kind of quick and staggering forward motion, stumbling like a wounded messenger who does not care if he lives or dies, so long as he speaks the words that he must. Those slaves and servants he cornered and questioned did not ask him his purpose nor what authority he had to make such inquiries of them. His desperation was authority enough.

He found Maia, at last, in a storeroom of the palace. She was pale faced, and thinner than he remembered. The march across the desert must have been hard for her; like him, she was no longer young. When she saw him, at first she seemed ready to deliver a rebuke or dismissal.

Then she saw the expression on his face. Without a word being passed, she led him away to a cellar of wine and grain. They sat down together, and she held his hands and let him speak.

He spoke as calmly as he could. From time to time he found himself wandering into silence, lost in the memories of what he had seen. Then he would start, like a man waking from his sleep, and speak once more, as though afraid he would forget what he had to say.

She did not speak when he had finished his story. He turned away from her, reached into one of the great clay jars, and slowly ran the grain through his fingers. A thousand-year empire, the great pyramids and temples, all founded on that simplest of things, the growing of grain, the baking of bread. The gift of the Nile.

He had heard it said that none knew why the Nile flooded, though all in Egypt and many beyond called it a blessing, a gift from the thousand gods of Egypt. He wondered if he believed that. For the rich soil had brought the farmers, then the kings to gather their wealth and hoard it jealously, then other kings to come and take it from them. All matters of pride and ownership had followed from this simple beginning. He wondered how differently the world might have been shaped, if the first farmer had never planted those first seeds. They had planted the beginnings of kings.

'Is he mad, do you think?' he said.

'I do not know, Croesus.'

'Neither do I. Perhaps a king will always go mad, given enough time. Even Cyrus, strong as he was. He almost lost his mind, at the end.' He paused. 'Was I? Mad, I mean, when I was king?'

Yes,' she said. 'I think that you were.' And she looked worried for him, if he could not see something so apparent.

Perhaps she was right, Croesus thought. Somehow he had not thought of his years as a king as being years of a quiet kind of madness.

'You would save him, if you could?' she said.

131

Croesus hesitated. 'Yes.'

'I do not understand.'

'You have never . . .' Croesus checked his words, but saw that she knew what remained unsaid.

'No. You are right. I do not know what it is to have a child. But this is not your son. You do not have to save him.'

'Yes, I do.'

She sighed. 'I heard that with the older peoples of the world,' she said, 'no man was permitted to rule for long.'

'Is that so?'

'A king married the queen, was given the power to rule as he pleased, every luxury he could desire. He ruled for one year.'

'What happened then?'

'He was sacrificed to the gods, to make way for the next.'

'Did these cults murder their queens too?'

'No. The queens lived to see many kings. It seems they thought the women could withstand such things better. But we live in a world of men, now.'

She looked at him with what he took to be an exhausted, affectionate sadness, and Croesus thought again how tired she looked. She's just old, like me, he told himself. We are all tired.

Slowly, the smile faded from her face. 'I will not be able to see you again, after this,' she said.

He did not reply.

'You do understand, yes?' she said. 'I should not have seen you now. But . . .'

'You will obey Isocrates in this?'

'Yes.'

'I did not think that was your way. You have made yourself a slave twice over?'

'That is not worthy of you. It is as he told you. You made your choice, out in the desert. He loves you. But he cannot forgive the king.'

132

'I understand,' Croesus said. 'He has made a choice too, though.'

'Yes. That is true.'

Croesus looked down at his hands, slowly rubbing one palm with the thumb of his other hand, as though trying to wipe away some stubborn stain. 'You love him very much, I suppose,' he said.

'I do not think about it.' She shrugged. 'Call it what you will.'

'That is something I have never had. I did not think of it when I was a king. If I wanted a woman I could have her. My marriage was an alliance. We were fond of each other, but little more than that. I suppose now is the time for regrets, when it is too late to change anything.' He paused. 'I look at you and Isocrates with envy.'

'I think you speak too highly of us.'

'No. I do not think so. It must be remarkable, to love and to have that love returned. I am sorry to have not felt it. But I am glad to have seen it, at least.' He shook his head. 'I am an old man. Much too old to speak of such things.'

'Perhaps,' she said softly.

She should have gone then. It would have been the right moment to leave. But she stayed, and seemed to be waiting for something.

He reached over and took her hand again. He turned it over, held it in both of his for a moment, like a man holding a bowl of water. Then he lifted her palm to his lips, and held it there.

She sighed. She curled her fingers around his and held them for a moment, then pushed his hand away. 'That,' she said, 'is another reason we should not see one another.'

'What must I do, for Isocrates to forgive me? For you to forgive me?'

'You already know, Croesus,' Maia said. She stood, and walked away.

He looked after her, and thought for a moment she might look back, but she did not. She went from the room, and he was alone once more.

*

The streets of Memphis were nearly deserted. No merchant drove his cart through the dust, no mobs of dirty children played in its alleys, and even the beggars seemed to be in hiding. A deaf man might have thought it an abandoned city, its people driven away by disaster, but one who could hear would make no such mistake. From many houses came the wailings of the mourners, crying out for the sons and daughters who had been taken from them, the thousands of dead inspiring twenty thousand voices of grief. They joined together, cacophonous, until it seemed that the entire city cried out.

Croesus went through these empty streets, moving slowly and carefully with neither purpose nor urgency. From the open doorways, he felt many eyes on him. Perhaps they took him for a beggar, or thought him mad. But none challenged the foreigner who walked amongst them.

Nearly two decades before, he had gone into the city of Babylon after the Persians had taken it. He had spent a last day of freedom there, wandering the streets, seeing the greatest wonders of the world. That should have been the happiest day of his life, or so a prophetic dream had told him. Maia had been with him then. Perhaps that had been why.

He turned a corner in Memphis, and there, at last, were people in the streets.

He could not count them all at first glance. Almost a hundred women stood there, each with a blanket-wrapped body in a cart beside her, so that two hundred, living and dead, waiting patiently outside the embalming houses.

Some had brought their sons from the execution grounds where Cambyses had put two thousand to death. The dead they bore with them seemed almost to be sleeping, if one could disregard the ragged spear wounds that had killed them. Others had the look of those who had travelled much further, accompanied by corpses that were grey and festering, that had lain unburied for weeks. Those mothers must

134

have travelled to the battlefield where the Egyptian army had been destroyed, Croesus thought. He wondered what could inspire such a bleak pilgrimage across the land, there and back, bearing the putrefied dead with them. What a fear they must have had of death, of decay, to do such a thing.

One of the women turned her head to look at Croesus. Then another, and another, until they were all watching him, a hundred sets of eyes fixed on him in silence. Not with anger, or grief. Perhaps, seeing his white hair and wrinkle-cracked skin, each was staring at him and trying to imagine the old man their sons might have become.

It was beyond the street of the embalmers that he reached his destination, a place that he had sought, half without thinking. Croesus had seen the great building from afar, a high-walled fortress of carved stone, ringed by statues of kings or gods. The great temple of Memphis.

It was dark inside. A few diagonal shafts of sunlight cut through the air, slow trails of dust turning within them, and it took Croesus's eyes some time to adjust. He looked over the carvings of animal-headed gods, reliefs depicting the deeds of kings long dead, the endless, alien lines of the Egyptian script. He found, deep within the darkness, what he was looking for. A priest, his head shaved in the Egyptian manner, his back bowed under the weight of his years.

Croesus hesitated, uncertain of whether or not the priest could be approached, or if even to look at the man constituted some unspeakable act of blasphemy. But the priest caught his eye and smiled at him, beckoned him closer. Croesus was prepared to be frustrated in his attempts to speak to the priest, to communicate only through mime and gesture, but he discovered in moments that the Egyptian knew Persian, the common language of their conquerer. When Croesus asked the priest how he came to speak it so well, the other man gave a little shrug.

'I thought that it might be useful. It seemed likely that Cambyses

135

would come to our land, sooner or later. Now, what brings you to my temple?'

'I do not know.' It was true. He did not know what had brought him to this place. It was not the consolation of a foreign religion. Their many thousand gods could give him no comfort. Perhaps it was quite the opposite, he thought. Perhaps it was not hope he sought here, but the ending of it.

The priest waited. From time to time an acolyte would come forward and begin to ask him some question or other, but the priest would smile at him and wave him off, content to wait for Croesus to find his thoughts.

'What god is worshipped here?' Croesus said.

'We know him as Ptah. The Hellenes, I think, know him as Hephaestus.'

'The forger of the world.'

'The maker of the world,' the priest said in gentle correction. 'He needed no tools but his thought and his words. The world was begun in this place.'

'Begun by words?'

'Yes.'

'I have heard many cities claim to be the centre of the world.'

'I am sure. But here, it is true. The world began when the god spoke in Memphis.'

'When was this? How long ago.'

'None can say,' the priest said.

'And do your gods still walk the earth?'

'As animals, sometimes. Once every thousand years, Ptah takes the form of a bull we call Apis. But the gods have not walked the earth since the world began.'

'I am a slave now, but once I was a great king in Lydia,' Croesus said, and waited to see what response this might provoke. If the Egyptian thought him to be some wandering mad man, claiming, like all mad men do, to be a god or a king, he gave no sign of it. 'I was told by my father that within sixteen generations,' Croesus continued, 'we could trace our ancestry back to the gods. That the world began sixteen generations ago, when the gods stood beside men. I was wondering what you thought of that?'

The priest smiled gently, as one would to a child's question. He did not speak, but beckoned for Croesus to follow him. They walked past the tall statues to a chamber deeper within the old temple, where the sun did not penetrate; fire gave the only light in this place, and a high wall loomed before them. It was decorated with collections of strange markings grouped together, separated by lines scored in the stone. There were more of them than he could count at a first glance, and though he knew little of the Egyptian script, Croesus knew them to be names.

The priest stepped forward, and tapped the lowermost marking on the wall. 'My name,' he said. He put his finger to the collection of symbols above it. 'The high priest before me.' Another tap, one higher again. 'And before him.' He gave another little shrug, and a wave of his hand. There was no need to say the rest.

Croesus counted the rows and the columns, and multiplied them against one another. There were more than four hundred names there – four hundred generations of priests who had worshipped in this place for tens of thousands of years. He checked his calculations again, thinking that surely he must have been mistaken. He was not.

He knew that the world was greater in size than he could fathom, that there were lands beyond the edges of the greatest maps that he had seen. Somehow this had never troubled him. But to see the world as so old, to think of the hundreds of generations that had passed and the thousands that were to come, filled him with sadness.

No, he thought, there is no fear in size. One need only stand before a single mountain to know that one is but a tiny creature in a world built for gods and monsters. But time, the age of the world, was fearsome to contemplate. If a man lives for close to a hundred years in a world that is only a few thousand old, that man's life is small, but it still matters. Cast into ten thousand, or a hundred thousand years, and it meant nothing at all. How little one life counted for, he thought, in that annihilating ocean of time.

'Thank you,' Croesus said.

'This sight pleases you?'

'No. But I am glad to have seen it.'

'I am sorry I cannot speak to you longer. We have much to do, to prepare for our new ruler. He is a good king?'

'No. He is not.'

'Ah. Well, we must do the best we can, no?'

As they walked back towards the entrance of the temple, Croesus spoke again. 'There is something else I wanted to ask you.'

'What is that?'

'The Second Death.'

'You fear it for yourself?' the priest said. 'That is not the custom in Lydia. I know an excellent embalmer, if you wish to make preparations.'

'No, you misunderstand. I do not know what it is.'

'I see.' He paused. 'We Egyptians do not fear death, for we may live on in another world after this one. But only if our bodies are preserved.'

'The body is destroyed, and the soul follows it?'

'Yes. The body cannot live without the soul, nor the soul without the body. That is the Second Death.'

Croesus thought about this for a time. 'There is no way of avoiding this?'

'Very difficult. Without the body, it is very difficult. But there are charms that can work.'

'Charms?'

'Yes, there are many of them. Places where the soul can take refuge. Those figurines with which we fill our tombs. A carving on a wall. Even a memory.'

'A memory?'

'Yes. The most unreliable spell of all. A last resort. But it is only when a man is truly forgotten, his body destroyed and his memory lost as well, that his soul will finally perish.'

Croesus nodded. 'Thank you.'

'Come again, Lydian. I would like to speak to you again.'

'I will not be free to come here again. I should not be here now.'

The priest nodded. 'Then I wish you good fortune,' he said, 'and hope you find the death you deserve.'

Croesus almost smiled at this morbid statement, spoken like a blessing.

'The same to you,' he said. 'And I hope you meet it well.'

Croesus returned to the palace, but he did not go in search of the king. Instead, through questioning those he passed, he looked for Psamtek. Croesus expected to find him in some communal chamber of slaves, but he soon found that the Egyptian had been given a chamber of his own, and had retired there. Quite the honour for a slave, he thought, and was surprised at the jealousy the thought provoked.

When he found it, in some near-forgotten corner of the palace, he saw to his satisfaction that it was not the grand private room of a nobleman. It was an old store chamber, a piece of rough fabric across the entrance converting the room to a private space. There was no guard there, and so Croesus at first assumed that Psamtek could not be inside. He would not have been left alone, unescorted. Yet, when he drew closer, he heard a gasp from behind the cloth, a little stifled cry of pain.

Croesus hesitated there, for he had no desire to intrude on the man's private grief. He remembered his own suffering when he had been taken as a slave – months where, seemingly out of nothing, a great and terrible pain would strike him down, the pain of a man mourning for his lost freedom, his lost future. But, whether it was from empathy or curiosity or through fate, he lifted the piece of cloth, and looked in on a scene from a nightmare.

Blood ran on the floor. More, impossibly more than it seemed a single man could hold in his body, yet Psamtek still lived, hunched over on his knees in the centre of the chamber, a red stream pouring from his left wrist. In his other hand was a broken shard of pottery, the only blade that he had been able to improvise. In a moment, Croesus took in the many shallow reddish scores on the Egyptian's arm, the tiny crumbled pieces of clay on the ground in front of him. He must have tried half a dozen times, each piece giving way just as he found the courage to make the cut, until he had found one strong enough to open the vein. He looked up at the intruder, his teeth bared, a man interrupted in a brutal, private act.

In a moment, Croesus was on his knees and at the other man's side. Psamtek tried to fight free of his grip, scrabbling back into the corner of the room. Croesus pursued him, slipping on the bloody floor, tearing a strip from his tunic and pressing it to the wound.

Psamtek had made a bad cut – deep but poorly placed. It was not surprising that he did not know the art of self-destruction, for what need did a king have of such knowledge? The Egyptian could not have imagined that dying could be so difficult.

Still, Psamtek fought to die, clubbing at Croesus with a closed fist, pushing at the old slave's face and trying to tear himself free. But he was not strong enough, in body or in will. His traitor muscles, knowing that they were fighting for their own destruction, gave no force to his blows. After a time, which could have been moments or minutes or hours, Psamtek stopped fighting. Whatever courage he had, he had used it up in a single cut. Croesus felt the Egyptian go limp, and lean against his shoulder. Keeping one hand pressed against the wound, he put his other around Psamtek's back, and held him close. He waited in that strange embrace for the blood to cease flowing, like a man waiting for the changing of the tides. At last, when the wound had closed, Psamtek slumped back defeated against the wall, cradled his head and wept.

From a jar of water in the corner of the room, Croesus poured out two bowls. He carefully washed the blood from his hands and arms and face in the first, then took up the other, and drank it down in a single long swallow. He refilled it, and brought it back to Psamtek, but the Egyptian would not drink.

'The Second Death?' Croesus said, after a long silence. 'Your father?'

'Yes.'

'Then you must live, and remember him. That will prevent it, will it not?'

'That is no use. I will die soon.'

Croesus tore more cloth from his tunic, and began carefully to bind the Egyptian's arm. Psamtek did not resist. 'I thought I would die when I became a slave,' Croesus said. 'But I have lived a long time.'

'Are you glad of it?'

'Yes. I do not know why, but I am. Perhaps it is nothing more than cowardice.'

'I think it is cowardice,' Psamtek said. He looked at his wound. 'But I cannot be brave again.'

'I will stay here tonight. I will not watch you after this.' He pointed to the wound on the other man's arm. 'You may try this again. But if you want to live, I can teach you. If you want to learn.'

'Why would you do this?'

'Because someone once taught me.'

They fell into silence.

'You do not need to stay,' Psamtek said, after a long time. 'I will not do it again.' He paused. 'What is it you live for? Why have you not done this yourself?'

Croesus drank again from the bowl of water, wiped the drops from his whitened beard with the back of his hand. 'Once, I wanted a happy life,' he said. 'Then I wanted a good life, and thought I had found a way to live it. Now it seems that will be taken from me as well. All I have left is the hope of a good death.' He passed the bowl to Psamtek, and the Egyptian took it.

'And what is a good death?'

'There are only two that I know of. One is to die an old man, with your children at your side. The other, to fall in battle, a great enemy dead at your feet.'

'And which do you seek?'

Croesus paused. 'I have no children left,' he said.

Psamtek drank the water, leaned back against the wall and closed his eyes. He was silent for so long that Croesus thought he must have fallen asleep. Then he said: 'I am not like you. Perhaps I do still have something to live for.'

'What is that?'

'That is my concern, is it not?'

'Of course. As you wish.'

'I am glad that you stopped me,' the Egyptian said. 'And I think you are fortunate, Croesus.'

'Why?'

Psamtek looked at him, his expression alien, unknowable.

'Because you are an old man,' he said. 'You will die soon, and will not see what is to come.'

6

In the months that followed the fall of Memphis, Croesus, old as he was, sought to learn a new art: the murderer's lonely contemplation. He had never thought before of how close death was, and now he saw it everywhere. Every piece of fabric seemed a garrotte to him, every hard surface – the stone hand of a statue, the pointed corner of a table – something to force a skull against. His hands wandered restlessly towards any object that might fit his hand, testing weight and sharpness. For all this, he did not yet know if he had the courage to kill, to die in the act of killing. He watched the king, empty of hope, waiting for some opportunity to find out.

Perhaps if they had left the palace of Memphis a chance might have offered itself. At night on the road, in the quiet corner of a temple, some moment in battle where all eyes looked outward, and none thought to watch the slave at the king's side. But Cambyses would not leave the palace. His brother and sister arrived by boat at the dock of the city, and he did not come out to meet them. A great festival was organized by some ambitious local men eager to gain favour with their new master, but the king refused to attend. Each time a courtier suggested, gently or indirectly, that he might wish to go out and survey his new kingdom, they were met with snarls and curses. He remained within the palace at Memphis, but he did not languish in his throne room, or remain in his bedchamber like an invalid. He was constantly on the move, like a man looking for something he had lost and only half remembered. As he stalked from room to room, it was as though the palace was his empire, each chamber an unruly province that threatened rebellion, in need of supervision and suppression.

His entourage followed him on these endless circuits of the palace, Prexaspes, silent and attentive as ever, with Psamtek taking the place of Phanes at the king's right hand. Croesus trailed a few spaces behind them all, for he could not match the king's rapid footsteps, and it was only when his master paused in one chamber or another that he could catch up with the group. As they walked in the corridors, Cambyses would sometimes look back and smile at him, and then increase his pace a little. It was as if he knew what Croesus was thinking about, knew he only had to stay ahead of him, like an antelope outpacing an old and starving lion for days on end, waiting for it to lie down and die.

Croesus was not privy to the king's business. Few were, it seemed. Each day, emissaries were dispatched, but he did not know to where they travelled or what messages they carried. One day, word came that a great part of the army had marched west from the city, the generals and captains given sealed commands. But none seemed to know where they marched, or why.

From time to time Cambyses would cease his wanderings and speak to Croesus, but the old slave seemed to hold scant interest for the king. He received only a few stilted questions, spoken more out of some sense of obligation than anything else, the way a man with little taste for riding will feel obliged to take out an expensive horse from his stable. They never spoke for long, and never alone.

It was not until a month had passed in the palace that the opportunity came.

When he went to the king's chamber that morning he found

Cambyses waiting for him without his entourage, a single bodyguard his only company. Croesus opened his mouth to speak, but the king shook a finger at him, then beckoned for the slave to follow. In all the king's restless wanderings, Croesus thought he had seen every part of the palace. But, as they walked, he soon found himself in corridors he had never been to. It might be, Croesus thought, that the king's movements were deliberately disorientating, that he wished to share every place in the palace with his followers except for this one.

They came to a guarded door, and one of the spearman who stood there started when he saw Croesus, looking at the king in surprise. It seemed he was not used to seeing the king come here in company. They passed through the door, working deeper and deeper into the palace, and as they walked, Croesus prepared himself for what the king would show him. A torture chamber, perhaps, some elaborate dungeon where the king practised the most secret cruelties. A mausoleum, where Cambyses would toy with the preserved bodies of the Egyptian dead, like a child playing with painted wooden dolls.

The last door opened, and he stepped not into some place of forbidden violence, but a balcony that overlooked a garden.

It was a Persian garden in its infancy – the trees were saplings, the grasses newly planted. Perhaps Maia had been at work here, had been commanded to Egypt for this sole purpose, to bring the gardens of Babylon and Pasargadae to the land of the Pharaohs.

It should have been beautiful, but Croesus saw the garden was ringed by high walls to keep out the unwanted and unworthy. Or to keep someone in: the garden had the eerie emptiness of a room designed and kept for one who is absent. He had heard of kings who constructed elaborate homes for rare animals, reproductions of jungles and deserts and steppes and oceans, a miniature of the free world they had been taken from. Yet no matter how elaborate these places were, no matter how comfortable and ornate, they were still cages nonetheless. Any animal put into them, after a month's restless pacing, would die.

He could see fountains of flowing water, a table filled with food, a place where musicians could play. But he could not see the person for whom this place had been built. It was not for the king, as Cambyses made no move to descend into the garden. Indeed, there was no way that Croesus could see of getting down to the garden from the balcony, nor any entrance below.

Croesus watched the king's weak eyes moving restlessly, seeking something. Croesus joined him the search, and at last, almost concealed in the shadows of garden, behind the tallest of the slender saplings, his eyes picked out the shape of a woman. She stood so still that at first he thought she might be a carved statue. Her head tilted up, and she looked back at him, her eyes shining from the darkness. It was the king's wife, the impostor they had called Nitetis.

'Do you see her?' the king said.

'Yes, master.'

'Where?'

'The far corner. To the left, master.'

Cambyses leaned forward, squinting. 'Yes,' he said, and seemed to relax a little. 'She knows I cannot see her without help, and so she hides from me. I have been bringing Prexaspes here, to be my eyes. But he does not understand. He looks at me in a way I do not like. You understand, do you not?'

'Yes, master,' Croesus said quietly, and did not take his eyes from the woman in the shadows.

During the bloody purge, when dozens of noblemen and hundreds of slaves had been put to death in a single night, the impostor Nitetis had vanished too. The people of the court had imagined a cruel death, spoken of how the king must have made her suffer for her deception. Croesus had heard some men insist that the king had spared her, that even in his great rage he did not have the heart to kill the woman he loved, but they had spoken like men who seek to convince themselves. After that deadly night, the long march across the desert, the bloody

146

parade outside Memphis, there were none who now believed that the king could have mercy.

'I cannot let others see her,' Cambyses said. 'And I cannot let her leave. They would laugh at me. Did you think that I had killed her?'

'It is not for me to have such thoughts, master.'

'Ah yes. The old slave's defence.'

Croesus said nothing for a time. 'Mercy can be the sign of a great king, master,' he said eventually.

'I do not think that is true. It is a sign of the weak. But, sometimes, even a king must be weak.' The smile on his face faded. 'I would like to have kept her as my wife,' he said. 'In secret. But I could see that she was afraid of me. That she did not want me in her bed.'

'There are none who may refuse the king his desires.'

Cambyses turned on him, a sudden rage in his eyes. 'I will not force myself on any woman. Do you think me so cruel?'

'Never, master.'

Cambyses seemed to grow calmer. He gestured to the seats on the balcony. 'Come. Sit down.'

Food and wine were brought to them, bread and meat and a knife to cut them with. The king sat down to eat and drink with great relish, seeming to forget that he had company. Eventually, he motioned to a slave to pour Croesus a cup of wine, doing so with a strange reluctance.

'Sometimes I wish I could stay in this garden for ever,' Cambyses said. 'With her. But there is much more to be done.'

'Master?'

'I have sent half the army west. They are going to destroy Ammon. And my emissaries have gone south, to spy on the Ethiopians. I must conquer them as well, it seems.' He shrugged irritably. 'A king's tedious tasks. But there is nothing else to do, is there?'

'You may do as you wish, master.'

'Again, you lie. Those kings who sought to become philosophers

147

or peacemakers or men dedicated to the gods, what happened to them? Butchered and replaced, to a man. And that will not happen to me. I must make war, and I will live because of it.' He looked away, his face solemn. 'But I will have love. They will not take that from me.'

There it was. The moment. The knife, kept sharp for the meat, on the table between them. The lone bodyguard a step too far away. Cambyses had turned his head to face down into the garden, and Croesus could even see the shallow, rapid pulse of the vein in the neck, calling to him with every beat.

Then Cambyses leaned further back, the bodyguard shifted a little closer, and the murderous instant had gone, almost as soon as it had come. To see, know and act in one moment without doubt was what he had to do, Croesus realized. An assassin could not hesitate. What use was a doubting man?

He said: 'Do you remember the desert, master?'

Cambyses blinked like a sleeper waking, and looked back at him. 'What?'

'The desert. Between Palestine, and here. You told me you wanted to go back there. To live with the desert tribes, and be free of this life. I said I would go with you.' Croesus stared down at his hands. 'Do you want to go?'

There was silence for a time, a silence so complete it was as if some god had reached out to hold the world still. Then, just as Croesus was starting to believe the strange dream might come to pass, he heard the king laugh. He closed his eyes against the sound.

'You are old, and stupid, Croesus,' he heard the king say. 'I would never say such a thing.'

'Master, I—'

'What have I to do in a desert?' Cambyses said, interrupting him. 'What work is there for a king in such a place? You are a fool. Look at me.' Croesus opened his eyes, saw the king's hand coming towards his face, and tried not to flinch.

148

Instead of a blow, Cambyses reached forward with an open hand. He stroked the side of Croesus's face and patted his jaw with his absent-minded, gentle touch. 'But I love you, for all your foolishness.' The king stood. 'We must go. There is so much for us to do together, Croesus. So much that you must help me with.'

Cambyses left, but the old slave lingered for a moment longer, looking again down at the woman in the garden, marking the image of her in his mind.

He turned away, and followed the king back into the heart of the palace.

7

The king's emissaries returned from Ethiopia, in a convoy of camels like a merchant's caravan. But they did not travel loaded high with spears or wine or grain. They carried only a single object, wrapped in scarlet cloth, a little shorter than a man.

They passed through the palace, one man carefully holding the crimson-wrapped gift close against his chest, the others ringed around him as if they were bodyguards defending a king. Prexaspes tried to delay them, to get some sense of what news they brought from the south, what gift they bore. But the emissaries, no matter how they were begged or bribed or threatened, did not speak of what they had seen. Their words were for the king alone.

Cambyses received them in his private chamber. Their audience did not last long. A matter of minutes, with no raised voices heard from within the king's chamber, no calls for others to come and offer their opinion. The emissaries left the room, their faces unconcerned. Their hands were empty, the gift left within.

Behind them, the chamber door swung closed, and, from the inside, they heard the bar come down.

*

Hours passed, and the hours became days. The king would not leave his chamber.

Courtiers came, one after another, to beg with the king through the closed door, but he would not receive them, nor even speak a word. The king's world, which he had already reduced to the size of a palace, now measured nothing greater than a single room.

The government continued like a beheaded animal, with lurching, senseless motion. But soon the empire would be paralysed, no man wanting to take a decision that the king might countermand, if and when he returned from his isolation. None wanted to think of what might follow, should the absence of command persist.

On the third day, Croesus went to sit outside the king's chamber. He saw a pair of slaves already stationed there, ears pressed to the door, no doubt put there by Prexaspes. Every breath and cough, each bout of weeping or muttered word, would be passed on to their master, who would try to find some pattern, to understand the mind and will of the king.

Croesus sat and spoke at the king's door for many hours. He pleaded, reasoned, and flattered, but received nothing but silence in return. At last he stood, the wooden stool scraping across the floor, and something stirred within the chamber. Croesus heard bare feet padding across stone, and the door creaked as weight was pressed against it from the other side.

'Send Psamtek to me.'

Then, not waiting for a response, Croesus heard the sound of the footsteps moving away again.

The following day, Croesus found himself summoned by royal command. He assumed he was being called on to reason with the king, as he had done the day before. Yet the man who led him did not turn towards Cambyses's quarters.

When he passed through the unfamiliar door, he found the king's sister waiting for him. He had not seen Parmida for the better part of a year, yet she seemed to have aged much more than that span of time would suggest. She was still beautiful, but her eyes were sunken, deeply scored with lines of grief. She had a face that had forgotten how to smile.

Parmida marked his arrival with a blank gaze, then turned to her personal slaves. 'Leave us,' she said. They hesitated for a moment, glancing at Croesus doubtfully. But, after brief and silent deliberation, they seemed content to leave their lady alone with him. Perhaps they thought an old man as safe as a eunuch.

'What has happened to him?' she said.

Croesus did not reply for a time. 'I wish that I could say that he was mad,' he said quietly. 'But if that is true, it is only part of the truth.'

'They say such terrible things about him. About what he has done. Are they true?'

'Yes. They are.'

She covered her face with her hands. 'I love him,' Croesus heard her say. 'But I do not know if I can ever forgive him.'

'You must try.'

'Why must I?'

'Because someone has to. And I cannot.'

'You will not have to live to see what he will do.'

'So others have told me. That is little comfort. You may live to see the end of this. I will not.'

'Perhaps none of us will.' She paused. 'I have heard from him.'

'You have seen him?'

'No. But he sent a message to me. To reassure me, I think. I don't know.' She stared down at her hands, which, as if of their own accord, had resumed their ceaseless motion. 'He is going to war against the Ethiopians.'

'Why?'

'He says they have insulted him. That they have shamed him, worse than the Egyptians ever did.'

Croesus tried to smile, to give some gesture of reassurance to her. 'You must not worry. He means to march through the desert next next summer, I take it? We will have the harvest. With the supplies from the Nile—'

'Croesus, he says the army must march tomorrow.'

Croesus did not reply. He turned the news over in his mind, to see exactly what it must mean, to see if he could be mistaken, if there were any other way that this plan of the king's would end. And then he felt the sudden, aching relief of a man relieved of a burden, who has had a terrible decision made for him.

'Will you do something for me?' he said.

'What is it?'

'There are two slaves. I will give you their names. Would you keep them here, with you? I fear he will take them with the army, old even as they are.'

'They are friends of yours?'

'They were once.'

She hesitated. 'It is much to ask. I do not know what he will do.'

'You will be safe. He loves you, Parmida. And they will serve you well.' He paused. 'Be kind to them, will you?'

'What will happen in the desert, Croesus?'

He did not reply for a time. 'Your brother once wanted to go and live with the people of the desert,' he said, 'and asked me to go with him. I had hope that I could take him away, that he might find some peace there. But in his sickness he forgot this wish. He wanted us to live in the desert. If we march tomorrow, we will die there instead.'

She nodded dully. Croesus reached forward, parted her restless hands, clasped them in his own. She did not show any surprise or outrage at this forbidden gesture, except to close her eyes. He held her hands for a moment, still, as if they were both in prayer together.

Distant, he heard the beating of the drums, like the great heart of a monster. All over the city, the spearmen and archers and horsemen would be taking up their weapons and marching to their places, hearing the call to war once again.

When the army gathered outside Memphis, the mood amongst the men was relaxed. They laughed and joked and sang their songs, surprised by the strange and sudden command to gather and march, but not fearful. They believed, with the trusting hope of a soldier for his commander, that there must be something that they did not know, that a caravan of supplies would greet them at the southern border, or that the land to Ethiopia was not impassable desert as they had heard, but land rich in grain and wine. They had crossed a desert before by using a trick – there must be another prepared. It must be so, they said to each other, for otherwise to march south would be madness. The king would not make so foolish a mistake that a spearman could see the error.

The soldiers waited beneath the burning sun. Some propped their wicker shields up to make shade to sit beneath, and stacked their spears in piles. Others sat cross-legged and took arrows from their quivers, inspecting fletchings and straightening bent shafts. They passed around wine and bread, eating and drinking freely. More supplies would soon be given to them, they said to each other – no need to march on an empty stomach. The captains gave no sign that anything was amiss. They knew that to admit the slightest doubt could not be countenanced, for nothing was so destructive as doubt to an army. Up to the very last moment, they would say nothing except give the lie of assured victory. They looked towards the walls of the city with the opposite hope to that of the men they captained. The ordinary spearmen hoped that their wait could be over soon and the march begin. The captains prayed silently that the king would never come.

But, at last, the king did appear, riding a white horse, and the army roared its acclaim. He shyly raised his hand to acknowledge them, and they roared again. The men had heard the rumours of his seclusion, yet it seemed to them more proof that their war would be blessed with good fortune. He had brooded on his own and communed with the gods, and now he was here to lead them to victory once again.

There were some who noted that Prexaspes was not there beside him. A few wondered why. If he were out of favour they would have heard of it; he must have chosen to remain behind. But Psamtek was there, and Croesus as well. They looked at the old slave, the lucky charm of Persian kings. No army had been defeated with Croesus as a part of it, and when Cyrus had sent him away, the Massagetae had killed him. They believed in Croesus even more than they believed in the king. They looked at him and saw his blank face, took it for confidence, for faith.

The soldiers picked up their shields and their weapons, and formed into their ranks. Forty thousand men, marching to the beating drums began the long march south, into an empty land.

'It is war again, then?'

'Yes.'

'You were right, Croesus. You said he would not stay in Babylon.'

'He lasted longer than I thought he would. I only wish we had been given more time here.'

'Well, I have never seen the plains. Neither has Maia. We shall see them together.'

'No.'

'No?'

'You both go west. With the stonemasons, to Pasargadae.'

'Your doing?'

'No. I would rather you rode with us. But Cyrus needs good workers to finish the palace. You have earned that reputation. You and Maia both.'

'That I have.'

'I suppose I may not see you again.'

'That is true.'

'Isocrates—'

'There is no need to speak. I know what you want to say. You can hide nothing from me.'

'And yet I can see nothing of you, beyond what you choose to show me. I wonder if that is why Maia agreed to marry you. To know your secrets.'

156

'You invent mystery in me where there is none. That is your way, I suppose.'

'You say you know me. I still do not know what you think of me. Whether I am a fool who keeps you entertained, or some kind of brother.'

'Do not talk this way, Croesus.'

'I am sorry. But if I live through this war, I shall not be parted from you and Maia again.'

'Then I must pray to the gods of the Massagetae to grant them victory, it seems, to finally be rid of you.'

'You see? Perhaps you truly mean that, I do not know.'

'A poor joke. Come, enough of this. You are not a fool or a brother. You know you are a friend to me.'

'Thank you.'

'You must go. The king will be waiting.'

'Yes. Good luck, Isocrates.'

'Croesus?'

'Yes?'

'I will see you again.'

'I hope so.'

'You hope. But I know.'

The City of the Dead

I

Out in the Ethiopian desert, the men gathered around the weak fire, huddling close with their arms around one another. A few thin pieces of wood, mummified by decades beneath the sun, burned reluctantly, giving smoke but little heat. These men were lucky. Few in Cambyses's army had even this scanty fuel for their fires. They were burning other things now.

Beneath their armour, their ribs were pressed tight against weak skin, like those of cattle in a drought land. Their muscles had wasted down to tendons, barely strong enough to hold their starving bodies together, and their faces were so deeply sunken that, in the light of the fire, they had only shadows where their eyes should be. They sat, silent together, and waited for someone to have the courage to begin.

Finally, one man lifted his helmet from the ground beside him. Another man handed him a bag of small pebbles. He counted them out, one for each of the men left in the circle. One pebble was unlike the others; the same shape, but entirely black in colour. He lifted this pebble up between his thumb and forefinger, and showed it to every man in the circle. The others nodded to him, and he cast the black stone into the helmet. He shook it, and listened to the gentle rattle of stone against stone and stone against metal, like the breaking of the waves on a pebble shore.

Around other fires in the Persian army, the decision was made by brute strength, or by allegiances and factions that shifted and changed every night. But these men, who had fought together in a dozen nations and shared everything equally together, could not break their brotherhood. All was decided by the lot.

Each man assumed that if the black stone fell to him, he would meet his end well. Not like the others who had been taken before. Yet none could truly believe, or allow themselves to believe, that when they reached into the helmet they would draw their death out of it.

This time, it was the fifth man to reach in who took the black stone.

He had dreamed of it every night, but had still believed it was impossible that it would ever fall to him in the waking world. He wondered, for a moment, if he was still dreaming. Weakened, almost hallucinatory with hunger, day and night, waking and dreaming, had all long since melded together for him. When he looked up, saw the famished eyes on him, he found that he could not go peacefully. He leapt up, and, with the last of his strength, he tried to run.

They chased him, the starving in pursuit of the starving. They could barely move faster than a walk, all feeling the emptiness within that somehow still had weight, dragging them towards the earth. A few of the pursuers collapsed, unable to go further or unwilling to do what had to be done. The rest pressed on, almost bent double, each folded over his hunger like a dying man over a wound.

At last, the doomed man could run no further. He stopped and went to his knees and bowed his head, and the others fell upon him, in relief more than in anger or bloodlust. One of them leaned in close and murmured a breathless thanks to him.

The daggers rose and fell and came up again, the blood black on the blades under the moonlight. The dying man didn't have the strength to cry out at their clumsy, exhausted thrusts. He lay mute as they murdered him.

The men collapsed around the body, their hands and faces dark with blood. Like an automaton, the first lifted his helmet again. Each reached inside once more, and the second man to pull a lot out was the one who took the black stone. He wept, as another man handed him the jagged blade. He knelt over the corpse, his knife working in the darkness, taking the body to pieces. The others waited, licking the blood from their hands, each man hating the saliva that flooded into his mouth at the sight of the dead soldier being prepared.

Theirs had been the first killing that night. Now men screamed all across the camp, first one at a time, then more and more, until hundreds seemed to cry out with a single voice.

Then there was only sound and smell of cooking meat. The army fell silent, and began to feed on itself.

The food lay untouched before her. Parmida found no desire for the rich meal that they had brought to her chamber. She had chosen this room in the palace for her own, purely because it faced south. Each day, Parmida sat by the window, pulled aside the thin fabric that covered it, and looked out across the funerary grounds and into the shimmering heat of the red sands, looking towards Ethiopia, waiting for them to return.

Maia sat beside her. The slave should not have taken her eyes from Parmida, while waiting for a command from the king's sister. But she too looked out into the desert.

'How long could we stay here, do you think?' Parmida said.

'There are stories among my people of those who waited twenty years to see their sons and husbands return from the wars.'

'It must have been a more patient time. They are gone two months, and already . . .'

'That is a long time in the desert, my lady.'

'Twenty years, you say. I could not stand to wait so long. I would go mad. I am afraid of that, sometimes.'

'You will not go mad, my lady.'

'If my brother has lost his mind, perhaps I will too. We share the same blood, after all.'

'That will not be your fate.'

'And what will be my fate, do you think?'

'That is not for me to say, my lady. Forgive me. I speak too freely.'

'I am glad that you do. Your old stories: I suppose they were full of princesses who did nothing but wait.'

'Only some of them, my lady.'

'Oh? There is another fate open to me?'

'I have heard there was a princess who did not want to marry. A great runner, restless and free, who would not wait for anyone. She would race any man who sought her hand, and kill those who lost.'

'I like that story. My mother was a good runner, I have always been told. What happened to her? To your running princess.'

'A man tricked her and caught her and made her his wife, of course. How else would such a story end?'

A noise from behind took their eyes from the desert. At the entrance to the chamber, Isocrates bowed to them. 'Bardiya has asked to see you my lady.'

'I wait for one brother, and another comes to find me. Isocrates?'

'My lady?'

'Do you think they will return?'

'I do not know.'

'Do you want them to?'

He hesitated, caught out.

'You want Croesus to return, I think,' she said.

'I wish he had told me that he was to go, and I was to stay.' His gaze drifted to Maia. 'But I do not know if I want him to come back. I wish he could have been braver.'

'You mean crueller,' Maia said softly.

'Yes. Perhaps I do.'

'Enough of this. I will see my brother,' Parmida said. 'Leave us now.'

When Bardiya came in she tried not to flinch at the sight of him – he looked so much like his brother, it was impossible not to think of Cambyses. She knew that Baridya hated the way that people would look at him with fear, as if he were some ghost of the king. Or perhaps it was something else they saw in him – the king as he should have been.

'Leave us,' Bardiya said to Maia.

'I have no secrets from her.'

'No? But I do.'

When they were alone, she said: 'There has been news?'

'No. Only rumours.'

'How long will the noblemen wait?'

'They are all too afraid of him. They will want to know for certain.'

'Are you afraid?'

'Yes. But I think he will return. He will see sense, and turn back.'

'I fear he may be beyond that,' she said quietly.

'I have heard others talking. Saying the same thing. That Cambyses should not be king. Sometimes I wonder, even if he does come back, if we should—'

'No,' Parmida said. 'Do not even think of that.'

'You are sure?'

'We cannot. We are Cyrus's children. We must protect each other. We must not turn against each other. No matter what happens.'

'Yes,' Bardiya said. 'You are right.' He sighed then, and some hidden tension seemed to unravel from his shoulders. 'I am glad that you said that. I was so afraid, that I might have to . . . But I could not bear it.'

'Will you sit with me?' Parmida smiled at her brother. 'You have chased away my slaves. I do not want to be alone.'

He sat beside her and looked outwards. They both knew that, if the army did return, he would be the one to see it first. Unlike his brother's, Bardiya's eyes had always been strong.

They let the silence return, and stared together into the desert.

2

'Horsemeat. Disgusting.'

Croesus flinched as the bone, still half covered in meat, clattered back to the plate. The king wiped the grease from his fingers onto a piece of cloth, and Croesus felt his eyes linger on each brown mark on the pale fabric. The words fought to be spoken, the words begging the king not to waste the slightest smear of food, and he swallowed them down, hating himself for it.

The king finished cleaning his hands, and looked down at the meat. He hesitated, shrugged, and picked it up once again. 'But I am hungry,' he said, laughing as he tore a fresh strip from the bone, 'so I shall not complain.' Croesus felt a sigh escape his lips, beyond his power to restrain it, and heard it echoed by the others. They had all wanted, more than anything, for Cambyses to leave that food untouched.

Each night the king would dine, and once he had retired, Croesus and the other members of the council would feast on the food the king had rejected. They did not brawl for it, not yet at least; they silently divided it amongst themselves equally, for what happened around the campfires at night had given them a fear of the rule of force. The food was not much; every waking moment Croesus felt the yawning, dulling hunger that left no other thought behind it, and each night he dreamed of nothing else. But they had not yet had to make the terrible choices of the other men.

Cambyses did not know what was being done for him. When he rode out at the centre of the army, his failing eyes could not see the starving men who surrounded him, growing thinner, growing fewer. He had not even noticed the sudden disappearance of his cavalry, two weeks into their journey, not connected that with the sudden preponderance of horsemeat. When the killing began at night, a general would gesture to the musicians to strike their drums and sing. Usually it was loud enough that they heard only the occasional, solitary scream, but Croesus had come to hate and fear that music. It was like perfume covering the smell of a corpse.

He looked around the circle, in the half-light of the fire, to see if, at last, any man would speak out. General and councillor and slave alike all looked to the ground. They waited, tense and miserable, for some miracle to free them. Only Psamtek looked calm, and did not seem to care. Perhaps he had already resigned himself to death.

'Why do you not eat, Croesus?' the king said.

'I am not hungry, master,' Croesus said dully. It was the same response he had given for days, now. He listened, for a time, to the sound of the king eating. 'I must speak to you, master.'

The king did not notice the shiver of tension that passed through his council. Nor did he stop eating. He waved a hand to Croesus, gesturing for his slave to speak, and continued to tear meat from the bone with his teeth.

'The men are starving,' he said.

'We are all starving,' Cambyses said, gesturing to his plate. 'You call this food? But we will be through the desert in another two weeks, I am certain of it. We will find supplies on the other side. These Ethiopians cannot live on air, can they?'

Croesus looked again at the others. They said nothing. A few muttered their excuses and hurried towards the entrance of the tent, not wanting to be present for what was to come.

'It is worse for the men, master,' Croesus said quietly.

'I should certainly hope so,' the king said, continuing to eat. 'I would have you all put to death, if the common men were eating better than their king.'

'They are feeding on each other, master,' he said.

A silence.

'What?'

'They draw lots. Some do, anyway. They all have different ways of deciding. It has been been going on for many days now.'

Silence came again. Cambyses looked down at the piece of horseflesh in his hand, as if seeing it for the first time. He dropped it back down again, and stared at the plate for a long time.

When he looked back up at Croesus, his eyes were lost.

'What do I do?' he said softly.

Croesus had been ready for disbelief, and rage. He had even been prepared for some kind of regret. But this, seeing his king utterly at a loss, looking for someone else to guide him and to take control, he had not expected.

Another voice filled the silence. 'Men die in battle in their tens of thousands, master,' Psamtek said. 'What does it matter if a few thousand more die to get us to the battle? It is a sacrifice the men are happy to make for you, my king.'

'Do you think so?' said Cambyses.

'I have heard that they weep with joy when they are chosen for the fires,' the Egyptian said. 'Remember the Ethiopians. Will you really let them shame you? Will you shame yourself, by running from battle?'

Cambyses bent to the ground and tore at the carpet with his long nails, strings of fibre collecting under his nails like ripped flesh. He howled, and the others affected to look elsewhere. They stared at the ground, or their hands, or closed their eyes, and waited for it to be over.

At last, the king sat upright once again. 'Croesus?' he said. 'Tell me what to do.'

Cambyses would be the last man left, he thought, if they continued. Croesus had believed that the king would be the first to die when the men began to starve. But some strange, impossible loyalty bound them to him. No mutiny would come, and when the last of the horse-meat gave out, the men would begin to give themselves up to feed their king. His entire army consumed, he would march on; one man, blind and ragged and almost starved to death, coming alone out of the desert against the Ethiopian army.

It would mean the death of the mad king, at the very last. But he thought of the army, the tens of thousands of men who remained, and he knew that he could not give them that death.

'We cannot win this war, even if we stay,' said Croesus. 'The men can barely stand, let alone fight. We will all die out here. Unless we turn back.'

Cambyses said nothing, staring down at that torn carpet with his dull, near-blind stare, weighing up the shame of living against a fear of dying.

'We will turn back,' he said.

The council, so long dormant, returned suddenly to life. Orders were prepared and dispatched, plans laid for the return to Memphis, all seeking to forget the horrors they had seen in practical action. Croesus remained still, and let the words of others wash over him like water.

When, at last, he raised his head, he found Psamtek staring back him. The Egyptian's face was unreadable.

The sun rose again on the desert, and the men of the army rose with it. No man would look at the one who stood next to him. What had been done at night was not spoken of in the day, and none liked to read his own guilt in the eyes of his companions. They bent over, slow and sighing like old men, and took their weapons from the ground. Weak as they all were, no fighting man would willingly leave his weapon behind – he would leave his honour in the sand with it. The pack animals had long gone, and the cavalry marched awkwardly beside the infantry, unused to walking. But all men now stood equal on the desert sand. All men except for the king.

The rumour spread – first to two men, then ten, then two hundred, until every one of the thirty thousand men that remained were speaking the same thing. That today, they would march with the rising sun at their right hand, not their left. They were going home.

They broke from their ragged formations, massing in a great mob around the king's tent. When Cambyses emerged, to see what remained of his army gathered before him, he turned his face away, and wept. Still not looking at them, he raised his arm, and extended a single finger towards the north. As one, what remained of the army gave a ragged, exhausted cheer. They had forgotten, or forgiven, that he had brought them to that place. They knew simply that he was the only one who could save them. He had done so, and they loved him for it, as they loved him for his tears.

The king mounted his horse, the sole one left in the army, and turned its head to the north, back towards Memphis. He rode out, and the soldiers marched behind him. Each man with the bone of a comrade in his pocket, to suck and chew on during the long journey home.

3

An army of the dead, skeleton men with a little flesh stretched over them, marched out of the desert. On the outskirts of Memphis they passed the stone tower that had once witnessed the humiliation of the Egyptians. There were no farmers working in the outlying fields, no children playing in gangs on the fringes of the city. Even the ditches were devoid of beggars. Confronted with the deserted city, in the fevered minds of the soldiers a fantasy began to take hold. Perhaps they truly had died in the Ethiopian desert and were returning to some mirrored Memphis in the afterlife. If they marched to the graveyards, they might discover the cemeteries teeming with ghosts to welcome them to their new home. If they broke into one of the pyramids, they would find themselves not in a tomb, but received in the splendid court of one of the hundred Egyptian kings who ruled in the city of the dead.

Deep within the city, they heard the sound of music, the sound of laughter. Some of the men broke away, to raid the houses and scavenge for food. Their captains let them go, too sick with hunger to call them back to order. The rest of the army stayed in line and marched on. Unified by their suffering, they moved through the empty streets, towards the source of the sound.

It was a festival.

The starving, cannibal army marched into the centre of Memphis to find the Egyptians in celebration. The whole city was gathered there, and many more besides, from the towns and villages for miles around, every one of them dressed in their finest clothes, dancing and singing. And above it all, pervading every corner of the city, the air was filled the familiar smell of cooking meat.

The people of Memphis stared at the arriving army in surprise, but not in fear. At first, they wondered if this horde of men was, in some way, part of the festivities. A parade of new slaves, starved for the march to weed out the weak. They stood on their toes and climbed on top of market stalls, looking behind to see the army that was driving this new force of slaves before them. It was only when they saw Cambyses on his solitary horse that they realized this was the Persian army, defeated by the desert, enslaved by hunger.

Cambyses stared out over the crowd. Gradually, silence fell, and the Egyptians gathered and stared at their ruler, more in curiosity than in fear, waiting to see what kind of a show Cambyses and his army would put on for the festivities.

When Cambyses spoke at last, it was in the quiet, steady tones of a man contemplating murder.

'You dare to hold a festival?' he said. 'We march out of the desert, like this, and you celebrate?' His face went pale. 'I will kill you all,' he whispered. 'I swear it.'

A shaven-headed Egyptian priest came forward from the crowd. Croesus recognized him – the high priest from the temple of Ptah – and felt fear tighten around his chest.

The Egyptian bowed deeply. 'Forgive our celebration. It is not to do with you, my king.' He smiled. 'Our god has come to us in the form of an animal. Only once each generation are we so fortunate. Perhaps,' he added, 'it is to welcome our great king back to Memphis. To give you his blessing. There could be no greater honour.'

'Is this true?' Cambyses said, turning to Psamtek. 'About this god?'

'A foolish superstition, shared only by the ignorant people of my country. They should have shown more respect.'

Cambyses nodded, and looked back to the priest. 'Bring it to me.'

'Master, I—' Croesus began.

'Bring it to me,' Cambyses said again. 'This animal. This god. Let me see your god.'

The priest bowed again. 'As you wish.'

The first hints of nervousness passed through the Egyptian crowd, at the thought of the king encountering its god. The soldiers broke order. Some lay down and slept in the street like stray dogs, too exhausted even to eat. Others busied themselves with gathering all the food, wine and water that they could. Some hesitated over the cooked meat, but ate it all the same, hunger overcoming their memories of the desert.

After a time, there was a clamour at the back of the Egyptian crowd, and the sea of people parted reluctantly to let the procession through. The god approached.

It was a black bull calf. It walked without a halter, flanked by a dozen priests who guided it with respectful taps on the rump and gentle clicks of the tongue. Even at a distance, Croesus could see the holy marks upon it: the perfect white diamond on its forehead, the eagle shape etched in white hairs along its back, like the blazon of an army. Had either of these marks been imperfect, it would have been just another animal for meat, breeding and labour. But they were flawless – mathematicians could have applied their instruments to the diamond to confirm its perfection, the most exacting artists could not have faulted the symmetry of the eagle. As the god came forward, the crowd, glancing nervously at Cambyses, reached out to it with quick, hesitant touches, seeking the blessing of their god, fearing the retribution of their king.

The calf trotted forward until it stood in front of Cambyses. The priests respectfully suggested that it stop, and it did so, sniffing curiously at the horse, then raising its head to face the king. The calf looked up at him expectantly, with the happy, anxious air of an animal that is made the centre of attention.

Cambyses dismounted and came forward. He stared into the calf's deep black eyes, looking, perhaps, for some spark of divinity there. He reached out a hesitant hand towards the diamond mark on the animal's forehead but stopped before he reached it. He pulled his hand back sharply, as if he had been stung. He screamed, reached down, and there was a flash of sun against bronze. Then the calf cried out, stumbled back with one leg lamed, and the dagger came out of its thigh followed by a flowing arc of blood.

A sound somewhere between a sigh and hiss broke through the watching crowd. For a moment, when the blade was in up to the hilt, all who were there could pretend that they had not seen what they had seen, could imagine that he had reached forward empty-handed, to receive the blessing of the god as thousands had that day. But the pouring blood confirmed the sacrilege.

The Persian soldiers locked shields and rapped their spears against them in a show of force, but the Egyptians showed no sign of anger. They looked on their king with pity, as one would look on an imbecile or god-cursed man, as the beast shrieked and hobbled away, dragging its lame leg behind it.

Cambyses laughed as he watched it try to run. 'There. This is your god? This shitting god?' He reached up and wiped away sudden tears. 'Let us go.' He waved an absent hand at the priest, almost as an after-thought. 'Put him to death. Put anyone who continues to celebrate to death as well.'

The Egyptian priest gave his familiar little shrug, as if receiving a piece of news that was of no real consequence, and went quietly with his executioners. The crowd stood defiantly for a moment in the face of the soldiers who began driving them away, looking at the retreating figure of Cambyses. They marked the image in their minds, then filtered back through the crowded streets to their homes. Every man and woman there, seeing their god defiled, wished Cambyses dead. A wish of ten thousand for one man's end. Belief that strong can take physical form, like molten iron pouring into a mould. This mould, in years to come, would take the shape of a blade sliding into the king's flesh.

But not yet.

When Croesus came back to the palace, he walked like a wounded man, staggering, stumbling, almost falling, only somehow to stay upright and take another step. He felt as though he aged with every movement of his body, like one of those men from the old stories who is blessed with eternal youth, merely to have the weight of his years come upon him in a matter of moments.

Around him, soldiers ran past, breaking order and raiding the kitchens, demanding food and wine from every slave and servant that they passed, but the very sight of food made Croesus retch. His hunger, a constant companion for so long, seemed to have atrophied entirely. It had gone as soon as the blade had struck the bull, as if the blasphemy had taken away some crucial inner part of him, cursing him never to eat again, to starve to death in the most fertile land on the planet. If this were true, at that moment the thought did not have the power to trouble him. He could think solely of the person he must see.

He went up stairs and through narrow corridors, past armouries and treasuries, until the chamber he had been searching for loomed large in front of him. He lifted a hand, shaking like a palsied man, and pushed the door open. Inside, he saw the woman's face, her eyes widening in shock. Then the face dissolved into the air around it, and the whole world swam away from him. He felt himself falling.

*

Time passed – days or hours, he could not tell. His world was reduced to fever dreams, to warm milk that was given to him by figures he knew but could not seem to name, to crying out in the dark and hearing no answer. He wondered, with the strange, specific clarity that sometimes comes to those struck down by fever, if he would lose a part of his mind to this sickness, the way Cambyses had lost a part of his. They would be a mad king and a mad slave, ruling a kingdom together. Perhaps, if he were to go insane, he would understand his master better. He thought of Psamtek. Then he thought of nothing at all.

When he returned to himself, the fever burned from his skin and shaken from his bones, he was in darkness. There was only a single source of light, hidden somewhere close by, a small fire placed out of sight to protect his eyes. He could smell the odour of stale sweat clinging heavy on his skin, and feel improvised bedding under him, empty sacks that still bore a few stray stalks of wheat. He had not noticed them in the depths of his fever, but now he felt them worrying against his back like insects, and could not ignore them.

He shifted, and as if in answer, a shape moved in the darkness. Even with so little light, he recognized who the figure was. He fancied that he could have had half his senses taken from him, his mind broken with age and destroyed by sickness, and he would still know that man in a moment.

'Has the king asked for me?' Croesus said.

'No,' Isocrates replied. 'He speaks to no one but Psamtek now.'

'How long has it been?'

'Five days. The fever broke last night.'

With difficulty, Croesus pushed himself up to a sitting position. 'That is too long.'

'Less than a week.'

'You do not understand how fast Cambyses moves from one idea to the next.'

'You forget. I do know how quickly he thinks. And acts.'

'That is true.' Croesus ran a hand through his thin, dirty hair. 'Why are you here, Isocrates?'

Isocrates did not reply for a time. He lifted the small brazier, and fed it another sliver of wood. Croesus flinched from this weak light, for it seemed to physically press itself against his eyes. Isocrates glanced at Croesus, and placed the fire out of sight once again.

'Was it as bad as they say, out in the desert?' Isocrates said.

'Worse.'

'Did they—'

'Yes. I do not want to speak of it.' Croesus looked down at his hands, found them trembling slightly, and thought of that disease of the mind that began with shaking hands. Concentrating hard, he made them go still. 'I do not even know why we were there,' he said.

'I do. The truth came out after you left, and the men of the court speak of little else.' Isocrates hesitated. 'Do you truly wish to know?'

'Yes. I do.'

'Cambyses's men went to the Ethiopian court,' Isocrates said. 'They said they were there to honour the Ethiopian king, though really they were spying. The king sniffed them out. I have heard they select their king by finding the tallest man in the land, but it sounds as if he was as clever as he was tall.

'They brought him gifts. A purple robe, a casket of myrrh, a golden necklace and bracelets, and a jar of wine. They said that he looked at the purple robe and when he heard it was dyed, he cast it aside and said that, like the messengers, it was pretending to be something it was not. He said the same thing about the myrrh, when he heard it was perfumed. He laughed at the gold, saying that gold was so common in their country that they used it to fetter the condemned.' Isocrates paused. 'He did like the wine, though. He said that was one thing the Persians did better than his people.

'He told them that Cambyses was a liar and a coward, who craved lands that were not his and had already enslaved one nation who had never wronged him. He told them to be thankful that the children of Ethiopia were not afflicted with the disease of ambition, or they would come and take Cambyses's kingdom from him. Then he sent them on their way. And he gave them a bow, of a kind that is common amongst their archers. He said that when the king of Persia could draw that back to his chin, that would be the day Ethiopia would fall.' Isocrates spread his hands, and shrugged. 'The messengers gave the bow to Cambyses when they returned, and he could not even draw it a finger width.'

'An insult,' Croesus said, and turned his head away. 'Ten thousand starved and murdered, for such an insult. I had hoped they had died for something more.'

'Wars have been started for less than that.'

'I suppose that is true. I do not know why he sent a force west, to Ammon. It might have been for nothing more than a whim. Has there been word from that army?'

'Yes. That is why you must attend the king tomorrow.'

'Why tomorrow?'

'A messenger has come back from the west.'

'Word from the army at Ammon?'

'They did not reach Ammon. No one has heard or seen anything of them since they left the city.'

Croesus did not reply at first. 'I do not know that the king's mind can withstand another disaster,' he said eventually.

'Is this the end, do you think?'

'No. Not after what I saw out in the desert. Cambyses once told me that the people respected the cruel more than the kind, the strong more than the wise. Perhaps he sees it more truly than I can bear. And now he has Psamtek to help him see.'

'Psamtek?'

'He wanted us to stay out in the desert. And at the festival . . . I do not know why he acts as he does. Why he encourages the king.'

Isocrates did not respond, and in the darkness, Croesus could not read his face to understand what this silence might mean.

'Has Parmida been kind to you?' Croesus said, to break to silence.

'Yes. I thank you for that. She is a good mistress.'

'And is Maia well?'

'She is well. She does not wish to see you.' Isocrates leaned forward, put his head in his hands like an exhausted or defeated man. 'When you came into the palace,' he said slowly, 'it was her you came to find, wasn't it? Not me.'

'Yes.'

Isocrates nodded absently. He stood, and walked to the door of the room, out of the reach of the dim light.

'You were right, Isocrates. In the desert.'

Isocrates turned back. 'Yes,' he said, 'I was.'

'I will do it. I will . . .' Still, he could not speak the words. 'Will you help me?'

'No, Croesus.'

'Why?'

'Because you will never get the chance again. Because it is too late.'

With that, he was gone.

Croesus lay back down in the silence for a time. When at last he rose again, in the corner of the room he found a clean tunic and a deep bowl of clear water, left behind by the slave who had once been his friend. He stripped off his dirty clothes and poured the water over his head, rubbing the dirt from his arms and chest and face, the old skin moving slack beneath his fingers like that of some lifeless thing.

He stood naked, trembling with the cold like a newborn calf. He slipped the clean tunic over his head and went in search of the king.

*

Walking with slow, confident steps, Isocrates left the corridors of the palace behind, passed through the gate, and went down into the city. He was gambling with his life to do so. Had any of the guards chosen to question him, looked past the initial smooth evasions he would have given and found that he had no true excuse to offer, his offence would be punishable by death. But no man challenged him. Most of the guards had come from the desert, and leaned hollow-eyed against the walls, their bodies only partially restored by five days of feasting, their minds still reliving the things that they had seen and done out on the unforgiving sands.

He walked the same streets that Croesus had wandered through many months before. He passed market stalls that sold bread and wine and salted fish from the Nile, past the embalming houses where the poorest paid for the crudest of preservations, hoped for some chance of surviving in the next life, and those the wealthy families paid for miracles, their corpses so unaging it was impossible to imagine that they did not, somehow, live on. He saw too the dentists' lodges, where every Egyptian went as inevitably as they went to the embalming houses, their teeth ruined by hard grains just as their bodies would be ruined by time. He walked next to the great temple of Ptah, but did not stop there. He walked on, until at last he found the place he was looking for.

It was a tradesmen's house with no markings on it, no sign hung outside. From it came the almost imperceptible scent of ink and papyrus, notable only when massed together, as if it were solely when these materials were gathered in some vast phalanx, countless thousands of rolls of paper and gallons of ink, that they had any kind of substance at all.

The scribe stood in doorway of his home, his thin fingers marked with ink, like little tattoos. Isocrates went to him, and began to try to speak. They stood for a time, each trading words that the other could not understand. They passed through half a dozen different languages, for in his long years of service Isocrates had learned pieces of speech from many nations. The scribe had such a knowledge himself, and slowly, switching between the fragments of language that each possessed, acting out in gesture when words failed them, Isocrates and the scribe pieced together some manner of speaking. They invented their own tongue, and when they had reached some common grammar, they began, at last, to try to understand each other.

It was difficult. Isocrates was asking for something that had not been done before; an idea that was hard to explain in a common language, near impossible in the improvised speech to which they were reduced. But they worked together, neither the slave nor the scribe showing any sense of rush or impatience, both men quietly confident that they could understand one another.

After hours of speech and gesture, at last the scribe clapped his hands together, nodded, and sat down to begin his work. Isocrates watched the man write, the ink marking out the strange pictograms that the Egyptians used instead of letters. He had heard tell of caves in the deserts that were covered with the paintings of ancient hunters, the first markings of thought made solid. Paintings of men and women making love, and swimming in seas in lands that were now parched of water. Paintings of great monsters of hair and teeth tumbling to the ground, bristling with spears, lost from the world and living on only in ash daubed on cave walls.

He knew that men now wrote down their taxes, debts, and inventories. There were rumours of poets, not trusting that their work would outlive them, who had begun committing their work to paper, fixing for eternity what had once been ever changing and told anew every night; of women writing letters of love on wax and clay and sending them to the men they desired. He wondered if any man had yet done what he sought to do, to commit murder with the written word.

The scribe finished writing. He looked up at Isocrates and smiled, revealing a mouthful of ruined teeth, worn away almost to nothing. Isocrates gave the Egyptian the last few coins that he had; a pittance, considering the quality and danger of the work, but the scribe received them with delight, it seemed at their novelty more than anything else. Egypt, somehow, was still a world without money.

He looked at the parchment in his hand, and at the alien script that was marked across it. He wondered if it said what he wanted it to, and if he would ever find the courage to put it to use. Then he rolled it carefully, placed it in a sewn pocket inside his tunic, and began the long walk back to the palace. Whether it was an omen or a trick of the mind, he did not know, but as he walked, Isocrates thought that he could feel the parchment burn hot against his skin. Like a newborn child, when you hold it in your hands for the very first time. Or like a weapon, still hot from the forge.

4

The next morning, in the throne room, they waited. Courtiers and generals, servants and slaves, all waited for the king to give the word, to summon the messenger from the west to deliver his report. But the king would not give the command. He had been told that the messenger had arrived as soon as he took his place in the court; later he was reminded once more, but Cambyses ignored both prompts. He sat on his throne, his brother at his left hand and sister at his right, and spoke only to them. He seemed most engaged with Bardiya, though Croesus could not hear what passed between them. Bardiya spoke more than the king, seeming to plead for something in an insistent undertone, but Cambyses shook his head and waved away his brother's concerns. At last, Bardiya threw up his hands, and turned away from the king. Whatever it was they had discussed, Bardiya had been defeated.

When this conversation had finished, there was a moment of expectation in the room – surely now the king would call for the messenger. Instead, Cambyses reached down beside the throne, and picked up the bow that he now kept there, the shorter kind that was favoured by the Persians. On the other side of the throne room, still wrapped in scarlet cloth, Croesus could see the great bow the Ethiopians had given to the king as an insult.

He had heard that Cambyses did not let that weapon out of his sight. Each day, he practised with one bow after another, each one of a greater weight on the draw than the last, and now Croesus watched as the king stood from the throne and began his daily practice. He had been well taught, though with his weak eyes he would never make a skilful archer. Croesus supposed that this did not matter. The king did not want precision or grace. Only the power to one day draw back the Ethiopian bow. To loose a single arrow with it, that would be enough.

Slowly, all conversation in the room fell away to silence. Most of the men of the court did not dare to look at the king directly, but all waited in the still quiet. Cambyses continued his practice with no sign that he had noticed, moving like some repetitive piece of machinery, a waterwheel that will move unceasingly for as long as a river flows. At last, on what might have been the fiftieth or the hundredth pull on the bow, his sister reached out and gently covered his hand with hers, just as he was about to draw the string back once more.

'Brother.'

He nodded in response, and, with an air of sadness, placed the bow carefully on the ground and sat back down in his throne. 'Very well,' he said.

The messenger entered the throne room, and for a moment Croesus thought that there must have been some mistake, that some madman or travelling soothsayer had bluffed his way into the king's presence, for this man did not look like a soldier or an emissary. His muscles had wasted away, his bones sharp and prominent against his tunic. His beard, while not long, had the wild, unkempt quality of a man who lives in the world of the spirit more than that of the flesh. Whorls of grime and dust were apparent on his skin, and when he walked past Croesus to kneel before the king, he carried the heavy stench of sweat with him, horse and man mixed together into the new scent of some alien, hybrid creature. Normally, guests were bathed and given the attentions of a barber before seeing the king, but this man had refused. Whatever story he had to tell the king, it seemed that he thought his appearance was part of the telling.

Cambyses kept him kneeling there for a long time. He stared at the man and frowned in thought, as though seeking for some alternative to letting the man speak freely, searching for some way that he could refuse to hear the soldier's story, regretting perhaps that he had not had the man silenced. It was too late now. The whole city was waiting to hear the man's words, to hear what had happened to the army in the desert. To deny them would be to provoke a riot. To hear him speak would be to confirm disaster.

'What news,' Cambyses said at last, 'do you bring the king of Persia?'

'Your army is lost, my king.'

'What?'

'The expedition to Ammon. They are all dead. Except for me.'

'How is this possible? Are you a coward, who ran at the first sign of battle?'

'I am no coward, my king.'

Cambyses mouth twitched. 'Tell me, then.'

The soldier stared at him with empty eyes, and began to tell his story.

'It started just as the men were sitting down to their midday meal. It began with a soft west wind.

'We tried to ignore it at first. My companions laughed and joked and cursed the fickle desert, dug the sand from their eyes, coughed it from their mouths, shielded their food and water from the attack. Eventually they gave up on eating altogether. They threw down their spoiled food, and stood in tight, protective huddles, braced against the wind, waiting for it to die down.

'It did not die. The wind grew stronger and heavier. Soon, none of us could see further than the man next to him. It was strong enough to carry twisting, solid columns of sand through the air as though it were bearing spears and battering rams. I saw men thrown to the ground, struck down by the airy force, some screaming with broken arms and shattered ribs.

'The captains blew horns and beat drums, rallying the army to fight against this enemy of nature. We stood in formation, shields locked against each other, to try and hold off the storm. Half by trained instinct, half in superstition, some even set their spears against the wind. But in moments, the army of sand broke the shield wall. And as the shield wall broke, the army broke with it.

'The cavalry ran first, hoping to outride the storm. The horses rebelled against their masters, shedding their riders to run faster, just as the infantry were casting down their weapons, scattering their shields, clawing off their armour to run naked and unhindered away from the killing wind. Weight was the enemy, weight pouring into every fold of our clothing, the edges of our armour, our hair and eyes and ears, dragging us to the ground to bury our feet and then our legs, forcing open our mouths and choking us with sand.

'The fortunate ones died quickly, choked and blinded, but far more were buried alive, trapped but still breathing, waiting to be slowly crushed and suffocated. The wind blew on until the army was covered over entirely, the dying men screaming beneath the ground, as though it were some cemetery of men brought cruelly back to life by the gods to die again in their graves. They died in their thousands, murdered by wind and sand. As the last screams faded away, the killing wind died away with them.

'I was alone in the desert. Buried up to my neck, I shook the sand from my face and gasped for air. Breathing was enough at first, for I wanted nothing more than the luxury of air, taking each breath as a thirsty man would swallow water. But then I wanted to be free.

'I fought for hours against the weight that imprisoned me, my skin and lips blistering beneath the sun, every muscle straining against the sand, each movement fractionally greater than the one before it. The ground grew hot and began to scald my skin. I wondered if I had been spared suffocation only to be slowly burned to death, half buried.

'One arm burst from the sand. I clenched and unclenched my fist, to prove to myself that the arm truly belonged to me, that it was not some cruel illusion of a dying mind. I curled it beneath my head and wept my thanks on to it, then began the long, slow struggle to free myself fully.

'After, I lay like a half-drowned man washed ashore, too weak to move. Then I dug through the sand, searching for water. When I found the first full waterskin I drank too greedily, coughing and vomiting sand and water.

'I dug carefully into the desert. Deep below me, I knew there to be entombed regiments of infantry, herds of camels and horses, frozen mid gallop in the sand by the killing wind, slaves and servants fixed in servitude for ever. I uncovered only a scattered few of the dead, and took all the water and wine I could. The rest will never be found.

'When the weight of water hung heavy from my back, I knelt and gave thanks to the gods for sparing my life, and asked them to look after my companions in the afterlife. I emptied one of my waterskins out on to the sand by way of sacrifice. I stood, and I walked out of the desert, back to Memphis, to tell this story that the gods have spared me to tell.'

When the man had finished his story, Croesus waited for the king to speak. To cry and scream, to shout and rage, to show any kind of response to the disaster. But he did nothing. He sat there, lost in thoughts of his own, and did not speak a word.

Slowly, the court returned to some pretence of normality. The messenger was taken away, doubtless to be cast into some kind of strange limbo, kept comfortable whilst they waited for the word of the king to bring him his fate: a reward, or torture, or death. The people of the court began to talk once more, half-heartedly discussing matters of state, though no one would say a word without half an eye on Cambyses.

Beside the king, Bardiya stirred restlessly. He leapt from his chair, and began to pace the floor of the court. He would reach one wall, then pick an angle at random, and following it along the floor until he reached the other side of the chamber. Before long this ceaseless crisscrossing brought him next to the wrapped Ethiopian bow. He reached down and plucked off the scarlet covering. 'What is this?' he said.

No one said anything. Though he trained with smaller bows openly, the king had been careful not to try to draw the Ethiopian bow in his brother's presence. He repeated the question, his brow creased with princely irritation, for he was a man unused to being denied his will. After another silence, longer than the one before it, a voice spoke out.

'It was sent by the Ethiopians,' Psamtek said. 'They say that no Persian can draw it.'

'Oh. Is that so?' And before any man could tell him to stop, he picked it up.

No one in the court had dared to touch it, as if it were some cursed weapon out of the old stories that would strike dead any who dared to take it from the ground. Bardiya turned it this way and that, admiring the quality of the wood, the perfect lines of the design. He gripped the bow in his left hand and stood in the archer's stance, shifting his weight from foot to foot until he had found his point of balance, and put three fingers to the thick bowstring. He lifted it, rolled his shoulders, and began to pull.

He was not a large man, no bigger of frame than Cambyses, but he had that hidden strength of the natural athlete. Croesus watched the string, impossibly, begin to creep back.

A sigh broke out across the room when he pulled the string past where Cambyses had drawn it, drew it back almost as far as his left shoulder. He held it there, unable to take it further, unwilling to let it go. He gave one last great pull that seemed to possess every muscle, his jaw tense, his feet flexing against the ground, seeking some greater purchase.

The string slipped from his fingers, and loosed a whipcrack that shuddered through the chamber.

Bardiya did not seem to notice the stillness his efforts had provoked. Laughing, he put the bow down again, ruefully stretching and rubbing his shoulders, shaking out the fingers of his right hand, the tendons strained from the force of the bow. 'It must be a land of giants,' he said, looking at his brother, 'to draw bows like this one.'

Cambyses said nothing. Neither his head nor his eyes had turned towards Bardiya during this trial of strength, and Croesus nurtured some vain hope that somehow the king had not registered what had occurred. Then Cambyses lifted his hands and brought them together, waited a moment, then did so again, in a slow series of hard claps that drove the amiable smile from his brother's face.

Cambyses turned to his sister. He lifted her hand to his face and kissed her fingertips. She went quite still. 'Are you well, brother?' she said.

'Yes,' he said. 'I am well.' He stood from the throne, and his failing eyes hunted through the men and women staring back at him in silence, like the faces of the dead. He found Croesus, beckoned once to the old slave, and then he strode away.

In the privacy of the garden, watched over by a single bodyguard, they sat together in silence. Cambyses still had the absent expression

190

of a man thinking of nothing at all, and Croesus found he could not open a conversation with the king. He was like a wrestler whose style demands that he must wait for the other man to attempt the first lock or throw, unable to make the first attack himself.

At last, the king spoke.

'There can be no more conquest, can there?' he said in a soft, resigned voice.

'No, master.'

'I was so proud of the war against Egypt. They seemed to give me so much respect for it. Now this. It is like Nitetis. Or Bardiya with that bow. First the honour, then the shame that follows the honour, that overwhelms it. Will this always be my fate, do you think?'

'I do not know, master,' Croesus said. 'Perhaps the gods do not wish your empire to grow any larger. It might threaten theirs.'

'Yes, I suppose so.' The king's hand began to pluck restlessly at the robe he wore. 'Psamtek tells me they have a thousand gods in this country,' Cambyses said. 'Do you think that can be true?'

'I do not know, master.'

'He says that only the king may hear and speak with them; that he heard them, when he was a king, and the moment that I took his throne from him, their voices fell silent.'

Croesus hesitated. 'Do you hear the gods, master?'

'No,' Cambyses said. 'I hear nothing.' He lifted his thumb to his mouth and bit into the nail. 'Did the god die?'

'Master?'

'That calf. The one I . . .' His voice faded for a moment. Then: 'I wish I had not done that.'

'Because of the blasphemy, master?'

'No. You think I am a fool, to believe an animal can be a god? But I have always hated those who are cruel to beasts. The priests deserved death for their stupidity. But that calf . . .' Tears surged to the king's eyes, hot and sudden. He wiped them away, then looked down at them and started in surprise, like a man who finds his hands bloody yet cannot feel a wound. 'I am glad that I have never killed a man,' he said.

Croesus tried to keep the disbelief from his face, but it must have shown, for the king immediately spoke again. 'It is true. I have ordered many deaths. But what of that? What does it matter what I say? It is the one who does the killing who bears the evil of it. Men like Prexaspes. Or perhaps he too has other men that do it for him. That would be better. Then I am twice removed from that murder.' He stared out into the air for a time. 'What an awful thing that would be, to kill a man.'

'Yes,' Croesus said. 'It is.'

'I wish that you had not done that, Croesus. That you had not chosen to taint yourself in that way.' Cambyses paused. 'Sometimes I think that you must want to kill me. For what I made you do.'

Croesus shivered in sudden fear. 'Master—'

'Do not answer.' The king leaned forward, until his milky eyes almost filled Croesus's world. 'Do you want to know the truth?'

'Tell me, master.'

'I do not care if you do or not. I do not fear you. You killed a cripple. What of it? I know you cannot kill a man.' He sat back in his seat. 'You are weak. It is why you fell from being a king to being a slave. But I love you for it. If only the world was filled with men like you. Gentle, weak, stupid men like you. Instead of men like me.' He beckoned for Croesus to rise. 'Leave me now. I have much work to do.'

'Let me help you, master.'

'On this matter, you will not want to advise me,' the king said, and there was something strange in the way that he spoke. He almost sounded like a sane man.

'Why, master?'

'Because I must do something other than a war. Something that I want, but am afraid to want.'

Before he left the king, Croesus lingered a disobedient moment longer, and looked over the balcony and down into the garden. It had grown much since he had last seen it, and it took a little time for him to be certain. He studied every shadow, each piece of thick foliage, until he was quite sure that his first thought had been correct.

The woman who had lived there was gone. The garden now held nothing but a ghost.

5

The season turned, and the flood began.

Of all the many hundred gods that the people of Egypt worshipped, the Nile was not one. It was too regular in its habits, its unfailing yearly floods. It lacked the capriciousness that any wise god must use to inspire fear and respect, and this made it something greater than a god.

There were none who knew where it came from, only that its origin lay deep within the uncharted lands to the south. Countless expeditions had been launched by one Pharaoh after another, each wanting to prove his brilliance above his predecessors' by solving the Nile's mystery. Some of these survey parties returned, their numbers depleted by sickness or starvation or bandit raids, always with no answer. Many never returned at all.

No one knew its origin, nor why it rose in such force each year. They only knew that, in the heat of the summer, when one looked up at the night sky and saw the star they named Sopdet appear, the flood would soon come. The waters followed the star as the moon followed the sun.

Now the Nile rose, advancing so quickly that some who could not run, drunkards and children and the infirm, were swept away and lost to it. The Egyptians did not mourn those taken in such a way. For these people, to whom a body lost to nature was usually an unspeakable tragedy, considered a drowning in the Nile to be a blessed death, a guarantor of eternal life.

There were a few radical thinkers amongst the Egyptians, often wealthy men tired of the yearly chaos and destruction, who spoke of stopping the flood. They said that the damage done to their property was unacceptable, the loss of life intolerable, and that exchanging a little of the land's fertility for peace and security would be a worthy trade. They devised remarkable engineering innovations, great dams and systems of channels that they claimed would tame the waters. But these men were treated almost as heretics by the people of Egypt, who would not wish to still the Nile any more than one would seek to stop a heart because it beat too loudly.

After the sudden advance, the flood waters reached their highest point and paused there, the way that even a conquering army that destroys all before it must stop for a time to tend to its wounded and bury the dead, and when the river stopped, all things ceased with it, an entire country struck still by nature. They waited for the river to draw back, so that they could minister to the flooded plains, plant the crops and pray that the harvest was a good one. They waited, and prayed.

This great lassitude seemed to still the king as well – even he, it seemed, was not immune to the mood of the nation. No word came of whatever new project occupied his mind, and like the rest of the nation, he seemed content to wait.

But this year the waters did not fall, and soon all of Memphis was alive with rumour. The priests said that it was a curse from the gods, a rejection of the new king like the sandstorm that had destroyed his army. Some said the flood would last for ever, and Croesus found himself wishing that it could be true. Then the king might never stir from his torpor, like those ancient warriors who have been perpetually charmed to stillness by the gods to prevent their fury from splitting open the earth and tearing apart the sky.

It was not to be. Just as it seemed as though the river would never recede, the waters vanished as fast as they advanced. The people woke one morning, looked to the west, and what had been so high and so strong that they might have mistaken it for a sea had become merely a distant glitter of water on the horizon, leaving behind a drowned land that was ready for the planting.

The people swarmed out from their homes, all thoughts of omens and inaction forgotten, and began to tend to their fields. And the king stirred at last, like some ancient creature awoken by ritual, and prepared to commit the worst blasphemy of all.

Even after all he had seen the king do, Croesus could not, at first, believe what he was told. Such were the rumours that the king's actions inspired, he had taken the news for some slander that a particularly vicious gossip of the court had spread. It was only when he saw the slaves and servants begin to dress the hall of the palace and prepare the wedding feast that he began to believe it could be true.

When he had been a king, half a lifetime ago, at the outset of a disaster he would rally his generals and his courtiers and his priests to his side, the way that Odysseus of the old stories, a greater recruiter than he was a warrior, had gathered the heroes of Hellas together to change the shape of the world. Now, as a slave, he sought to do the same with what little influence he had.

He went in search of Bardiya first, hoping, in spite of everything, that the ties of blood might still hold some power over the king. But the king's brother was not to be found in his chamber, the throne room, nor any other place that Croesus could think to find him. Most of those he asked simply ignored his question, though one or two thought that the king's brother had been sent back to Persia on some matter of state. At last, Croesus gave up the search for the king's brother, and went to find Prexaspes in his private chambers.

There were few who came willingly to these rooms. Those that did came fawning, seeking protection by denouncing their companions, the way that some seek to buy the gods' favour through sacrifice. But those that hoped to win protection through friendship did so in vain, for Prexaspes had sent as many friends of his to their deaths as he had enemies. If the king gave a name to him, there was no appeal that could be made. The king could not be wrong, and so that man disappeared and none would speak of him thereafter.

When, at last, Prexaspes received him, it was as though Croesus looked upon a different man. He was no older than thirty, his thin beard still the mark of his youth, and he had always had an unaged appearance that suited him to his role: the king could look on his face, unlined and innocent seeming, and not think of what this courtier did in the king's name.

Now he had the manner of a much older man. It was as though he bore a year for every man he had put to death, and they had come upon him all at once. Croesus wondered how much longer he would be able to remain in his position, now that Cambyses would have to witness the record of his crimes, marked on the face of the man who had committed them.

'You have heard, then,' Prexaspes said.

'He will not do it.'

'He will. I am sorry, Croesus.'

'After all you have done, you are sorry now?'

'Every king kills, Croesus. But few act like this.'

'Then you must stop him.'

'She has tried to speak with him herself. She has pleaded with him. What can you or I do that she cannot?'

'The judges will not allow it. It is against Persian law.'

'He has spoken to them already. He gathered six of them together, and asked . . .' Prexaspes faltered for a moment, hesitating to speak the crime aloud. Then, in a quieter tone, he said: 'He asked if the law would allow him to marry his sister.'

Neither man spoke for a time. Croesus had yet to say those words himself, and he wondered if it was the first time that Prexaspes had given voice to the king's blasphemy. All of those who had informed Croesus of what was to come had spoken obliquely. The wedding was only days away, but perhaps only half a dozen times had those words been spoken aloud.

The gods would not stir against a war or a murder or a rape. What were these crimes to them, these gods who killed on a whim, raped as if it were sport? They were transgressions for men to forbid, not the indifferent divinities. But parricide, and incest – these too the gods practised, but did not permit mortals to indulge in. They were the privilege of the divine alone. Prexaspes and Croesus waited, as if disbelieving that such blasphemy could be spoken and be uncorrected by some higher power. And yet, the gods remained silent.

'What was their decision?' Croesus said, breaking the silence.

'They said nothing, at first. We waited, and I thought the king would have to repeat himself. Then one of them, the eldest, said there was no law that permitted a man to marry his sister. The king was furious. I thought he was going to have them all killed. Then one of them said that, while what the old man had spoken was true, neither was there a law that forbade such a marriage. They all nodded, and gave their assent, and the king was satisfied.'

'I knew men could be cowards,' Croesus said. 'I did not know the law could be a coward as well.'

'It would have done no good for them to resist.' He hesitated, then concluded: 'Or for us to resist.'

'You must stop him.'

'I do not know how.'

'It is a little late to speak like that.'

'You remember that night, in Pasargadae? When . . .'

'Of course I do.'

'He summoned me, and said that he would give me names. He did not tell me what I should do to those named. I knew it well enough. I thought it would be a handful. A few dozen. I never thought it would go so far.'

'You have been well rewarded for it.'

Prexaspes raised his hand and touched the jewellery that hung from his throat, as if it were blood that had been transmuted into gold. 'I follow his commands,' he said. 'I cannot change the will of the king.'

'You must try.'

'You forget. I am merely the replacement of another man. And simple enough to replace myself.'

'I have not forgotten.'

At this, Prexaspes turned from him. He went to a chair and sat in it heavily, rested his head in the palm of one hand. Croesus felt like a youth as he looked at Prexaspes, a man less than half his age.

A flicker of motion distracted him from deeper within Prexaspes's chambers. He turned his head slightly, and found a child staring back at him. The boy was perhaps nine or ten years old, born before his father had become a murderer. Croesus remembered his face now, for the boy was one of the many sons of the nobility who served in the court of the king, learning their fathers' trade first-hand. The child looked at them with a shy curiosity. He would have to unlearn that, Croesus thought, if he were to survive. The king's palace was no place for the curious.

Prexaspes turned around, and angrily waved his son back into the chamber. The child gave one last, fearful look at Croesus, then he slunk away.

'You understand?' Prexaspes said, when the boy had gone. 'It is different. For a man like you . . .'

'A man with no family, you mean. An old man. My life is worth less than yours.' Croesus nodded towards the empty doorway, the absent child. 'I wonder if he knows that his father is a coward.'

'You cannot shame me, Croesus.'

'So I can see. Very well. Go and be with your family.'

'Good luck, Croesus. I will save you, if I can.'

'I think your protection is worth little.'

'You are right. But I will try.'

'Why?'

'Harpagus asked me to.' Prexaspes dropped his head, unable to hold Croesus's gaze.

'Do they always confess?'

'Yes.'

'Even though they know you will kill them when they do.'

'They know we will continue until they do.'

'Does it lessen your guilt,' said Croesus, 'to hear them speak those lies? Perhaps you tell yourself they might even be true.'

'I do not believe them. But to see how they all give up their friends, their family . . . I suppose I think less of them for that.' He lifted his head again. 'All men are cowards, Croesus. That is what I have learned. There is no ideal that will not be sacrificed for fear of pain, and death.'

'They all give names when they are asked?'

'Eventually. All except Harpagus. He did not give your name. He was a man from another time.' Prexaspes paused. 'Where will you go?'

'To the king.'

'You should not do that.'

'There is no choice.'

'No. I suppose not.'

Croesus waited for a time, to see whether Prexaspes would speak again. But he did nothing but sit there in silence, his eyes blank, perhaps reliving some crime or another. Croesus wondered if it were the most recent killings that haunted him, or if it were the killings from years past that grew and grew in significance the older they were, as if the dead became more restless the longer they were sealed beneath the ground. Croesus left him sitting there, lost in his memories, and went in search of the king.

Outside Cambyses's chamber, Croesus stood in silence. Within, the king would be reviewing the preparations for the wedding. Perhaps he had commissioned a poet to tell him stories of the ancient kings and gods who had married their siblings, or the beasts in the fields that cared nothing for the taboo of kinship.

Croesus had heard that great heroes meeting on the battlefield will pause in silent confrontation, fighting through every possibility in their minds before either man throws the first spear. In this way, they already understand the outcome of their duel, who will live and who will die, before they begin to fight. As he stood there, he thought of what he might say to the king – whether he would beg and plead, or reason, or shout and rage. The words now came into his mind unhindered, and he imagined each of these conversations through to the end. They all concluded in the same way. Every one, pursued long enough, led to his own death at the hands of the king.

But that should not matter. He should still make the attempt, he thought, as he stared down at his hands, the skin slack and near translucent. Most men did not live to be half his age. His heart might go still in his sleep that very night, his lungs close with sickness, his mind be blanked with fever. If he should run from this place only to die tomorrow, he would have preserved his life for the sake of a single day. To live was to acquiesce to the blasphemy, to give it his silent consent. He should be like those warriors who fear cowardice more than death or defeat, their great Law commanding them to stay in formation no matter what happened, to fight and die with no thought of retreat. Why should he still seek to cling to life?

He looked up at the door and tried to find the will to enter, to speak his way to the death that waited for him behind it. But he could not do it. The king had gone to a place where words could not reach him, beyond hope or reason. Croesus knew then, at last, that words had failed.

6

No public feasting accompanied the wedding day. It was barely spoken of inside the palace, let alone in the streets of the city. The rumours had reached the people of Memphis, but meant little to them, for it was not unknown for the Pharaohs to marry their sisters. Some of the Egyptians said if the king were to become more like the Pharaohs, perhaps he would be kinder to the people of Egypt, others that, if Cambyses took on their customs, it meant that he would never leave.

In the palace, the nobles were divided. There were a few who could not stand to witness the ceremony and who pleaded sickness, or invented emergencies that they had to attend to. Most who were present saw the chance to demonstrate their loyalty, or else were too afraid to stay away, and so they put on their greatest finery, fixed smiles on their faces, and prepared to applaud the king's choice. There were some who celebrated for themselves, for every man with a daughter had dreaded that she might be taken as a wife of the king, had lived in fear of the day that the king might summon them and request a betrothal which they would be unable to refuse, had even hidden their daughters away on private estates, or denied that they even had daughters at all. This blasphemy, at least, was some temporary protection.

It was not until the hour before the ceremony that Croesus, at last,

203

found the courage to see Parmida. Doubtless it was supposed to be forbidden, but the guards did not seem to care as he passed them, and neither Parmida nor her slaves acted to expel him. And so, in silence, he watched as a slave painted her face, and clasped pieces of jewellery to her wrists and throat as if they were golden shackles. Another scattered perfume over her, the way one might offer incense for a sacrifice. Parmida sat quite still. She wore the look of one who knew that they were coming to a point of ruin; the moment where all happiness will be taken from them, but that they will still live on afterwards, defeated. Croesus wondered if he had looked like that, many years before, when he had been condemned to die.

At last, she turned her painted face to look at him. 'It is time, isn't it?' she said.

'Yes.' He glanced again at the slaves in the chamber, but did not find the two faces he was afraid that he might see.

'They asked to attend on me,' she said, in answer to his thoughts, 'but I did not wish them to be here. To see this.'

'They serve you well?'

'They have become dear to me,' she said. 'I understand why you wished for them to be saved. And I understand, now, why they wish to have nothing more to do with you.'

'He told me once he would never force himself on a woman.'

'And you were a fool to believe him.'

'I did all that I could to prevent this.'

'Did you speak to Cambyses?'

'He would not have listened.'

'You did not speak to him.'

'No,' he said. He wondered how it was that she did not cry. Perhaps it was the thought of weeping the kohl to black rivers, of being painted again, and weeping again. She had withstood this dressing, this sham of a celebration, once already.

'Should I have taken my life, do you think?'

He did not reply.

'I think I should have done,' she said. 'But I am too afraid to die. Even though I know that I cannot endure this.'

'You will not have to.'

'You cannot stop this.'

'Yes. I can. I will.' He paused. 'Do you understand?'

She looked at him, confused, but after a moment, he saw that she did. Her mouth parted slightly; perhaps to ask him questions, to ask him if he was sure. But she did not speak. She was afraid, he supposed, of the answers that he would give. Afraid that he would, at the last, change his mind.

She could not meet his gaze any longer, and looked down at the rings on her fingers. 'Will it be tonight?' she said.

'Yes.'

She closed her eyes. 'Do you want me to give them a message? After . . .'

'Maia and Isocrates?'

'Yes.'

'No,' he said. 'They will know what it means.' He shifted where he stood, suddenly restless, eager to begin and for it to be over. 'You must go now. He will be waiting for you.'

She stood then, and, her head held high like a condemned man showing defiance at the last, she went to meet her brother.

Croesus watched the wedding in a kind of trance. From time to time he would try to look more closely, to mark what was happening, but he always felt his gaze sliding away, refusing witness. At last, he closed his eyes, and tried to experience it as the near-blind king might, listening to the chants of the priests as they called on the gods to sanctify a crime, the hollow cheers of the crowd as they acclaimed the king that they feared so much.

He waited for the ritual to conclude, for the toasts to be drunk and the sacred words said. He waited for the guests to disperse, stumbling and dull-eyed, like men returning from battle. He waited until he was almost alone in the great chamber of the palace, as other slaves moved around him extinguishing the fires and taking away the wine. He left the chamber, and followed the path his master would have taken a little while before, through the corridors of the palace, towards the king's private chamber.

He wandered past walls that had once been marked with the names of ancient kings, now scratched out at the king's command, bringing ten centuries of Pharaohs one step closer to the Second Death. He looked at the statues of gods that had been beheaded and defaced. They might have been taken to the dungeons, he thought, and put to whatever tortures one could inflict on stone, to draw speech from gods that had fallen silent. The king had tortured a corpse. Why not a statue?

The palace was still and silent. It reminded him of his own palace, so long ago, when the Persians were storming the walls and his city burned around him. Then too he had wandered the corridors alone. Such silence was rare in the palace of the king, a place of a thousand conspiracies and intrigues, feuds and love affairs. Only in celebration or disaster, or this celebration that was a disaster, did the palace return to stillness.

As he drew nearer and nearer to the king's chamber, his pace began to slow. He wondered if he would ever reach his destination, or if he would wander the palace endlessly, the way one does in dreams, exploring labyrinths with the impossibly slow pace of one walking underwater; if his cowardice would lead him astray, making him forget the path.

But he turned into the passage that led to the king's chamber, and saw that all was as he had expected. The bodyguards stood at the end of the corridor, not outside the chamber door where they normally stood. For one night only, they gave the king his privacy.

Now would be the time for them to stop him, to ask him questions to which he could give no answers. But they did not stop him as he walked past, and he saw that their heads were nodding with the strong wine they had drunk. Perhaps even these men, inured to the worst kinds of violence, needed to forget the blasphemy that was being committed.

They paid no attention to him. What harm could an old slave do?

His traitor heart beat hard, as though it sought to break within his chest rather than allow treason. Croesus forced himself to walk slower still, as though he were half asleep, wandering to his sleep rather than to his death. The door was close now. He found his breath coming in shallow rasps, the world swimming before his eyes. Life was waiting for him beyond this place, a world of thought and sensation that it was madness to abandon, and he almost walked on, past the door and towards whatever months or years might remain.

Instead, he stopped in front of the door, his breath steady and vision clear once more, and felt the courage of a hopeless man. He knew they would break him afterwards, as they had broken Harpagus. He wondered whom he would name, in the terrible, unknowable depths of pain that he would discover before the end, that place where all courage, hope and love are lost.

He knew he would not give up Isocrates, or Maia. That was all that mattered.

He rested his hand against the door, and readied himself to go within.

'Croesus.'

The voice came from behind him. He went quite still, not believing it at first.

'Croesus,' the voice said again, and now there could be no doubt.

Croesus let his breath out, a little gasp of loss. He turned slowly, and his fearful gaze found the man who was calling to him.

It was not a guard or a slave, a god or a ghost that had stopped him at the last. It was Psamtek, staring back at him from the shadows of the passageway.

'Come with me, Croesus.'

Croesus could not speak. His eyes flickered back towards the door.

'Come with me, Croesus,' Psamtek said again. 'Or I will call to the guards.'

Psamtek began to walk away, not even waiting to be sure that Croesus would follow him. Perhaps he had seen the relief in the old slave's eyes.

The moment before he followed the Egyptian, Croesus thought that he could hear something from deep within. A woman's voice, soft but distinct, crying out for help.

7

Bardiya stepped up the gangplank on to the ship and left the land behind him. Immediately, as was his habit, he went to the prow, so that he could stand so far forward and tilt his head in such a way that not a single piece of the ship could be seen; so that he could look out and feel that he was travelling unassisted across the water.

They were to sail downstream, following the flow of the Nile to the northern cities of Egypt. What business he had there he did not yet know, but Cambyses had been insistent that he must go. Perhaps some rebellion was stirring, or there was some stubborn local governor who needed to be flattered with a royal visitor. Whatever it might be, Bardiya had been hurriedly dispatched that morning, with the promise of more commands to follow.

He heard a sound behind him. He turned, and on the dock he saw one of his sister's slaves, a man whose name he did not know, calling out from the dock of Memphis. He seemed to be calling to the ship, a roll of parchment in his hand, and for a moment Bardiya considered asking the captain to stop, to row back. But he kept silent; the message would follow them on the next ship out. Doubtless it was merely some last farewell from Parmida. It had all happened so quickly, he had not had the chance to say goodbye.

He had heard rumours in the hours before he left that a wedding was coming. Perhaps it might even be hers. He wondered whom she would be married to, which of the nobles of the court had finally won her hand. He supposed that it was likely to be someone that he disapproved of; he had noticed the noblemen avoiding him in the past few weeks, conversations falling silent when he approached. He suspected a secret was being kept from him, but Memphis was a city of many such secrets – a man did not have time to unravel them all.

They had not been sailing for long when Bardiya noticed that something was wrong with the motion of the ship. It was drifting out of line, heading towards the shore. At first, he assumed that it was a random eddy of the water that was pushing them aside, that the sailors would notice and correct their course. There was no port near by, no reason for them to stop. But they persisted off course, and when he looked back, he saw that the steersman was, quite deliberately, turning towards shore.

Something else had changed. His bodyguards were staring at him. Their eyes should have been anywhere else; studying the sailors to watch for an assassin hidden amongst them, staring up or downstream, to observe other ships that could have been a danger. But they looked only at him. They were drawing close to the shore now, and, rounding a dune and riding to the bank of the Nile, Bardiya could see a single man on a horse, his face covered against the sand and sun. Bardiya did not understand yet what that lone rider could mean, but he found himself afraid. Trapped as he was on the ship, he wanted to get as far away from that man as possible.

But when he turned, he found the bodyguards drawn up in a silent line against him. Bardiya stepped forward, and for the first time in his life, the men did not part before him. He stood there, disbelieving for a moment. He put a hand between them and tried to force them aside, convinced that they would surely part at his touch. No man moved. Bardiya half drew his sword, and in an instant a hand was at his throat, and a foot swept his legs for under him and sent him to the deck. They took his sword from him as easily as one would take a stick from a child.

It was an impossible blasphemy. It was death to lay hands on the brother of the king. But they stood in a circle all around him, and, at last, he understood. He tore at the deck of the ship with his fingers, as though hoping, impossibly, to break his way through to freedom, or to dig his own grave. He cried out, begging for a mercy that he knew could not come, for a brother who was not there to hear him. He waited to see which one would come forward, but none of them moved. Bardiya stood and hurled himself against them, and they forced him back again and again. But none drew a weapon. The true blasphemy was reserved for another man.

The ship touched the shore and shuddered, and Bardiya fell to his knees once more. He heard the creak of the wood, as the rider came aboard the ship and walked forward to the prow. The circle parted, and Bardiya looked at the face of his executioner. He knew this man from the king's table. They had shared wine together, laughed together, hunted together.

Bardiya saw the blade the other man carried. He could see the killer's hands trembling.

When they came to Psamtek's quarters, Croesus could not help but look first to the floor, to see if any trace of blood was there – some drop that had dried between the stones, a tiny, unwashed smear in some dark corner of the room. But there was none. It had been cleaned with forbidding exactness. He wondered if Psamtek had another slave do this for him, or, trusting no one with this secret, if he had done it himself. A man who was once a king, and one of his first acts as a slave would have been to get to his knees and wipe his own blood from the floor.

'How did you know?' Croesus said.

'It was not so difficult to guess. You are a predictable man.'

'Why would you stop me?'

Psamtek did not reply.

'Do you hope for power? That he will return to Persia and give you your kingdom back?'

'No. He will never leave Egypt. He is afraid to leave this place.' Psamtek paused. 'What did you think would happen? Afterwards, I mean.'

'I would die. They would kill me. What would matter after that?'

'You are a man who always thinks of the after, I suspect. Every assassin dreams of a better world.'

'Bardiya would take the throne,' he said.

'Did you see Bardiya at the ceremony tonight?' the Egyptian said.

Croesus did not speak for a long time. He understood then why Prexaspes had looked so broken when Croesus had seen him the day before. Doubtless he had men who usually did the work for him, but Prexaspes would not have trusted anyone but himself with a killing of such significance. At last, with many hundreds dead at his command, Prexaspes had become a murderer with his own hands.

'We could have saved him, you and I,' Croesus said. 'You know that, don't you?'

'Yes, we could have,' Psamtek said. 'But I did not want to.'

'You owe your life to me.'

'You need not worry. I have no desire to seek your death.'

'You are the second man to offer me my life today. I suppose you expect gratitude.'

'No. I do not expect that. Your death would not hurt him. It would mean nothing to him. So it means nothing to me.' Psamtek paused. 'What a terrible thing it must be. To be willing to sell your life, and yet find it can buy nothing of value, that it will change nothing.'

The Egyptian turned from Croesus, his manner still that of a king dismissing a subject. There was nothing more that could be said.

The marriage passed, like some natural disaster that is so great that all know it will become myth in time, but in the present is merely to be endured. Within the palace, the king fell into silence and absence, rarely seen by any.

The old jokes, of new husbands lost for months at a time in the bedchambers of their wives, went unspoken, though all thought of it and shuddered. Yet whatever happened in the private chambers of the king, it seemed to have calmed Cambyses. He no longer wandered restlessly through the palace in search of an insult to counter. He came to the court, gave passive acceptance for what his advisors suggested he do concerning the governance of his kingdom, then disappeared again.

This, at least, was what Croesus heard. He did not see it himself, for he went no longer to the throne room of the king, nor attended on him in privacy. Quietly and suddenly, he withdrew from the business of the court. He wandered through the palace, at no one's command, going where he pleased. He went to find the high balconies and look out at the teeming city he could not go to himself. When, from time to time, a servant came across the old slave on these balconies and took a moment to study the movement of his eyes, they noticed that Croesus seemed to be looking towards the youths who ran errands for their parents, and the packs of children who swarmed and played in the streets and alleyways, and who seemed oblivious to the tyrant who lurked in the palace.

Croesus became the subject of gossip in the court. There were those who felt that it was improper for other slaves to see one of their number standing idle. Yet he was of no use to anyone save the king, and the king did not call for him. His idleness could perhaps be excused. Some even began to speak of it as a good example to show to the slaves, to show them that if they worked hard and earned favour, they too might be permitted to retire into meaningless obscurity. It was not a vision of the future that any free man would want, but a better tomorrow than most slaves could hope for.

Croesus was sitting in the empty garden the king had made, many months after the wedding, when the summons finally came. As he dozed in the sun, he became aware of another presence on the balcony. He lifted his head and found the eyes of Prexaspes's son staring back at him once again. The boy stood there hesitantly, acting with an unnecessary shyness, for he should have known that as the son of a noble he was far above a slave, and that no respect for age was needed in a time where the old were prey for the young.

'What is your name?' said Croesus.

'Artabanos,' the boy said, coming forward.

'And what message do you bring? A summons from your father? You are young, to be doing his work.'

'No. From the king. You are to dine with him tonight.'

Croesus nodded. 'Very well. You may tell him I will join his table. That it will be an honour.'

The boy made no move to go.

'Why do you stay?'

'Will you tell me about my father?' Artabanos said.

Croesus glanced down at his hands. 'You hear the other children speaking of him?'

'They do not say anything to me, but . . .'

'No. They would not dare to bully you, would they? Their fathers would not let them. But these boys, they talk to each other? And sometimes you overhear?'

'Yes.'

'It is true, what they say. He has killed men. Or rather, they die at his command. Perhaps that makes you feel better?'

'Did they deserve to die?'

'No.'

The boy fell silent. Croesus looked at him, and thought of how

214

another more brutal, or braver, man might have taken revenge on this child. The boy's father had killed innocents. When Prexaspes had killed Bardiya, he had killed all hope with him. Should not Prexaspes pay the price himself? It would have been no blasphemy. Croesus thought of infants thrown from the battlements to spite their dead fathers, heirs to captured thrones who were castrated and blinded to remove them as future threats. The child was but an extension of the man, a part of him like any other. You would not shy from hurting it, any more than you would ignore a gap in an opponent's armour.

'You may have wanted me to tell you a comforting lie,' Croesus said. 'But I will not lie for him.'

'No. I wanted the truth,' the boy said, as he blinked back tears. 'Did he choose to do it?'

'He had a choice. But it was the choice that few men are willing to make, the choice between living badly, and dying well. Do you understand?'

'I think that I do.'

'Now you wonder, perhaps, what you should do.'

The boy nodded solemnly.

'You must get away from the court,' Croesus said. 'As soon as you are able, though it will be some years yet. You must get away from the king, whatever it costs you in honour or position, whatever your father or your friends say to you, to shame you into doing otherwise.'

'What will happen if I stay?'

'You will grow rich and powerful. You will marry a beautiful woman. You will commit terrible acts, and witness them. And then you will die.'

'Will my father die?'

'Yes.'

'At the king's hand?'

'At the command of the king. Not by his hand.'

The boy fell silent, locked in that serious, concentrated way of thinking which is unique to children, who can lay their minds entirely open to a new thought without prejudice.

'I will do as you say,' the boy said.

'I am glad.'

'But you should go too. Is that not true?'

'I cannot run. Even if I could, I would not. I think there might be something left for me to do here. But I do not know what it is.' He regarded the boy for a time, and some deep, buried knot in his mind seemed to loosen a little. 'Thank you,' he said.

'What have I done?'

'It is difficult to explain. One day, you may understand.'

The boy left, and Croesus sat alone for a time in the garden with the ghosts of the disappeared, looking upon the verdant replica of Persia. A beautiful land that he would never see again.

At last, it grew dark. It was time to go.

8

In Persia, the king had insisted on dining in almost total darkness. In Memphis, the great hall was brightly lit, the walls hung with polished artefacts of gold and brass. His perpetual indecision, between subjecting others to his darkness or providing as much light as he could for his failing eyes, had swung once again towards the latter.

To an outsider, the table might have offered a semblance of companionship. The nobles and generals spoke to one another, interspersing discussions on politics and ethics with raucous, obscene stories. But, looking closer, one could begin to see the real games that were being played. Calculations were being made, shown in the brief hesitation before each man spoke. Every man there watched and probed for the weaknesses of others, guarding against a mistake of his own, his conversation a form of self-defence. A single mistake would, at the least, cost him his position. It might well cost him his life.

Each man struggled to keep a clear head, fighting against the wine and his own exhaustion. There was no hope that Cambyses would become tired before them. Whatever other qualities he was lacking as a king, he never seemed to grow weary, rarely slept, and never seemed drunk, in spite of all the wine he swallowed. Sometimes, Croesus wondered if he drew sustenance from his time awake in the same way that normal men were refreshed by their dreams. If Cambyses regarded the waking world as a dream to be shaped to his will, it would explain much.

The noblemen's sons worked around the table, bringing private messages and taking them away, pouring wine for those that needed it or, more commonly, those whom Cambyses decreed had not drunk enough. They were learning first-hand from their fathers how to survive at the king's table: how never to say anything that one might be held to firmly at a later date, how to speak only in empty, abstract constructions, how to trap one's rival in a conversation that he could not escape from, and how to silently form alliances around the table in a matter of moments, and break them in half that time. To be witty, but not stand out, to be insightful, but not to show a dangerous intelligence. To be shadow men, taking shape as the king willed it. Amongst the boys who served, Croesus could see Prexaspes's son, and Artabanos looked up at him only briefly before averting his gaze. Good, Croesus thought to himself. He has learned not to associate with those who are out of favour.

There were some that Croesus recognized at the king's table, and many he did not. He was grateful to see Parmida was not there.

'My wife is unwell,' Cambyses said, with his uncanny habit of answering unspoken thoughts. 'You have been long absent, Croesus.'

'Forgive me, master.'

'Oh, it means little to me. In truth, I had not noticed that you had been gone. But Psamtek says that he has missed your company.'

Croesus turned to the Egyptian, who silently inclined his head in greeting. 'I see,' the old slave said. 'It is a blessing, to be missed.'

'Sit, Croesus. There is better food here than the kind you are used to.'

'As you wish, master.'

Cambyses said little, and even at the table, Croesus could see he kept a short bow propped against his chair; occasionally his hand would stray down and brush against it, as if he were about to launch into his exercises even as he ate. But for now, the king contented himself with listening to the conversation, accepting the compliments that regularly came his way and offering the occasional comment of his own. He seemed to enjoy the discussions and the jokes, but did not contribute to them. All could see that, as was his habit every night, he was working on a question to ask them. A single, dangerous question that they would all have to answer.

When a few men's heads were nodding from exhaustion, and all had drunk too much, the king cleared his throat to bring silence.

'So,' Cambyses said. 'I have a question for you.' He smiled. 'Who do you think is the greater king? My father, or myself?'

The men said nothing.

'You must present your case, master,' Psamtek said from the king's side.

'Oh I will.' Cambyses leaned back and drained his cup. 'He may have formed his kingdom from nothing. He may even have conquered such trifling kingdoms as Babylon, and Lydia.' Polite laughter at this. 'But I have retained all of my father's lands,' he continued, 'and I have added Egypt to his conquests. He never conquered so great a kingdom as Egypt. There has never been an empire as great as mine. What do you think?'

Croesus said nothing. He stared down at his plate, hoping that perhaps they would think he had fallen asleep at his meal, and that he would not have to perjure himself for the king's vanity.

'What do you say, Croesus?' the king said. 'You served my father. You should know, better than anyone. Am I the better king?'

'I cannot agree,' he said quietly.

Silence fell around the table. Croesus looked up. Cambyses still smiled, but it was a ghastly smile.

'Oh,' the king said, his voice still light. 'And what makes you say that?'

Croesus stared at him. 'Because you have not yet been blessed with a son to match yourself.'

Relieved laughter burst out around the table, led by Cambyses. 'Very good, Croesus, very good,' the king said. 'Even as old and ugly as you are, it is good to see you still have a few wits left.' The king smiled. 'But you are wrong. You shall learn so shortly.' He turned to look at the last man at the table. 'And you, Prexaspes. What do you think?'

'I think Croesus speaks well,' Prexaspes said, 'though in truth, I think you have already surpassed your father, son or not. You are a great king, and your people love you.' He paused, then smiled. 'Though I have heard that they say you are a little too fond of wine,' he said, raising his goblet in an ironic toast.

Laughter broke out again, stronger than before, but this time Cambyses did not join them. He smiled patiently until the laughter died away. 'Who says this?' he said.

'They say . . . I spoke in jest, my king. I apologize.'

'If they think I drink too much, they think I am a drunk. If they think I am a drunk, they must think I am mad. You dare to call me mad?'

Prexaspes opened his mouth to reply, but no words came out. Psamtek leaned in and whispered to the king. 'Quite right, Psamtek,' Cambyses said. 'Prexaspes, where is your son? He is here, isn't he?'

Prexaspes hesitated.

'Answer me. Where is your son?'

'By the door, my king.'

Croesus turned to look. The entire table, silent, turned with him.

The boy looked uncertain, with every gaze in the room suddenly on him; shy, like any other boy his age. Artabanos glanced at his father for some indication of what he should do. *Run*, Croesus thought at him.

'Excellent,' Cambyses said. 'Let us ask him, shall we?' He peered towards the doorway. Croesus realized that, in the king's near-blindness, he couldn't see the boy. 'Where are you? Speak to me.'

Croesus shook his head at Artabanos, but the boy did not notice. His eyes were fixed on Cambyses.

'I am here, my king,' the child said softly.

Cambyses squinted. 'So you are. Good, good.' He nodded once. Then he picked up the bow that lay beside his chair and, turning sideways in his chair like a mounted archer in the saddle, he nocked an arrow and shot the child.

The boy stood tall, and for a moment Croesus thought the arrow had gone astray, that the near-blind king had missed his shot. But, looking closer, he could see there was something wrong with the boy's chest. A protrusion. A sudden, spreading darkness.

Artabanos sighed, and leaned against the wall. Croesus thought he heard a choked sob before the boy fell to the floor.

'Bring him here,' Cambyses said.

The guard at the door did so.

'Cut him open.'

The guard hesitated for the briefest of moments, then took his knife and cut the boy's chest open.

'Tell me,' Cambyses said. 'What has it pierced?'

The guard looked up at him. 'The heart, my king.'

Cambyses turned to face Prexaspes. The other man shook silently in his chair, and the king smiled. 'You see? I am not drunk. I am not mad either. No mad man could ever shoot so straight. Do you not agree, Prexaspes?'

Croesus thought he would never forget the expression on the other man's face. It was the face of a man who will be forever lost to the past, who will relive a single moment, again and again, for the rest of his life.

'It is so,' Prexaspes whispered. 'I was wrong. Forgive me.'

The king, half blind as he was, somehow felt Croesus's eyes upon him. He turned to the old slave and, once again, answered his unspoken question. 'A child is not a man. I still have not killed a man.'

Cambyses turned away. But before he did so, just for a moment, Croesus saw Cambyses look again at Psamtek. The briefest look, a child seeking an acknowledgement of good behaviour. And he saw Psamtek nod, and give his approval of what the king had done.

They went from the dining chamber in silence, no man allowing himself to speak. Even these practised actors would struggle to voice the words of praise that would keep them safe. The slightest intonation, the faintest expression of censure, these would be noted and recorded by the others. No one could be trusted, for even a close companion might become a rival in a year for a woman or position at court. An almost innocent comment would be remembered, and turned against the one who had spoken it. It was better not to speak of such things. Better, by far, to forget.

Most returned to their own chambers at once. Some would confide in wives and lovers, the desire to confess outweighing the fear of betrayal. Others would lose themselves in drink, for there were many who had grown practised at drowning horrors with wine, like blood washed in water. The few who would go furthest in the court, who would survive every purge and rise to the greatest positions of power, would return to their beds and sleep soundly, unmoved by what they had seen.

Croesus had no wife or lover to go to, and what slave could find wine enough to still the mind, day after day? Instead he walked, with the resigned air of a beaten warrior going to offer his surrender, to Parmida's chamber. Outside the door, he waited for the slave to take his message to the queen, waited to see whether she would say yes or no. He thought, with sudden dread, of the king coming here, finding his slave outside this chamber, what he would have to say. Worse yet, to have to see the king disappear into the chamber, to think of what would follow. But the king did not appear, and, at last, the slave beckoned him inside.

It took some time for his eyes to adjust to the darkness of her chamber. A single torch, almost burned away to nothing, gave the only light in the room, for now it was she who lived in shadows, and the king in light. Perhaps, he thought, she sought to hide from the king in this darkness, to win a few moments free of his advances when he came to this place.

She sat up in her bed, the blankets gathered around her, and he did not know if she had retreated there already, or had not left it all day.

'Why have you come here, Croesus?' she said.

'I have come to ask you to do something for me.'

'You would dare ask anything of me?'

'I do not know what else to do,' Croesus said. 'He killed a child tonight.'

'What?'

'Your brother. He killed a boy.'

A pause. 'You want me to reason with him?'

'No. I have no hope of that.' He hesitated. 'I want you to speak to Isocrates and Maia. To ask if they will see me.'

'For what purpose?'

'For no purpose. Just to speak to them. They may listen to you.'

'I thought you might have come here to help me. How foolish of me.' She tipped her head forward, and her untied hair fell about her face. She was silent for a time, then raised her head, and, almost defiantly, said: 'I am with child.'

As soon as she said the words, Croesus shuddered. He wished that he had not, for even in the darkness he could see the pain in her eyes, and knew the wound he had inflicted. 'I had hoped it would not come to this,' he said.

'All your hoping can do nothing for me. Though I suppose it eases your conscience.'

'No. It does not.'

She put her hand to her stomach, as if to hide it, though she showed no sign of her child yet. 'It is an evil thing,' she said. Then: 'Will you help me?'

'I do not know that art.'

'Would you help me if you did?'

He hesitated. 'I do not know if I could do that.'

'You would allow this to happen?'

'Perhaps.'

'I can feel my child in me, longing to die. To not be born a monster, the son of a monster.'

'You must speak to Isocrates and Maia,' said Croesus. 'They may know more of such things than I.'

'Why do you flinch from this?'

Croesus felt a sickly weariness descend on him, the way a warrior, exhausted by killing, will collapse where he stands at the end of a battle and sleep a night amongst the dead. He found a chair to sit in, and rested in it for a time. 'I think of those who are children now,' he said, 'or are born now. I think of how they may outlive us, outlive the king, and see a different world. At least, that it what I used to think. But I saw today that is not true. Now children die as men do.'

'I would have it that none were born. Until this time has passed.'

'Until Cambyses is dead.'

'Yes.'

'I tried, the night . . . the night of your wedding. But I was stopped. I am sorry.'

'There is a part of him that used to long for death. That knew what he would become. But he did not have the courage. He wanted to die. I wish you could have helped him.'

'I do not think I believe that.'

'You still think that all crave life,' she said, 'as you do. He would have thanked you for it, if you had given him that death. But now

224

it is too late for such things. He wants to be as the gods are now. Witnesses to death, again and again. But never to suffer it himself.'

'Yes. You are right.'

She lay down on the bed, and turned so that she no longer faced him. He waited for a long time, but she gave no sign that she intended to break the silence. It was only when he stood to go that she spoke again.

'I will tell Maia and Isocrates what you have asked for,' she said. 'But I cannot promise what they will say.'

'They are Hellenes. A stubborn and proud people. But kind too. Perhaps they will take pity on an old man. I do not know.'

'Leave me now, Croesus.'

'I am sorry I could not do more. I wish . . .'

'I know. Leave me.'

He did not bow to her as he left. It would seem a mockery to one who, in spite of her royal birth, was more of a slave than he was.

After he had gone, she sat there in silent thought for a long time, one hand absently gathering up the cloth of her bedding into a bunched fist, then releasing it and beginning the process anew. At last, like one waking from a nodding half sleep, she raised her head, and looked to one of the heavy hangings at the side of the chamber.

'He is gone now,' she said.

From behind this heavy piece of cloth, Maia stepped forward. She sat down beside her mistress, gently taking one of the queen's hands in both of hers.

'You heard how he spoke,' Parmida said. 'What will you do?'

'I will speak with my husband.'

'I asked what you would do.'

'That does not matter.'

'You obey him?'

225

'No. We will decide together.'

'Of course,' the queen said, then lapsed into silence.

If one were to enter this chamber, knowing nothing of who these two women were, one would not have thought that the first was a queen and the other a slave. The way they spoke held no sign of command or servitude. Parmida wore none of her finery, and, in the near darkness, one might not notice Maia's simple clothes, the callused hands that marked her as a slave. One would have thought them mother and daughter.

After a time, Parmida spoke again. 'I look on you with envy, sometimes,' she said. 'What kind of a world is that, where the queen looks on the slave in that way?'

'That is a foolish thing to say, my lady.'

'It is?'

'I have endured many times over what you have suffered, my lady.'

'I did not know. You have never had a child, have you?'

'No.'

'Is it true, what they say? Of children that . . . of a child like this. That they are born weak or crippled?'

'Sometimes.'

'That they are cursed by the gods?'

'No. I do not believe that can be true. It does not have any choice in how it is born.'

'I had no choice, either.'

'That is true.'

'So you think I am not cursed?'

'No.'

'Perhaps I would rather that were so. That I was the plaything of the gods.' She looked away. 'Do you know how this can be stopped?'

'I wish that I knew how. I would help you that way, if I could. I cannot. But I will help you to raise this child.' She hesitated. 'I have always wanted to do such a thing.'

'Thank you,' the queen said. 'But it will not come to that.'

After that, they sat together in silence, knowing that there was nothing more that could be said.

9

They met some days later, at dawn, in an old armoury that had long since fallen out of use. Croesus had been there for some time, amidst the rusted and broken-down relics of old wars fought many centuries before, and had begun to think that Isocrates and Maia had changed their minds, that his old companions had chosen not to come. But, just as he was about to rise and wander slowly back to his chamber, he heard the footsteps approach.

Isocrates and Maia entered the room, and the three of them stood in silence for a time, gathered in that forgotten place like some group of aged conspirators. What a notion that was, Croesus thought. Conspiracy was for the young, those driven by desperation or ambition. What ambition could an old man have?

'I am glad that you have come,' Croesus said at last. 'You are both well?'

'Well enough,' Isocrates said.

The silence returned. Isocrates seemed almost unchanged since Croesus had last seen him. His movements were perhaps a little slower and stiffer, but he could not tell if that were some mark of age or simple discomfort. But Maia looked exhausted – perhaps she had fought long and hard to get Isocrates to agree to come here.

'It is a strange thing,' Croesus said, 'to live in a cursed time. It does not trouble either of you, I suppose.'

'No. It does not,' Isocrates said shortly.

'It haunts me. But then I think of other places. Lands where they may yet be piecing together a different way of living, and have not made the mistakes that we have. Or I think of other times, when these will be stories to scare children. Be quiet, and go to sleep, or Cambyses will come for you.'

'And Croesus too, perhaps,' said Isocrates. 'You too may find your way into such histories.'

'Yes, I would deserve as much. Cambyses said I am a man for another time. I think I am not cruel enough for this one. Or brave enough. I do not know what I believe. I do not know what to do.' Croesus looked away. 'He killed a boy.'

'Cambyses?'

'Yes. Or Psamtek. I do not know any more. Which is the hand and which is the mind that guides it.'

'Why are we here, Croesus?' Maia said.

'I have shown you both too little gratitude. For all you have done.'

'And now you wish us to do something for you once more, I suppose.'

'No, no. That is not what I want.'

'Then what is it?'

'I do not want to be alone.'

They did not reply.

'I want us to take care of each other,' Croesus said. 'I have no greater ambition than this. I spent my life in this world thinking that I might reshape it. Even as a slave, that was what I wanted. Now I want only some comfort before I die. And I find nothing matters to me more than both of you.'

Croesus could see some silent conference occurring between them, for Isocrates and Maia had known each other so long and so well that words were no longer necessary. He thought that it was Isocrates who still held back, that it was Maia who, in that silence, fought hardest for his cause.

At last, they turned back to him, and at first Croesus thought that his plea had failed. Then Isocrates said: 'Very well.' Perhaps there was the barest trace of a smile on his face, Croesus could not tell. 'You tend to get your way, after all.'

'Not in all things.'

'No. But when it comes to me, you do.'

Maia nodded once, tired but satisfied, like a priestess concluding some long and difficult ritual. She came forward, gestured for Croesus to rise, and embraced him.

'I have missed you both, very much,' Croesus said.

'We have missed you as well.'

'There is a garden. A Persian garden, hidden within the palace.'

'I know. I helped to plant it, when we first came to this place. But are we permitted?'

'I often visit it now. They will not stop us. Would you like to go there?'

Isocrates nodded. 'Yes. You should both go.'

'You will not come with us?' Maia said.

'Not yet. I have something to attend to.' He tried to smile. 'Perhaps I will join you there when my work is finished.'

'Will you know where to find us?' said Croesus.

'Yes. I will find you.'

Croesus clasped the other man on the shoulder. He turned back and took Maia's hand, almost without thinking, and led her away into the palace.

Isocrates watched them go; another man walking away with his wife. He imagined that, once again, he could feel the invisible chains of servitude settling upon him, heavy as they had always been. He had spent decades of his life in service to Croesus. Even all the time that they had spent as slaves together could not erase those instincts. As the other man commanded, or even requested, he felt himself obeying. He knew that he would never be free of it. And he knew what had to be done.

When Isocrates reached his destination, the guards at the door would not admit him at first.

'Whom do you serve, in coming here?' one said.

'I serve no one,' Isocrates replied. He waited for a moment to let the guards think about this impossibility, a slave acting without a master's command, then spoke again. 'But I come with knowledge that the King's Eye will be glad to receive.'

'You must tell us, and we will pass on your message to him ourselves.'

'I cannot. My words are for Prexaspes alone.'

'Then we may not admit you.'

'As you wish. It means nothing to me. But, if I were you, I would fear his displeasure when he learns of this.'

One of the guards still eyed him doubtfully, but, after a brief and whispered discussion with his companion, went within to deliver the request. Soon enough, the summons came, and Isocrates was taken inside.

He found Prexaspes sitting on a cushioned chair. His gaze was aimless, marked with the ghostly aura of the bereaved, those who look as though they have almost followed the lost to the next world. From somewhere deeper within the set of chambers, Isocrates could hear a soft insistent sobbing. Prexaspes's wife, he supposed.

'What do you want?' Prexaspes said.

'Forgive me for intruding on your grief.'

'Has Croesus sent you?'

'In a manner of speaking,' Isocrates replied.

For a moment he did not act, permitting himself one last moment of hesitation. Then, from within his robe, he took the parchments that he had commissioned many months before, but had not found the will to use.

'Can you read the Egyptian script?' Isocrates said.

'Yes.'

'Then you may look at this for yourself.'

Prexaspes took the papers from him, but did not read them immediately. He fixed the slave with a steady gaze, perhaps looking for some sign of nervousness or doubt that might colour his reading. Isocrates could not help but be a little impressed at this composure, a day after the death of his son.

At last, Prexaspes began to read, careful and thorough, like a merchant studying a contract, or a priest consulting a prophet's written words. After he had read it through for a second time, he gave a small nod.

'It is good work,' Prexaspes said, without taking his eyes from the parchment in his hands, still seeking some flaw in what had been written. 'I commend you. When did you have this done?'

'Some time ago. I thought that it might one day be necessary.'

'Why wait so long?'

'I hoped it would not come to this. Will the king believe it, if you show it to him?'

'I think that he will. But it is a risk. He is unpredictable.'

'As you well know.'

'Yes. I do.' At last, Prexaspes looked up from the parchment, and studied Isocrates. 'Why do you think that I will do this thing for you?'

'I would have thought it obvious.'

'Perhaps I value my life more than you think, and will not risk it for anything.'

'Perhaps. But I think you will do it, because you are a little like me.'

232

'In what way?'

'We are the men who do what others will not.'

Prexaspes's eyes dimmed for a moment, in pain or recognition. 'Yes, we are,' he said. 'Tell me, why do you do this? Is it for revenge?'

'No. A sort of kindness, I think.'

'Kindness?'

'Yes. For a man like this, I think death may come as a kindness.'

'You justify yourself well. You should take my place.'

'In another lifetime, I might have done. But I am glad this is not that life.'

'And I wish that it was.' At this, Prexaspes stood, and made ready to go.

'Was he your only child?' Isocrates said.

'Yes.' And Prexaspes left the chamber without another word.

Isocrates stood still and waited, counting his breaths to mark the time. He waited until he had marked five hundred of them, until he was certain that Prexaspes would have reached the king's chamber, and that what had been begun could not be reversed. Then, with the slow steps of a tired old man, he began to make his way towards another part of the palace.

When Isocrates entered the chamber, the man within did not acknowledge his visitor. The slave who had once been a king sat in his chair, poring over his papers and in no hurry to finish what he was doing. And so Isocrates waited.

Finally, Psamtek, last ruler of the ten-thousand-year dynasty of Egyptian Pharaohs, rose from his chair and looked at his visitor.

'You are Isocrates,' the Egyptian said. 'I have heard a little of you.'

'What do they say?'

'Some say you are in love with Croesus. And that there is a woman who acts as a wife to you both.'

'Is that what they say?'

'It is. Though I do not believe it.'

'No? Why not?'

'I cannot think you would be that taken with him. You are a man of intelligence. Croesus is a fool.'

'Oh, many men have thought that of him,' Isocrates said. He paused for a moment, and idly ran a finger across the stones set in the wall. 'It might even have been true, a long time ago. But not any more. Still, there are some things that he cannot bring himself to do.' He looked back to the Egyptian, and folded his arms. 'But he has me to do them for him.'

'You still serve him? A slave to a slave? Perhaps the habit is a difficult one to break.'

'That may be so. But he does not know that I am here.'

'Why are you here?'

Isocrates did not reply.

'You have come to threaten me, I suppose,' Psamtek said. 'But none will lay hands on the favourite of the king. And the guards are within earshot.'

'You will not call for them.'

'No?'

'No,' said Isocrates. 'Will you answer a question of mine?'

'What is it?'

'Why do you toy with the king? I would understand if you sought to kill the man. I would kill him if I could. But it is a strange revenge, that kills the innocent, and spares the guilty.'

'What did you think I would do? I am not a coward like Croesus. Like you. To fawn and beg for favour from a conqueror. They will always remember him, now. Remember what he has done. There can be no revenge greater than that.' Psamtek paused, for a moment, then said: 'Why are you here?'

'To tell you that Prexaspes will come for you today.'

234

There was silence for a long time.

'What have you done?' Psamtek said.

'You have been conspiring against the king.'

'That is a lie.'

'Yes, it is. But he is being given letters, written in your name, that prove that you are a traitor to him. '

'I do not believe you,' Psamtek said. But there was doubt in his voice.

'I am not a skilled liar. I never learned the art. So you may believe what I say.'

Psamtek said nothing, and Isocrates watched his eyes go dim, his mind searching for a way out. 'I will speak to the king,' the Egyptian said eventually.

'You of all people should know the futility in that.'

'Then let us talk. We can reach terms. What is it that you want?'

'It is too late. The letters have been given. Prexaspes will take your death sentence from the king. He may already be on his way here.'

'Then why are you here?'

'To let you choose how to die.'

Silence fell once again. Psamtek looked down and stared at his hands, lying limp at his sides. Isocrates wondered if he were trying to remember, once more, what it was to turn them against himself.

'You want me to have the death I deserve?' said the Egyptian.

'Few of us get that. But you will get the chance to choose. There are not many that have that privilege.'

Psamtek did not move for a long time. He stayed seated, his eyes dull and body tense. Then he seemed to sink down slightly into his chair, some tautness in his shoulders going slack. The smallest gesture of defeat.

He stood and went to the corner of the room, and opened a small wooden chest. From it he took a wineskin, and poured out a thick red liquid into a clay cup.

'You are prepared, I see,' said Isocrates. 'What is that?'

'Bull's blood.'

'Like in the old stories.'

'Yes. Like them.'

'Not the blade again?'

'Croesus told you that, did he?' Psamtek shook his head. 'The body refuses a death it has faced before. I cannot endure that again.' He took his eyes from the cup, and looked back at Isocrates. 'When the king has you put to death – which he will eventually, I promise you – will you remember something for me?'

'What is that?'

'Remember that it is I who am killing you, with his hands.'

'I will try to keep it in mind,' said Isocrates. He pointed to the cup. 'You had better drink that. They will be coming for you soon.'

Psamtek stared at the cup in his hand. His mental rehearsals must have brought him to this point a thousand times, Isocrates thought. Perhaps he had even poured the blood out once or twice, and held it there in front of him. He had never gone further, but always imagined that it would be a simple enough choice, given the alternative. But now, faced with swallowing death, he hesitated.

He closed his eyes. Perhaps he imagined that it was a dream he had to wake from. Perhaps that was the only way he could trick his mind and body into accepting this death. He breathed steadily, and raised the drink to his lips.

'You will have to put something in that,' Isocrates said.

Psamtek opened his eyes once again. He lowered the cup and looked down at the bull's blood within it.

'It will not kill me?' he said.

'No. The old stories are wrong. It is just blood.'

Psamtek shuddered once, and put the cup down on the table with a strangely careful gesture, as though afraid to spill it and see the blood run loose. 'What will I do?' he said.

236

Isocrates did not reply. He took a small, sharp piece of flint from within his robe, and held it up between a thumb and two fingers for Psamtek to see. Isocrates had carried it with him for many long years, and thought he would have to use it for himself one day. He reached out and offered the blade to the Egyptian.

The moment that Psamtek took it, his muscles seemed to go weak. Perhaps his body truly did remember what it was to feel sharpness in its hands, to know that that sharpness would be turned against it, and stole the strength from his limbs in one last attempt to prevent this act.

'Will you help me?' Psamtek said. 'Please.'

'No,' Isocrates said. He pointed to the blade. 'That is a better death than the one that the king's executioners will give to you. Do as you wish. It means nothing to me.' With that, Isocrates turned and walked away. He closed the door softly behind him.

As he walked down the corridor, he could hear the rattling stamp of the soldiers approaching. Perhaps Psamtek heard them too. A moment later, the first choking screams came from behind him, as the blade began its slow work.

'I did not think I would see you again.'

'You cannot escape me so easily, Croesus. Even if you were to travel one way, and I another, we would always find each other.'

'You have heard?'

'Isocrates told me. I am to go east to be a gardener, it seems.'

'Yes. I go to war, and you go to paradise.'

'To build a paradise. An important difference. From the stories I have heard of the gods, building a world can be hard work.'

'I wish I could go there with you.'

'You will come there in time.'

'So Isocrates says. I hope so. I sometimes wonder, you know, what would have happened if I had been born a slave, not a king.'

'Oh yes?'

'Had we met then, I would have married you, I think.'

'If you had been born a slave, maybe I would have been born a queen. And I would have the pick of handsomer men than you.'

'A man like Isocrates?'

'Handsomer than him, too, I would hope.'

'But if I had been a slave and you a slave, or I a king and you a queen, do you think—'

'You would not have been happy, Croesus. I could have given you no children.'

'My sons are lost to me.'

'What of that? We are all lost, in time. You must be glad to have seen them. To have had what time you had. I wish that I could have known such a thing.'

'Does it trouble Isocrates? He would have been a good father.'

'A hard father. But yes, a good one. I do not know. I do not want to speak of it.'

'I am sorry. I wish we could stay here longer. I wish that we did not have to leave Babylon. I wish that we had more time.'

'So do I. But there is no time left.'

The Second Death

I

When they heard of Psamtek's death and the rumours of conspiracy that came with it, the people of the court expected another purge, more great and terrible than the last. They sent their families into hiding, and began to think of whom they might denounce to save themselves. But the days passed, and the king did nothing.

They watched him obsessively, as priests study omens, and every man had differing thoughts on what this inaction might mean. Some said his cruelty might have died with his advisor, that he seemed in some way relieved, like a man who is at last freed from some terrible burden or heartless duty.

But most did not believe that the king had changed; it was merely that his attentions were elsewhere. For though none had seen her leave her chamber for months, all knew that Parmida must be growing heavy with child. The king spoke of little else now, so excited was he by the coming of an heir. The city waited for the birth of the child, the beginning of a tainted dynasty. All feared what would come to pass when the child was born. The king had taken no chances when it came to his own safety; a single misplaced word that might hint at disloyalty would earn a death sentence. What lengths would he go to protect his child? The noblemen implored the priests to take countless auguries, seeking some sign of what was to come. But no matter how many sacrifices were made and prophets consulted, all were inconclusive. The future, it seemed, was not set.

In the slaves' quarters, Croesus listened to these rumours and stories with little interest as they made their way down the corridors and staircases, passed from noble to servant to slave. He had surrendered his stake in the future, grown weary of trying to understand the cruelty of the king, like those tragedy-struck men who have given up hope of fathoming the will of the gods. But, one day, a rumour came from a different place; not descending from the court, but rising up from the slaves themselves. And the moment he heard it, he knew that it was true.

Word came to him, spoken of amongst the slaves and servants as nothing of consequence, but it was news that meant everything to him – that somewhere within the depths of the palace, an old slave lay dying.

It did not take Croesus long to find them. He searched the forgotten parts of the palace, storerooms that had long since been abandoned, half-collapsed side chambers that none had seen fit to repair. He knew every one of these places, and, more importantly, he knew the minds of those he looked for, knew where they would take shelter at a time like this.

And so, he came at last to a chamber that had fallen out of use, pushing aside a hanging of rough fabric that should not have been there. He found Isocrates sitting on a broken stone pedestal, dull-eyed with lack of sleep, beside him a jar of wine and a heavy piece of wood to serve as a club. Behind him was a doorway with another fabric partition.

Sitting there before that second chamber, Isocrates resembled nothing more than some ancient sentinel, a warrior who might have been assigned to guard this place decades before in some long-forgotten war, abandoned at his post and left to grow old there. He looked up at Croesus and offered no greeting, his eyes empty of hope.

'She is in there?' Croesus said.

'Yes.'

'And she still lives.'

'Yes. For now at least.'

'When were you going to tell me?'

'I do not know.'

Croesus tried to find anger, but could not. Instead, he sat down on the ground at Isocrates's feet, leaned back against a tall, empty clay jar. He had not seen Maia for many days, but he had paid it no mind, thinking that, as the birth drew near, she must be kept busy in service to the queen. He wondered whether they had both known for a long time, or whether some sudden collapse or overnight fever had brought about this crisis.

'Has she asked for me?' Croesus said.

'Yes.'

'And still you would not send for me?'

'I hoped . . .' Isocrates faltered. 'I hoped that it was not true. Though I suppose I knew. A part of me has known for a long time.'

'You could be wrong. Perhaps it is not true.'

'I have seen the wasting sickness before. She has been exhausted for months. I thought it might be something else. It is not. No one recovers from it.'

'You are certain?'

'Yes.'

Croesus bowed his head. He wondered how he could feel such grief as this. He had known that one of them must die soon. It was a strange stroke of fortune that had kept the three of them alive for so long, and it could not go on for ever. Yet somehow he had always thought that he would die first, that he would not have to think of continuing his life without them, the way a child, so needful of his mother's love, will believe, against chance, that she must out-live him.

'Can I speak to her?' said Croesus.

'Yes.' There was something in Isocrates's tone, a sense that this was a statement that was unfinished, and so Croesus waited. At last, the other man spoke again. 'But this will be the last time,' he said.

It took Croesus a long time to understand. 'No,' he said.

'If you have heard, others will have too. They will come for her soon. A dying slave is sport for the cruel. I would spare her that.'

'When?'

'Call to me when you are ready. When she is ready. We will . . .' He faltered for a moment, then spoke again. 'We will do it today.'

When Croesus parted the fabric, he stepped into near darkness, a small fire casting the only light in the room. He wondered if the light pained her, or if it was one of Isocrates's precautions against discovery. Someone glancing inside would have seen a storeroom like any other, but if they had lingered for a moment longer, a vague scent would have revealed that something was not right. The smell of urine, soaked and dried into bedding. A childish smell. And beneath it, another odour, a subtle, stale scent that did not have a name.

He found Maia huddled in the corner, wrapped heavily in blankets. He sat down beside her and took her hand, pale and dry, into his. 'How do you feel?'

'As if I am dying, of course.' He looked away. 'It is the truth, isn't it?' she said.

'I do not know. Are you afraid?'

'Yes.'

'You will get better. You could get better.'

'No, I will not,' she said. She paused. 'You must know, Croesus, that I love you.'

246

He did not reply at first, not trusting himself to speak. 'As a brother, not a husband, I think,' Croesus said.

'Yes.'

'I do not know why. I have never done anything for you. I always thought I would find the time to help you, some day.' He hesitated over the words, the admission that they contained. 'And now it is too late.'

She did not reply at first. He realized, with a surge of disgust, that he'd hoped for reassurance, hoped to use her one last time, imagined that she might give him some kind of absolution. She cocked her head, a gesture he knew so well, and considered the problem he had presented to her. 'You are an interesting puzzle,' she said. 'You want so much to be happy. More than anyone I have ever met. I tried to help, I suppose, but I treated you as a curiosity. Perhaps I was not as good a friend as you think I was.'

'Have you been happy?'

'From time to time, perhaps,' she said. 'Looking after your son, yes, I was happy then. I sometimes wish I had died when Sardis fell. That is another thing we might have in common. But I was glad to see Babylon with you. That was a good day. I am glad I lived to see it.'

Croesus closed his eyes, felt the tears seeping down. When he opened them again, he saw her looking at the doorway.

'I know what he is going to do,' she said quietly.

'What?'

'He thinks he can hide everything from me. But he is not the liar he wants to be. He is an honest man, like you.'

'Do you want him to?'

'I trust him,' she said. 'Even with this.'

'You love him.'

'Oh,' she said, 'I do not know about that. But we helped each other along the way. We tried to be good to each other. And that will have to do.'

'Maia—'

247

'There is nothing more to say. I am tired.' She hesitated, trying to find some other words to speak. 'I am tired,' she said again. She reached out, with effort, and touched his face.

When he felt that he could speak again, he said, 'Shall I call to him?'

'Yes.'

Croesus called out, and heard the curtain part, the heavy footsteps approach, felt a presence kneeling on the ground beside him, a reassuring hand placed on his back. Croesus bowed forward at this touch. That his friend would think to comfort him at a time like this, faced with what he was about to do.

Isocrates placed both palms to the ground and, like a supplicant prostrating himself before a king, brought his head down and pressed it to her shoulder. She turned a little, put both arms around him, and gently stroked his neck. Isocrates shuddered once, like a man run through, then rose again, took her hands in his. They stared at one another in silence, sharing their thoughts, wordless, for the last time.

Croesus made to rise, to leave them alone together, but a hand reached out and took his elbow.

'You must stay,' Isocrates said. 'I cannot do this on my own.'

Isocrates got to his feet and went from the chamber. In his absence, Croesus took Maia's hands, like a sentry replacing his companion at the watch. They did not speak.

When Isocrates returned, and knelt once again beside his wife, he had a cup of wine in his hand. Even in the dim light, Croesus could see the discoloration, the presence of some foreign element in the cup, and that Isocrates's hands were trembling.

'What is it?' Maia said.

'Hemlock.'

'A shame to spoil the taste.'

Isocrates bowed his head at this; she reached forward and touched the whitened stubble on his crown.

248

When he had recovered, she struggled upright in her blankets and took the cup from him. She paused for only a moment; then in two long swallows drained it almost entirely. She threw out the last of the wine on the ground in the way of the Hellenes, giving the lees as an offering to the gods. From another it might have seemed a desperate action, one last bribe of faith offered to the divinities in hope of their protection. From her, it seemed like a gesture of farewell.

'What should I do now?' she said.

'You should . . . I think that you should walk. It will . . .' But Isocrates could not continue.

She nodded. 'Will you help me?'

They lifted her to her feet, and, leaning on both of them, she began to pace the room, the way that a woman close to birth will be helped walk to speed the delivery, as if she is wandering in search of the child that lies within her. At the thought of that, Croesus wished that she could have known what it was to bear a child, that he could have looked at the son or daughter of his friends, have helped to raise it as a second father. To have held their baby in his arms, just once.

She stumbled, and her feet dragged uselessly on the ground.

'My legs,' she said. 'I cannot walk any more.'

They carried her back to the bedding. She seemed to weigh nothing at all now; perhaps, Croesus thought, he and Isocrates had found some last reserves of strength to carry her, the way that a wounded warrior, hacked and bleeding and soon to die, will rise from the ground one last time to defend his closest companion.

She began to gasp for breath, the air whistling and rattling in her throat, and for the first time, there was panic in her eyes.

'Do not be afraid,' Isocrates said.

She sank down into the bedding, her hands pressed against her chest, as if hoping she could reach under her skin and work the lungs that could no longer move by themselves. Her eyes were still focused and in motion, but she no longer seemed to see him. For a moment, Croesus thought that she might, at the last, bring back some sight of the other side, might have a chance to speak of what she had glimpsed there. She opened her eyes a little wider, and seemed about to speak.

She had been so still for so long, her every living movement only fractional, that it took Croesus a long time to realize that, with a quiet kind of grace, she had cast off that most valuable of gifts as if it were nothing.

She was gone.

That night, in an alley behind the palace, they built a pyre. It was a strange collection of everything they could find that might burn; broken pieces of furniture scavenged from the palace, dried cattle dung, a scattering of hay, rags and cloth. They hoped that it would be good enough.

Stray dogs began to gather, sensing the presence of death, and they chased them away with thrown stones and curses. They could not dismiss the beggars who came to the pyre, eager to feel the warmth of a fire. But it did not matter, Croesus thought to himself. She would not have minded. Perhaps she would even be happy that at the last, even in death, she could give out one last gift, the comfort of heat. And so they did not act against this strange funerary procession of the lame and the mad and the blind, but left them gathered around the unlit pyre, and went inside to bring her out.

They washed her together, one last moment of shared intimacy. They marked her cold skin with oil, and then, these tender ministrations done, Isocrates took a knife and cut the tendons in her limbs, to prevent the fire from contorting the body into some gruesome reanimation on the pyre. Isocrates did this butcher's work without hesitation, yet when it came to placing the coin between her lips, he could not do it. Perhaps for him, this token for the next world, more than anything, seemed to signify that she was truly dead.

Croesus took the coin. It was an old Lydian *stater*, marked with the bull and lion, minted in Sardis, in his home, long ago when he had still been a king. This might have been what had made Isocrates hesitate; he and his wife had met in that place, fallen in love there. In some way, the three of them had all longed together for that city, the home that none would see again.

He placed the coin gently between her lips. He brushed the hair from her face and rested his fingers on her closed eyes, tempted to open them and look at them one last time. He took his hand away, and he and Isocrates wrapped the thin body in what rags of cloth they had found, and carried her to the pyre.

They had no time for prayers or sacrifice. The guards would notice the gathering soon, drive them all away and cast her in some communal grave. It was a waste of wood, to burn a slave. A dangerous precedent, too, for what right had a slave to such sacred rites? And so Croesus lit the torch quickly, and gave it to his friend. It was the husband's duty to light the pyre.

Isocrates held the torch limply in his hand, and made no motion to advance. The crowd of beggars fell silent and looked at him, expectant. After a time, Croesus reached forward, intending to take it back from him, but Isocrates shrugged him away, and with a careful, gentle motion, he reached down and touched it to the wood.

For a moment, Croesus felt the mad urge to undo what could not be reversed, to stamp out the flames and be sure that Maia was truly dead. He wondered if those stories of husbands throwing themselves onto their wive's pyres showed that they too sought to beat down the flames, driven not by self-sacrifice, but a last, inconsolable desire for certainty.

The crowd sighed when the fire reached the body, and Croesus closed his eyes. He could hear Isocrates speaking in the Ionian tongue, but whether they were prayers or words of love, his own or borrowed from others, Croesus did not know, and was glad. They belonged to Isocrates alone.

Afterwards, they sat on the ground together with a skin of wine between them, waiting for the fire to cool so that they could gather the bones and ash. They passed the strong wine back and forth until the world pitched and yawed beneath them. In the dim light, Croesus could see Isocrates staring at the embers. He wondered if his friend had some impious desire to rush forward, to raise handfuls to his mouth and taste the ashy kiss of it. Perhaps he wanted to go further, to shape a body from the wood and ash and pray for it to return to life, the way an ancient sculptor, sick with love, had once created a woman of marble that the gods had made flesh. But this was not one of the old stories. There would be no miraculous undoing here.

At last, the fire died. They gathered what remained into a clay jar, sifting the ash for bone. They made their way through the corridors of the palace, staggering with wine and grief and leaning on one another for the comfort of it as much as necessity. Exhausted as he was, his age heavy upon him, to Croesus the palace seemed gargantuan, a kind of endless labyrinth. Perhaps this was what the next world was like, he thought, wondering if at this moment Maia's spirit wandered restlessly in a place like it. He discarded this thought as soon as it came upon him, for it was too light in the palace. He could imagine the afterlife only as a place of darkness.

In the slaves' quarters, they made their way to an empty corner, and lay down beside each other, in a mutual embrace. Croesus thought of the night, only a few years before, when the three of them had slept beside each other. Now, close as they were, there was a ghostly absence there between them. There always would be.

Whether it was for hours or moments, whether they talked or remained silent, whether they fell asleep against one another or remained awake, Croesus could not afterwards have said. He only remembered the comfort of another suffering soul placed beside him, the moment kept in his mind like some half-remembered dream that resists all recollection, yet shapes the life that follows it.

2

Afterwards, they spent barely a moment apart.

With Psamtek dead and Prexaspes cast out of favour, Croesus had
expected the king to summon him. But no word came, for the king
was entirely concerned with the coming of his child. A son: Croesus
had heard that the king insisted it would be a son. He had no use for
an old man, when a new life was so close to being born.

The old slave remained with his friend in the belly of the palace,
part of the machinery of cooking and cleaning that kept the royal
court running. Croesus, as old as he was, learned to work with his
hands. In truth, he knew himself to be more of a hindrance than a help.
But none would deny him his place at Isocrates's side. They passed
most days in silence together, for nothing more, it seemed, needed to
be said. When they did talk, they spoke of times long past, preserv-
ing memories they seemed on the verge of losing. They never joined
the gossip of the other slaves, concerned as it was with the present.
What in that world could be of consequence after Maia's death?

It was only after a month of this, when they rested between tasks,
sharing a bowl of drinking water as if it were wine, that Croesus
found the courage to ask what had truly happened to Psamtek.

Isocrates took a long swallow of water. 'You do not believe he was
a conspirator.'

'No,' Croesus said. 'He had no such ambitions. What did you do?'

'I did not kill him, if that is what you think.'

'But you made him take his own life.'

'Yes.'

'Why?'

'For you, I suppose.'

'For me?'

'I thought that he would have you put to death, eventually. I could not allow that.'

Croesus did not reply, at first. He regarded his friend, and wondered how it was possible to know a man for decades, and yet feel that you scarcely knew him at all.

'What have I done to earn this from you?' Croesus asked.

'Psamtek told me that I had a slave's mind. That I cannot break free of it. That every act I perform is one of subservience to a master. That could be true. But I think we love the people that we love. We will do anything to protect them. And there is nothing more to it than that.'

Croesus tried to find something to say in response, but other words, distant and indistinct, made their way into the chamber. They both went still, and listened. Sound carried far within the stone-lined corridors of the palace. Those with private business to discuss had often been undone by the echoes of their speech reaching unfriendly ears. There were even rumours that the near-blind king had stripped hangings and altered the architecture, converting the palace into an echo chamber that no words might escape from.

And so, with the rest of the slaves, Croesus and Isocrates listened to the king and his sister argue. These screamed altercations had become so common over the past month that all had learned to ignore them, as those who live by the sea no longer mark the rolling of the waves, or the mountain people become attuned to the echo of the wind.

Croesus and Isocrates could not make out the words, only the tone and rhythm of what was being said: the way that a sharp comment was seized upon, an explanation demanded and an insult given in return, building like a gathering storm. It was a pattern that Croesus and the slaves were well familiar with. But this time the voices did not fade, instead reaching a new intensity, speech giving way to wordless cries of hate, as if some transformation had occurred above them, the way the gods were said to sometimes change men into beasts at the height of their passion. There was a final pitched scream of rage or despair that could not be identified as belonging to a man or a woman. Then, there was silence.

Those who had prayed for argument to end now prayed to hear the voices begin again, to hear footsteps moving above them, to hear anything instead of that absence of sound. But there was nothing.

Eventually, a single set of footsteps made its way slowly through corridors and down staircases. The slaves listened to this, and argued where the messenger might be headed. Some said towards the priests' quarters, others that the sounds were headed towards the gate of the palace. But one by one they fell silent, as they realized that the footsteps were making their way, unmistakably, towards where the slaves worked.

At last, the servant, pale-faced and trembling, came into view.

'You must come to see the king,' he said to Croesus.

'What has happened?'

'You must come to the king at once.'

As he followed the servant up through the palace, he knew what must have occurred. But he still could not let himself fully believe.

He passed the king's bodyguards, and came to the corridor before the king's chamber. At the other end of this corridor was a set of stairs, and it was here, sitting on the top step like a child at play, that

Croesus could see Cambyses. The king seemed to be staring at something at the bottom of the stairs. It took Croesus a long time to find the courage to walk to the king. He could see that Cambyses did not sit there shaking with grief or rage, and he did not speak. He sat with a particular kind of stillness, as if afraid the slightest motion would startle the world back into life, as if by remaining entirely unmoving, he might somehow undo what had been done.

At last, Croesus walked twenty paces forward, and stood beside the king. He looked down at the broken figure at the bottom of the stairs. The pale ankle, crooked upright in an inhuman geometry. The arms that were curled, instinctive and maternal at the last, around the full, unwanted belly. He hoped that she had died quickly.

'So,' said Croesus. 'You still have not killed a man.'

'No.' The king's face was twisted in pain, but he did not weep. Croesus wondered if this was the next stage in the degradation of his eyes. Cambyses had little sight left, and now it seemed that tears were lost to him as well.

'I never wished for this,' the king continued, speaking softly, as though afraid he might wake the woman who lay at the bottom of the stairs. 'I have always hated those who hurt women. I thought them the worst of men.' He stopped, and wiped at his dry eyes, as though imagining the tears were there, willing them to flow. 'But she would not be quiet. She said such terrible things. She was cruel to me. I told her that I loved her, and told her to be silent, to think of her child, if she would not think of herself. But she would not listen. I did not mean to.' He paused for a moment, then asked: 'Why did she do it?'

'She wanted to die.'

'It is more than that. She wanted me to kill her. Wanted her death on my hands.'

'Yes, she did.'

'I wanted the child. The love it would give to me. That is truer than anything else in the world, the love of a child for its father, is it not?'

'It is the mother that is loved in that way, Cambyses,' Croesus said. 'The father must earn that love.'

'Is that true?'

'Yes.'

'I see,' Cambyses said. 'Leave me, Croesus. You are a comfort. But you cannot advise me on what I must do now. You are a creature of empty words.'

'Master, you should . . .' *Not.* The word hung there, unspoken. The utterance that would take a moment to say, and that would bring his death.

The old slave turned, and began to walk away. Then he stopped and looked back over his shoulder, down the stairs to the body at its base. At Parmida, and her unborn child. She must have brooded on this plan ever since the wedding, thinking over and over of the words that she would use, refining and perfecting them like a bladesmith at the forge. The arguments that he and the other slaves had heard had been experiments, testing her brother's boundaries, finding the words that would drive him to murder.

He wondered what, at last, had made her do this. Perhaps she had heard of Maia's death, and could not face the thought of raising her child without the slave's kindness. Or perhaps a bond between them had kept the queen clinging to life, the way that a grief-stricken man may be kept from suicide at the thought of how his mother would suffer. Now that Maia was gone, she had been free to die herself.

'This must stop,' Croesus said quietly.

The king lifted his head. 'What?' he said, like a man waking from deep dreaming.

'You are a butcher of your own people, Cambyses. Of your sister. Of . . .' Cambyses raised his hand, his palm towards Croesus, his face strangely imploring, but Croesus continued, 'Of Bardiya.'

'Of Bardiya,' Cambyses repeated.

'If you are to kill them all, whom will you rule over? Will you hold court with ghosts?' Croesus felt tears in his eyes, but he blinked them back. 'Let me teach you,' he said. 'Please. There is still time.'

Cambyses did not say anything. He sat there, his weak eyes alive with thought, and Croesus wondered if, perhaps, the king saw clearly for the first time the world that he had made. How it could be remade in another way. Cambyses looked up at him. 'Wait here, Croesus,' he said. Then he stood, and, with a deliberate calmness, walked to his private chamber and went inside. Croesus stood still, his mouth parted a little in surprise.

He heard the footsteps returning, hurrying a little faster now. It was that hint of eagerness that betrayed the king's intentions. It was then that Croesus remembered the bow.

Cambyses came from his chamber, his bow in his hand and an arrow already nocked. He stopped and leaned forward, his eyes wide and straining. His failing gaze picked Croesus out, and the king howled, raised the bow and drew back the string.

But Croesus had already started to run. He heard the straining of the wood, the whistle and snap of the arrow, but he was halfway down the stairs by the time the king could loose his shot. He almost stumbled over the body of the queen, catching a last glimpse of the terrible expression on her face. He heard that howl again from behind him, but words came with it. The king's voice, over and over again, screaming out a death sentence.

Through chambers and down staircases, past the terrified, startled faces of noblemen and slaves alike, he ran without hope. There was nowhere that he could go to, no place he could hide where the king would not catch him, no words of reasoning that he could use to buy back his life. But there was nothing else that he could do but run, and listen to the heavy tread of the guards pursuing him, drawing ever closer.

At last, he reached the place he had, almost unthinkingly, been heading towards. Isocrates was there waiting, his eyes wide in alarm, his mouth moving and forming words, imploring Croesus to tell him what had happened. But Croesus could not speak. He could only bend double, drawing breath into empty lungs, wondering at how his body, so soon to die, could still be so hungry for air. Over the pounding of blood in his ears, he could still hear the running steps of his pursuers. Isocrates heard them too. He took his place at the doorway, feet shoulder width apart, and knees slightly bent, like a wrestler waiting for the signal to begin. Two guards came running, slowing to a halt in front of Isocrates.

'You'd better step aside,' one of them said. The guard looked past the slave, to Croesus. 'We will do what we must. But you will not suffer.'

'Let them past,' Croesus said, his voice cracking. 'I should not have run.'

'What happened?' Isocrates said.

'He offended the king.'

'How?'

The other man smiled bitterly. 'How else? With honest words. But he will take our heads if we do not execute him.'

Isocrates nodded. 'Listen,' he said. 'Report that he has been killed.'

'Isocrates . . .' the guard said reproachfully, shaking his head.

'Just listen. You know how Cambyses favours Croesus,' Isocrates said. 'The king might change his mind. He might regret his decision. Think of the reward, when we present his favoured advisor back to him, alive and well, returned from the dead.'

'And if he does not change his mind?'

'Then you can come back and kill him later. I will keep him here, in this storeroom. Have men that you trust stand guard, if you like. He has nowhere to run to. Any punishment for this, it falls on me. Any reward I receive, I will give to you. What do you say?'

The guard looked at his companion. The second man shook his

head. Isocrates reached into a fold in his robes, and took out a small, heavy pouch. 'How long will this buy me?' he said.

The first guard weighed it speculatively in his hand. 'Four days,' he said.

'Four days it is,' Isocrates said. 'Thank you both.'

The guards turned to leave. The first man hesitated, then looked back. 'Good luck, Croesus,' he said.

Croesus put his head into his hands. 'Thank you,' he said.

'Come on. Lie down here. Try and get some sleep. I will have to bar the door, but I will be back tomorrow with some food.'

'Isocrates . . .'

'Quiet, Croesus. We can talk tomorrow.'

3

On the first day, Croesus slept.

For the first time in almost thirty years he could rest without fear. No king would summon him to a midnight counsel. No assassins or rivals would come into his room to smother him. The next day would bring no more choices between life and death – in four days he would live or die, and there was nothing he could do to alter that. So he delighted in sleep, wandering from dream to dream, drifting occasionally to the half-awake state where the mind is alive, but without fear. On one of these sojourns into the waking world he woke to find food and wine placed next to his bedding. He ate and drank as quickly as he could, and returned to his dreams.

The next day, his sleep was lighter. The scrape of the plate against the stone woke him, and he looked across to find Isocrates there, replacing the food. Croesus sat up.

'No word yet?' he said.

'No.'

'What does he say about me in the court?' Isocrates hesitated, and did not reply. 'Tell me honestly.'

'He laughs,' Isocrates said. 'He says he is glad to be rid of an old fool.' Croesus looked away. 'But who knows what will happen?' Isocrates continued. 'He will come to miss you.'

262

'In four days?'

'Who can say?'

Croesus nodded. 'Perhaps it does not matter. I would have only a few years left to live. Nothing else will happen in that time. Nothing that will change the way my life has been.' He looked up again. 'Are you happy, Isocrates?'

'Should I be, do you think? How does my life appear to you?'

Croesus smiled. 'Ordinary. A life of hard work. Much suffering, and little to show for it.'

'Ordinary,' Isocrates said, weighing the word. 'I have never thought of that.'

'I remember talking to Cyrus once. About what we were afraid of, as kings with all the wealth and power in the world at our command. The one thing that scared us both.'

'What was that?'

'An ordinary life. A life spent doing nothing new, nothing remarkable, nothing that would mark a place in history. I was always afraid of this, afraid that I would come to the end of my life, and have nothing to show for it.' He shook his head. 'But I have always been a fool. I never learned to be wise, as you said I should.'

'You think differently now?'

'I think every life is remarkable. When I was a king, I squandered lives as I wasted my wealth: on shows of vanity, on grasping at immortality. But even if I could be remembered for the rest of time, what would it matter? Surely, this world will end. The last man will die, and I'll be forgotten with him. What difference if I am forgotten tomorrow, or ten thousand years from now? What is ten thousand years, against the eternity that will follow?'

'You do not believe there is another world?'

'No. That is easy to believe, when death is far away. But I can feel the truth, now that I am close. There is nothing beyond.'

Isocrates stood. 'I must go. Some of the others have begun to suspect.'

Croesus nodded absently. 'Thank you, Isocrates. Please do not risk yourself by coming back here again. I do not need any more food. I have two days left to live. If he pardons me, well, we shall eat a good meal together. If he does not, then what does it matter?'

Isocrates nodded. He placed a hand on Croesus's head, like a priest giving a blessing, then he walked away.

Croesus did not weep, or return to his dreams. He lay back down, and tried to lose himself in memories.

On the third day, Croesus woke to hear the bar being lifted from the door. When it opened, Isocrates alone entered the room. Croesus wondered if Isocrates meant to put him to death himself — a last act of kindness for a friend.

'Well?' Croesus said.

'It is time.'

'Time for what?'

'The king wants you,' Isocrates said.

'Are you sure?'

'He did not sleep last night, and spent all day crying out for you. He will not make any decisions, receive any emissaries. The men of the court do not know what to do. They pray for a miracle.' At last, Isocrates smiled. 'It is time to come back from the dead, Croesus.'

'He might change his mind again when he sees me.'

'He might. But that is a chance we will have to take.'

Croesus closed his eyes, and was silent for a long time. 'Thank you, Isocrates,' he said at last. 'Let us go and see the king.'

A collective intake of breath announced his return to the court. The king, slouched despondently on the throne, looked up in alarm at the sound. With his eyes as weak as they were, he could not tell what could have provoked such a response. He saw only that a new pair of dim shapes had entered the room. 'What is it?' he said. 'Tell me what is happening!'

Silence followed his demand. Croesus and Isocrates looked around the court, but saw that none would announce them. 'Croesus is here, master,' Isocrates said.

'That's not possible. He is dead. I killed him.' Tears swelled in the king's eyes, and Croesus saw that he had been wrong before. The king could still cry.

'You are trying to trick me,' Cambyses said. 'Make a fool of me. I will kill you for it, I swear.'

'I am here, master,' Croesus said softly.

Croesus felt a tight pain in his chest at the love, the desperate, needful love he saw in Cambyses's eyes. Croesus was quite certain that Cambyses still could not see him. The king was simply deciding what he wanted to see.

'I am glad,' the king said. 'I am so very glad that you live, Croesus.' He smile grew broader. He turned his near-sightless eyes back to Isocrates. 'You . . . what is your name?'

Croesus saw the trap closing. He opened his mouth, trying to find the words that might turn aside the king's will. But nothing came. 'Isocrates, master,' his friend said.

'You,' Cambyses said. 'You lied to me. You betrayed me. My soldiers told me what you said. You're the one that told me that he was dead.'

Cambyses stood, and extended a single finger, levelled at Isocrates. 'Tomorrow, you die the way traitors die. You die by fire.'

4

In the cell, dressed in the white robe that he would die in, Isocrates slept. It was shortly before dawn, though day or night meant little in that windowless chamber. Only faint torch light, seeping in from around the frame of the door, offered any illumination. A rich stink came from one corner of the cell which generations of prisoners, by common consensus, had chosen to use as a latrine, and in the opposite corner, Isocrates was curled up against the bare floor. In spite of everything, he seemed to sleep soundly. And from the shadows, Croesus watched his friend dream.

Croesus's bribe had been taken by the guards some time before, and yet he found he did not have the heart to wake his friend. Somehow, even hours before his death, nothing seemed so right as this, to treat it as any other night, to refuse to extract every sensation from his final moments. Even at the last, Croesus thought, it seemed his friend still had something to teach him.

At last, Isocrates woke on his own, one side doubtless numbed by the hard ground. He rolled over, and found Croesus watching him. 'I hoped I would see you again,' said Isocrates.

'Are you afraid?'

Isocrates closed his eyes. 'For a long time, I thought I was ready to die.'

'Yet now you are afraid.'

'Yes,' Isocrates said.

Croesus watched him for a time. 'Can I tell you something, Isocrates?'

Isocrates nodded.

'For a long time, it has been impossible for me to be happy,' Croesus said. 'Yet I still want to live. Even locked away in that cellar, waiting and hoping for Cambyses to change his mind. Even now, with you about to die in my place, I still want to live. Even though there is no happiness left for me in this life. Do you know what that means?'

'Tell me.'

'It means that happiness is not why we live.'

'What do we live for, then?'

'I do not know.'

The silence returned. Isocrates sat with his back against the wall, head bowed. Croesus stood, irresolute, trying to make his decision. More than anything, he wanted to leave that place. To live. But he knew that he could not do it.

'Give me your robe,' Croesus said. 'We do not have much time.'

'What?'

'I have bribed the guards. They will let you out. Come on, give me your clothes.'

'What am I to do when I am free from here?'

'You are going to take my place, and I will take yours.'

'We look nothing alike.'

'Cambyses is the only one that matters,' Croesus said. 'He is mad, and he's almost blind now. If he says you are Croesus, who will dare contradict him? The truth is what he says it is.'

'Why would you do this, Croesus?'

Croesus looked away. 'I have lived long enough,' he said slowly. 'I was not much of a king. I was not a good father to my sons, or a good husband to my wife. I have not been a good friend to you. But this is something I can do.'

Isocrates shook his head. 'Croesus . . .'

'Do you remember Solon?'

Isocrates hesitated. 'Yes. I remember.'

'To die for what you love is a good thing. A good death.'

'You are afraid,' Isocrates said. 'I can see it. You must not do this.'

'Yes, I am more afraid than you are. You are brave, and I am a coward. You have tried to do much for me, Isocrates. It was not your fault that I turned out this way. A miserable old man at the end of his life. Let me do this for you.'

Isocrates tried to speak. He sobbed instead – a sudden gasp of shame and grief. 'Forgive me,' he said softly.

'What for, you fool? Come on, give me your robe. The guards will not stop you. But there is no time left.'

Isocrates pulled the white robe up over his head and handed it to Croesus, felt the old man press his own simple clothes into his hands. They stood together naked for a moment, each holding the identity of the other in their hands. Then they dressed, and each became another man.

Isocrates could see the world only dimly through his tears. Like Cambyses, he thought suddenly. He saw a shadow that was the shape of his friend moving towards him, felt arms tighten around him in a brother's embrace. Then, feeling the shame might drive him mad, he stumbled to the door, past the guards who looked away, not wanting to be to witnesses to the deception. He heard the door close behind him.

He ran out into the corridors of the palace. He had just a few hours before dawn.

Croesus lay on the floor of the cell, and waited for the sun to rise. This will be the last time I wake, he thought. The last time I will feel my mind coming to life. I will never sleep again. I will never have another dream.

He heard the footsteps scrape to a halt outside the cell, heard the bar being lifted, and knew that it was time. He stood as the door opened, and recognized the guards who had come to take him: the same two men who had pursued him through the palace, whom Isocrates had bought his life from. They nodded to him in greeting, and understanding. One of them silently handed him a skin of wine.

Croesus took it, swallowed a mouthful of the strong, bitter drink, and tried to hand the skin back. The guard shook his head. 'You had better drink it all,' he said. 'We still have time.'

They waited as he finished the wine, showing no sign of impatience or boredom. They did nothing but lean against the cell wall and stare into space, enjoying a rare moment's peace.

'Come on,' the first guard said when Croesus had drained the skin. 'We had better go. Can you walk?'

'I think so,' Croesus said.

Without asking, the soldier put his arm under Croesus's arm. 'Lean on me,' he said. 'There is no shame in it.'

As they passed through the dark corridors of the palace, Croesus tried to recall the moments of his life, to enjoy them one last time. But no memories came. It was as though he had been born in the cell that morning, to die an hour later. It did not matter, he thought. What did his memories count for, when they would soon cease to be? Had he died an hour after his birth, his life would have counted for just as little.

Outside the palace gates, Croesus saw the crude pyre looming. He remembered that other pyre, when he had been saved at the last moment by the king's reprieve, and felt the first tears of fear rising up and spilling from his eyes. He knew then that he would not be able to die well, that he would not find the courage he needed so desperately. That he would die begging for his life.

The guard at his side felt his fear, and Croesus felt the arm around him tighten, a brotherly half embrace. 'Courage, Croesus,' the man whispered to him. They tied him to the pyre, and waited for the dawn.

Croesus looked out, and saw that only a small crowd had gathered. There was scant spectacle in the execution of a slave. There were a few curious traders, willing to lose a little business for a free morning's entertainment, but most of them were children who had slipped away to watch something forbidden. He looked at the crowd, examining each face in turn, but he could not see Isocrates. The tears flowed more freely from his eyes. He had hoped that his friend would be there.

The dawn came. The guards lit their torches and placed them at the base of the pyre. The dry wood caught, and the crowd fell silent in anticipation. The first coil of smoke reached Croesus and he recoiled from the scent.

Almost three decades had passed since the pyre in Sardis, yet the smell, the sensation was so suddenly, immediately familiar that Croesus was seized by a paralysing fear, by a thought that would not let him go. It was the thought that perhaps he had never escaped that first pyre, that his life with Cyrus and Cambyses, Maia and Isocrates, had all been nothing more than a final, feverish imagining, the last desperate effort of a dying mind to save itself.

But something was different this time. He could not feel his hands or his feet. He felt cold. He ran his tongue over his lips, found some last drop of wine hiding in the cracked skin. When his tongue touched the liquid, he felt a metallic taste growing strong and heavy in his mouth. He remembered the secret tastes of poisons he had learned as a king, and had forgotten as a slave. How could he have drunk the wineskin without noticing that old taste? How had he not guessed that Isocrates would give one last gift to him at the very end, that of a gentle death?

His head hung heavy, and fell against his chest. He would sleep

270

soon, he realized. Perhaps, in the moments before the poison took him, he would have time to dream again. A dream spanning years, maybe even decades, in that impossible way that one can sleep for moments, but seem to imagine a lifetime. One last dream before he died. A whole life lived again.

With a wrenching effort, he lifted his head to look at the world a final time. Out there in the crowd, he saw Isocrates looking back at him. He tried to open his mouth to speak, to thank Isocrates, to thank the world, perhaps, for letting him live and dream there for a time, but his heavy lips could not form the words. He let his head drop down again, and found he could no longer even see the fire that was growing beneath him.

At the very last, he might have managed a bare fraction of a smile.

'Croesus?'

The voice was hesitant, uncertain; a child calling for a parent in the darkness. There was no answer.

'Croesus?' Cambyses said the name again.

For a moment, Isocrates wondered if he should mimic Croesus's voice and mannerisms, to truly play the part of his dead friend. But no, he thought. Let us see how mad this king truly is.

'I am here, master.'

Cambyses turned his milky eyes towards the sound. In that ruined mind of his, Isocrates thought, there is a mind that dreams, that imagines a better world. Perhaps, in this, he is the happiest of men. He has only to dream it, and for him it is so. He wants me to be Croesus. And so I am Croesus. His mind can work miracles. He has brought a dead man back to life.

Cambyses smiled shyly. 'I missed you, Croesus. I could not sleep when they told me you had been killed. Come here, let me touch you and give you my blessing.'

271

Isocrates let the king run his fingers over his face, and Cambyses nodded in satisfaction. 'Yes. It is you.'

'How can I serve you, master?'

'Tell me a story of my father. Tell me,' Cambyses said, settling back comfortably in his throne, 'what kind of a man was he?'

Isocrates looked at Cambyses for a moment, trying to think of what to say. In his life, he had taken on many roles. He had been whatever his masters had wanted him to be. But he had never been asked to be a storyteller.

He sat for a moment longer, collecting his thoughts, searching for a memory that he might shape to his master's satisfaction. He opened his mouth, and began to tell a story.

5

Soon after Croesus rose from the dead to take his place at Cambyses's side, another dead man breathed again. Word came, first travelling by rumour, then confirmed by a messenger, rowing up the Nile against the flow of the river. The impossible had happened. The king's brother Bardiya had returned from the grave to take the throne at Pasargardae.

Cambyses's rage was terrifying, and even the bravest men in the court knew better than to attend to him. Finding his court deserted, the king stalked the palace with an arrow nocked to his bow, looking for someone to punish for the betrayal. They cowered in quiet corners of the palace, running away from their blinded king. Eventually, Cambyses grew tired of the hunt. He called for his horse to begin the long ride back to Pasargardae at the head of his army.

Isocrates was there as the king leapt into the saddle. He heard the sound of warping metal, saw as the cap of the king's scabbard fell off, worked loose by the gods or by assassins or by chance, and watched as the blade cut a jagged wound in Cambyses's thigh. The king stared in disbelief at the blood that poured from his skin. Then he screamed. Isocrates watched, and said nothing.

The king should have recovered quickly from the cut, and yet within a few days, his thigh was stained with the blackish green of a rotten wound. All remembered Apis, the divine calf that Cambyses had murdered years before. Some said it was divine revenge on a blasphemer, the wound appearing in the same place the king had struck the god, others that the surgeons had been bribed to smear excrement into the wound and make it rot. Whatever the truth was, divine vengeance was blamed, and Cambyses's murderers, if ever they existed, escaped notice.

None of the nobles lingered at the king's side as he died. Perhaps they feared, even to the last, that he would take one final harvest of the court, that he would rise up from his deathbed and condemn them to the execution ground. Only Isocrates was there, listening to the rantings of the dying king. Even after all Cambyses had done, Isocrates would not let him die alone.

Once, towards the end, Isocrates looked at Cambyses and, rather than the madness he had grown used to, he found a sane man staring back at him. 'You are not Croesus, are you?' the king said.

'No. He took my place on the pyre. I am the man you wanted killed for sparing him.'

'You are brave, to admit that to me.'

'I do not think you will remember. In an hour or so, when the fever returns, I will be Croesus to you again.'

'You could die in an hour. I could call my guards now.'

'You could. But you will not.'

'Why not?'

'Because you do not want to die alone.'

A silence.

'Am I going to die?' Cambyses said quietly.

'Yes.'

The king nodded, tears running silently from his eyes. 'I am afraid.'

'We all have to die.'

'I do not want to die like this.'

'None of us gets the death we want.'

274

'They despise me. The people, I mean. As Croesus said they would.'

'You made them hate you.'

Cambyses closed his eyes. 'I am sorry.'

'That may count for something,' Isocrates said.

'Do you really think so?'

'Not much, mind. Not much. But it is better than nothing.'

'Do you forgive me?'

'No. I cannot forgive you for what you have done.' Isocrates paused. 'But I do not hate you. Not any more.'

'Thank you,' the king said softly. He drifted off to sleep, and returned to his madness.

In the months after the king's death, the noblemen of the court made their way to Pasargadae to beg for a place at the court of the new king. Some were given minor postings in distant corners of the empire. Some were quietly disappeared, Prexaspes amongst them. Of them all, only Isocrates was granted a private audience with the new king. Alone in the royal chambers, Isocrates and Bardiya stared at each other without speaking. After a time, the king broke the silence. 'I saw Croesus several times when he served Cambyses,' Bardiya said. 'And you are not him.'

Isocrates considered this. Then he said: 'I saw Bardiya many times when he was growing up in Cyrus's army. You have a good likeness, it is true. But you are not him. Bardiya died years ago, at his brother's command.'

'I see.' The man who called himself Bardiya nodded once, then lapsed again into silence. They looked at one another, the impostor slave and the impostor king, each trying to imagine if they could trust one another.

'I do not care who you are, or how you managed to steal the

throne.' Isocrates said. 'I need a master to serve. You need someone who knows the court well. Perhaps we can help each other.'

Bardiya nodded slowly. 'Perhaps we can. What is your name? Your real name?'

'Isocrates. And you?'

'My name is Gaumata.'

'Very well. Let us begin.'

From the moment he took power, Gaumata must have known that another, more powerful group would inevitably try to take the throne from him, but he had been willing to trade his life to enjoy a few short months as a king. When the inevitable coup came and they searched the palace for the king's closest advisor, he was gone. Isocrates had spent a lifetime reading the mood of one court after another. He had known the betrayal was coming long before it happened, before the thought itself had even fully formed in the mind of the conspirators. The night before they stormed the palace, he took two horses, some simple travelling clothes and what little gold he could steal from the treasuries.

He headed west. Every night, he dreamed of the red cliffs of Thera, the island which had been his home six decades before, and so he made his way towards the coast, hoping to see the island again. He did not think he would live long enough to see it. Sometimes in the night he woke up gasping, his left arm aching, his heart beating sluggish and slow. Soon it would stop altogether. He told himself that it did not matter if he saw Thera again. He would try, and that, perhaps, might be enough.

After a week alone on the road, Isocrates bought a slave. He spent days agonizing over the decision, but he was growing older and weaker. He needed the help, and, in private reflection, he could admit that he also needed the company. He understood now, for the first time in his life, the desire to own a slave. The craving for the loyalty that is bought and owned, that is beyond doubt. At the first auction he came to, he bought a quick-witted boy from Halicarnassus, sold to pay off his father's gambling debt.

The first night around the campfire, the boy looked at him warily. 'I know what you must think, an old man buying a boy like you,' Isocrates said. 'I'm sure the other slaves told you what to expect. But that is not my intention.' Isocrates broke off, and fed another piece of wood to the dying fire.

'While I live,' he continued, once the fire was roaring again, 'you will serve me. Think of yourself as a servant, not a slave. Serve me well, and I shall teach you everything I can. I have learned a little about surviving in this world. And when I die I will give you your freedom, and whatever gold I have left. You can go back to Halicarnassus, or wherever else you please. This, I promise you.' He looked at the boy. 'Do we have an agreement?'

The boy nodded, and smiled shyly.

Isocrates's stolen gold did not last long, and so he had to find some other way to earn a living. He spent many nights pondering this particular problem, wondering how it was that an old man, useless to the world, would be able to live, other than as a beggar. Now that he was a free man, he had slowly begun to dream, for the first time that he could remember. Some forgotten part of his mind, rendered dormant through servitude, was slowly coming back to life. It was in one of these dreams that he found his answer.

He wandered from one court to another, as Solon had half a century before, telling stories to kings, princes, satraps, and archons. He told the only stories he knew, the stories he had lived and witnessed for himself. His reputation spread, travelled faster than he did, and soon kings were vying for his favour, sending ever more generous gifts to tempt him to their courts. They asked for stories of Cyrus and Cambyses, of Persia and Lydia, of battles and intrigue at court. He spoke of the wonders of Babylon, the fall of Sardis, the wild plains of the Massagetae, the ancient tombs of Egypt. But above all, again and again, he told stories of Croesus.

He told them of Croesus the king, and Croesus the slave. Of the man who had lost an empire but saved his people from slavery, who had hoarded wealth but craved only happiness. He embellished the stories for those who wanted myths, told them truthfully to those who respected the truth, made them more plausible for those who would never believe the things that he had seen with his own eyes. He taught them all to the boy, to earn a living with when Isocrates was gone, to spread amongst his own people in Halicarnassus when he could finally return home. He told every story of Croesus that he knew except one.

At night, before he slept, he thought of the thousand deaths he could give his friend. Some heroic, some tragic, some quiet and peaceful. But none of them would do. In all the stories he spread amongst the courts of the Cappadocians, the Assyrians, the Medians, and the Lydians, he never once spoke of Croesus's death. He left the stories to spread and breed amongst themselves, as stories will, to find a hundred thousand different endings without him. To evolve and live on, to make his friend immortal in story.

He let Croesus slip quietly from the pages of history, and into myth.

Acknowledgements

First, my most sincere thanks are due to Caroline, Sara, James, Ravi, and to everyone at Felicity Bryan and Atlantic Books for their invaluable help in creating this book. My faithful band of early readers has been of great assistance: Gill, Michael, Vestal, Sho, I thank you all. Finally, many thanks to Jeff Fisher for another wonderful cover, and once again to Herodotus, the wandering historian who couldn't resist a good story.

A writer has many great debts to pay, one dedication at a time. This book is dedicated to the teacher (and friend) who was first to believe.

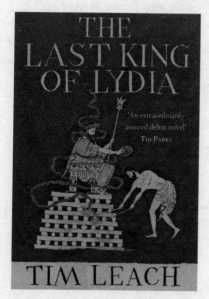

Shortlisted for the Dylan Thomas Prize

If you enjoyed *The King and the Slave* you will love Tim Leach's first novel, *The Last King of Lydia* – a brilliant imagining of the bloody rise and fall of Croesus, 'the richest man on earth', which powerfully shows how happiness, even for those who have everything, is so often elusive.

Out now in paperback and e-book.